Also by Carolyn Brown

Dear Readers,

Spanish Fort really does exist in the northernmost part of Montague County, Texas. After the Civil War, the Chisholm Trail, a route to drive cattle to the stockyards in Kansas, cut its way to Spanish Fort, which back then had a population of about one thousand, and provided the cowhands with lots of wine, women, and song. Spanish Fort had four hotels, several saloons, bordellos—of which the Paradise was one—and a few specialty shops, including the first store of that famous cobbler H. J. Justin. Once the railroad made the Chisholm Trail obsolete, Spanish Fort lost its glory.

By the turn of the century, the rough trail town quieted into a laid-back, tiny community and is now considered a ghost town. But in my imagination, the family of seven sisters and now three brothers are rebuilding the town, and soon it will be restored to its original glory. I must admit that my imagination is sometimes exaggerated—a lot—so bear with me through this story about the first brother of the Paradise, as he settles down on his organic farm.

I hope you all enjoy going back to Spanish Fort, Texas, and to the Paradise as much as I did and that after you finish the last words in this book, you are already wanting to read Tripp's story. As usual, I dragged my feet while writing the final chapter of Brodie's story. I so hate to leave my characters behind, but alas, Tripp has been whispering in my ear for a while now, so I'm off to see what he has to tell me.

Until next time,

Carolyn Brown

Meet Me
in the
Orchard

CAROLYN BROWN

Published by Sourcebooks Casablanca, an imprint of Sourcebooks
P.O. Box 4410, Naperville, Illinois 60567-4410
(630) 961-3900
sourcebooks.com

Cataloging-in-Publication Data is on file with the Library of Congress.

Printed and bound in the United States of America.
KP 10 9 8 7 6 5 4 3 2 1

This one is in memory of the three Brown brothers,
Charles Brown, William (Bill) Brown,
and Dennis Brown
One called me Sweetheart,
and the other two called me Sister!

Chapter 1

THE SOUND OF A freight train coming right at him was so loud that Brodie could barely hear his brothers, Tripp and Knox, yelling from the cellar door. A chunk of ragged wood stabbed the ground right in front of him. He dodged it, and a hog spun through the air above his head so close that he could smell it.

When pigs fly, he thought as he ran toward the storm shelter.

"Get in here!" Tripp's voice came through the noise.

A violent wind pushed him hard from behind, and suddenly he was being thrown forward with such force that his feet left the ground. He groped for balance, and then Tripp hugged him like a bear. The next thing he knew, he was sitting on the bench that lined the back wall. An oil lamp on an old wooden table dimly lit up the room. Brodie clasped his hands together to keep them from shaking.

"Pigs *were* flying," he whispered.

"What did you say?" Knox hollered above the noise. "With all the pounding out there, you've got to speak up."

"I saw a full-sized hog flying through the air," Brodie answered between bouts of catching his breath.

"Everything was flying." Tripp raised his voice. "Even you. If I hadn't caught you when I did, you'd be halfway to Arkansas by now. Thank God we've got a storm cellar."

"Thank Ira," Brodie said. "He's the one that built this storm shelter."

Brodie's heart was still pounding, and he wasn't sure his legs would support him if he tried to stand up. From the sound of things, the cellar door was taking a severe beating. Knox, the carpenter in the family, might need to build a new one next week. Audrey Tucker and her ninety-year-old aunt were his neighbors who had shown him nothing but disgust because he wouldn't sell his farm to them, but he hoped they were safe.

"Oh, no!" he whispered, but evidently neither of his brothers heard him. "What if this storm blows the Paradise away or hurts one of my seven half sisters, or my biological father?"

"I can see your lips moving, but I have no idea what you are saying," Knox shouted.

"Nothing," Brodie said loudly and shook his head.

Would his heart ever stop pounding, or was this his new norm? Did the force of the wind cause a problem in his internal organs? Brodie was no stranger to destruction. He had done a couple of tours in countries with bombed-out buildings. He had seen—up close and personal—what an IED could do. He'd served on the Bandera, Texas, Volunteer Fire Department and seen and been through atrocities that gave him nightmares. But coming so close to being swept away in a tornado affected him worse than anything he had ever experienced before. If he had been a child, and not thirty years old, he would have definitely needed years of therapy.

"Are you alright?" Knox asked.

Brodie glanced over at his brother. "Why do you ask?"

"You've been staring at the lamp with a blank stare on your face," Knox answered.

"I thought I was a goner," Brodie admitted.

"So did I when that piece of wood flew out of the air and stuck in the ground right in front of you," Tripp yelled.

Suddenly an eerie silence filled the place. The lamplight flickered a couple of times before it went out completely, leaving the cellar in darkness so heavy that made Brodie shiver. He stood up and felt his way around the shelving to his right. He moved slowly toward the thin streak of light on the steps, possibly coming through a broken board on the weathered old wooden door. A sticker in the palm of his hand was payment when he searched for the rusty bolt that would unlock the door. He ignored the stinging pain and slid the bolt to the side. Then he pushed hard with his shoulder, but it did not budge.

"Need some help?" Knox asked.

"Only if y'all want to get out of here," Brodie answered.

Even with three strong men giving it all they had, the door would not open. Brodie was so winded on the third try that he sat down on the step and groaned. "We are stuck until someone comes along to help us from the outside."

"Everyone may just drive by and think that we were blown away like you nearly were," Tripp groaned.

"Brodie! Tripp! Knox!" Voices blended together, but in among all of them, Brodie recognized Joe Clay's.

"In here. In the cellar," he yelled.

"Hush! Everyone be quiet!" Mary Jane's voice sounded like it was coming from the bottom of a barrel.

"We are trapped," Brodie shouted.

Shadows covered up the tiny streak of light, and the scraping sounds of something being dragged off the wooden door filled the cellar. Brodie didn't realize how tight his chest had been until he could actually take a deep breath without pain.

"Anyone got a chain in their truck?" Joe Clay's voice came through plain and clear.

"I do," Shane answered. "I'll get it so we can drag this tree away. Looks like the tornado ripped away the electrical wires to the house, but they're not lying around anywhere. Remy is calling the power company now to get them out here to fix things."

Brodie sat down on the top step. "I hope that's not one of the apple trees on the door."

"We're working on things out here," Mary Jane yelled. "Are y'all safe?"

"We are fine," Tripp called out.

"That's good," Joe Clay said. "We're wrapping a chain around the tree and using my old work truck to pull it off the doors. Y'all might want to stand back away from everything in case the wood splinters and flies. If this don't work, we'll go back to the Paradise and get chain saws."

"We'll get you out of there," Mary Jane assured them in a worried voice.

The crunching sound of the tree being dragged away was deafening, but immediately a beam of light flowed into the cellar. Joe Clay's face appeared first when he opened up what was left of the splinters and shattered doors.

"Are y'all sure you are all right?" he asked.

Brodie was the first one out, and Joe Clay grabbed him in a fierce bear hug. "When we saw that the house was gone, I thought I'd lost you."

"I'm fine except for a splinter in my hand," Brodie assured him.

When the other two brothers came out of the cellar, Joe Clay left Brodie and wrapped them up in a three-way hug. "We are so lucky that you made it to shelter on time."

"Brodie just about didn't," Tripp said and then pointed toward where their house used to be.

Disaster lay all around the place. The roof, all except for shingles scattered around the yard, was gone. Three walls of the house, along with everything but the bathroom fixtures, had been blown away. The water hose, hooked up to the well house, was still coiled up like a sleeping snake. How could a storm so violent that it picked him right up off the ground not even disturb a lightweight hose?

Brodie closed his hazel eyes, but when he opened them nothing had changed. He stood to the side of the cellar steps, looked out across the farm, and stared at broken boards and shingles scattered every which way.

"What do we do now?" Tripp asked.

His brother's voice sounded as if it was coming from a mile away.

Lightning lit up the sky behind Brodie and thunder rolled. The tornado had left a chilly wind, drizzling rain, and shock in its wake. Now it was traveling north toward the Red River, most likely destroying whatever got in its way.

"We will rebuild." Knox's statement seemed flat and unsure.

"That will take months," Tripp said.

"I've already got the plans drawn up," Knox said. "We were going to build a bigger house this summer, anyway. Until we get it ready to move into, we can live in my travel trailer."

"We don't have anything but the clothes on our backs," Tripp snapped.

"We'll go to Nocona this evening and get whatever we need—toothbrushes, soap, and that kind of thing. We'll figure this out," Knox said.

"Thirty minutes?" Brodie whispered.

"I can't build a house in half an hour," Knox declared.

"I know," Brodie said, "but half an hour ago Tripp was..." he paused and glanced over to see if the grill was still there—it wasn't. "Tripp was grilling T-bones."

"We can buy more steaks," Knox barked. "We can buy

anything we need or want. Three pieces of meat are the least of our worries right now."

"And what are we going to do for supper tonight?" Tripp asked.

"We'll eat at the Dairy Queen, buy what we need, stay in that little hotel east of town, and figure things out tomorrow," Knox answered.

"We need to see if we still have a truck that will take us to Nocona," Brodie finally got the words out, but his feet wouldn't move.

A cardinal lit on a bare pecan tree branch above him and began to sing. His mother Jolene always said that when a cardinal lands close by, it means that someone who has passed away is thinking of you. If that was true and his mother was thinking of him, then why would there be a song in her heart? She should be weeping, not putting out a joyful sound.

Somewhere off in the distance the sound of more vehicles coming down the dirt lane drowned out the bird's happiness. Dark clouds covered the sky to the northeast, but to the southwest, the sky was clear blue, and the sun was slowly making its way toward the western horizon.

None of it made any sense.

The noise of lots of trucks and cars took his attention toward the road, where they lined up like a funeral procession, which seemed fitting to Brodie at that time. Family members were hurrying out of seven more trucks and coming toward him.

"Family," he muttered.

"Are you guys hurt?" Parker asked as he and Endora ignored the rain and ran across the yard, sidestepping all the debris.

"We're fine, but we don't have a home anymore." Brodie could talk, but his feet didn't work anymore. "Did the tornado hit any of y'all's places?"

"We are all safe and our homes are still standing. Houses can be replaced," Mary Jane told him. "Sons can't."

But I'm not your son. Neither are Tripp and Knox. Brodie was glad he had just thought the words and hadn't spit them out.

He still hadn't moved a single step when all seven of his sisters surrounded the three of them, all talking at once and getting soaked by the drizzling rain.

"When we drove up and saw that the house was gone, we were scared that y'all were in it when the tornado came through," Parker said.

Mary Jane gave Brodie an extra-tight hug before she turned him loose. "Y'all are coming home with us. There are seven empty bedrooms at our house. You have a place to go."

"Knox has a travel trailer..." Brodie paused.

The sun was in front of him. The storm clouds behind him. Did that have some significance? How was he supposed to look forward when all he had to do was glance over his shoulder to see nothing but destruction. Then he looked over to his left and saw that Audrey Tucker's place was still standing. It didn't look like even a single shingle had been disturbed.

Of all the luck, he thought. *She's been a thorn in my side ever since I bought this place, and all she has is some debris lying around in her yard and a few blooms blown off a rose bush.*

The oldest sister, Ursula—the tall one—draped her arm around his shoulder. "Did it take your vehicles? We've got an old work truck y'all can borrow if it did."

Remy pointed toward the edge of the orchard. "There's three all crammed up together at the edge of the orchard. They look like they've been in a losing battle, but they might still run."

"Thank you, Ursula. We might take you up on that offer if our trucks aren't running when we get all that trash off them."

He wondered how he sounded so calm and collected when he wanted to shake his fist at the sky and demand that God explain to him why this had happened. He wanted to stand in the middle of the place where the house used to be and scream until his voice gave out.

Mary Jane raised her voice above all the clamor. "Okay, everyone, let's dig these boys' trucks out enough and see if they are drivable. Once we do that, they are all three going home with us until they can rebuild."

"We could drive into Nocona and get motel rooms," Tripp suggested.

"Or live in my travel trailer. It's tiny even for one, but we can make do," Knox said.

Joe Clay shook his head. "Family takes care of family, and besides there's not a one of y'all—me included—that will go up against Mary Jane."

"That's the truth," Ursula said with a smile.

Too bad that family included Aunt Bernie, Brodie thought when he was finally able to take a step forward. He followed everyone to the three trucks that had been pushed up against a barbed-wire fence that separated his farm from Audrey Tucker's.

Considering all the experiences Brodie had had in the past, he should have been prepared for anything life could throw at him. But he kept replaying the events of the past hour in his mind—the funnel cloud coming right at them, hearing what sounded like a freight train passing over the old cellar, then coming out to find total destruction just plumb knocked the wind right out of him.

"We are three lucky dudes," Brodie whispered as he threw pieces of boards and bits of shingles away from Tripp's truck.

"Our house is gone," Tripp looked back over his shoulder at the place where their home used to stand. "Where's the luck in that?"

"We are all three alive, and it looks like the storm left us with three vehicles," Brodie reminded him. "And only a few leaves are blown off my orchard trees. From what I can see, the gardens look good. That makes us lucky."

"And we are about to move into the Paradise," Knox whispered for Brodie's ears only. "Where Aunt Bernie is in and out all day with her matchmaking business. Still think your lucky Irish blood is calling the shots? She's going to have you standing at the front of the altar waiting on a woman in a big white wedding dress before you can whistle 'The Eyes of Texas are Upon You.'"

"Watch and learn, little brother," Brodie said with half a smile and then wondered how he or either of his brothers could find a bit of humor in their hearts.

"You can bet I *will* be watching, but I'll be the one picking out the women for my own dates." Knox had always been able to lighten the mood—evidently even in the aftermath of a tornado. He was the outgoing twin, the life of the party, and ready for a good laugh. Tripp was the introvert, happy to be left alone to do his leather work or even help out in the orchards and strawberry, watermelon, and cantaloupe fields.

"Don't worry," Brodie sighed. "Aunt Bernie seems fixated on finding a woman for me, and if history is repeating itself, Tripp will be next. So, you've got a little while to bask in your self-proclaimed bachelorhood."

"Did I hear Aunt Bernie's name?" Ursula asked.

"Where is she? I've seen everyone here but her." Knox asked.

"She's watching my baby take his afternoon nap," Ursula answered and then lowered her voice. "Don't try to live in a travel trailer stacked up like sardines or go to a hotel. The Paradise has lots of empty rooms, and the folks have been lonely in that big house, so let them help you."

"Are you sure?" Brodie asked. "We don't want to impose."

Ursula laid a hand on his shoulder. "You would probably offend them if you didn't take them up on the offer."

"Okay, then," Brodie agreed. "We'll go for a couple of days until we can make up our minds what to do, but before that, we need to make a run to Nocona and get a few things. Everything we had was blown away."

"I understand," Ursula said. "But don't be late for supper. Tertia is bringing over food from the restaurant. They had to close down early because of the storm, and there were lots of leftovers."

"Yes, ma'am," Brodie replied with a nod.

———

Brodie slid into his truck and grasped the steering wheel until his knuckles were white. His heart pounded and his pulse raced as he turned the key. It seemed like an hour went by before the engine started up and purred like a kitten, but in reality only a couple of seconds had passed.

"All three are running, but they look like they're the losers in a fight with a briar patch," Knox said when he crawled into the passenger's seat. "We can all go in one vehicle, right?"

"Right," Brodie agreed.

Tripp settled into the back seat. "Beware the Ides of March."

"Amen!" Knox agreed.

"I had forgotten that it was the fifteenth of March," Brodie whispered.

"I bet none of us ever forgets again," Knox said. "I thought for sure the tornado would suck up the cellar and dump us in the Red River. I don't think I've ever been so scared."

"Me, either," Tripp said. "Good thing that Brodie stayed calm during the whole thing. If he had freaked out, I would have started bawlin' like a baby."

"I was terrified," Brodie said. "I just couldn't find my voice to say anything. My whole body felt like it was frozen."

"Thank God!" Knox said with a long sigh. "If I'd known you were scared, I would have lost it."

"Me, too!" Tripp said from the back seat. "When Brodie's feet left the ground, I just reached out and grabbed him. I didn't even think about the fact that the tornado was strong enough to take us both and suck you up out of the cellar."

"Whew!" Knox gasped. "I'm glad y'all didn't tell me that while we were still in the cellar."

"Why would it scare you more then than it does now?" Brodie asked.

"There's no bathroom in the shelter." Knox's tone was dead serious.

"There's not one anywhere on the property right now," Tripp reminded him.

Brodie backed out away from the trees and fell in behind all the other vehicles. When the oncoming truck from the electric company passed them, he chuckled.

"What's so funny?" Tripp asked.

"What do we look like all going slow like we are down this gravel road?" he asked.

"A funeral procession," Tripp answered.

"No people were hurt in the filming of this disastrous tornado," Knox joked. "Do you think they'll put our names on the credits when they roll?"

"It's not something to joke about," Brodie barked.

"We just saved about ten thousand dollars," Knox snapped right back. "We were going to have to tear down the old house anyway once we got the new one ready to live in. The tornado did it for us except for the bathroom, but I don't expect any of us want to use the toilet or take a shower right out in public, do we?"

"Depends on the level of desperation," Tripp muttered.

Brodie had always been calm under fire—either the kind with blazes or with bullets—by keeping it bottled up inside. But like all volcanos, every now and then everything erupts and comes flowing out.

He slapped the steering wheel in anger, gritted his teeth, and growled.

"Let it out, brother," Tripp said. "If you don't, you're going to explode all over this truck and wind up killing me and Knox when you have a wreck."

"I hate this," Brodie said with a long sigh, "and I can't do one thing about it. In the blink of an eye, we lost our home and everything we own except for three trucks that look like they've been beat all to hell with green briars and boards flying out of the sky. We don't even have socks and underwear, or a clean shirt."

Tripp reached up and patted his brother on the shoulder. "We can buy what we need for a couple of days and go have supper with your family. That's two things we can do about what just happened."

"They are not *my* family. They are *our* family," Brodie snapped. "They took me in because Joe Clay is my biological father, and y'all both got kind of adopted a second time since you are my brothers."

"At least you know who your father is," Tripp said. "Our father died in a car wreck before we were born, and our mother died from complications two days after we came into this world. Like I've told you before, I'm a little bit jealous."

"Do you ever wish that Mother hadn't told us about our biological parents before she passed away?" Knox asked.

Tripp shook his head. "Nope. Now I know that there's no need to go looking for my father or the mama that birthed me, I'm just glad we had such good folks like Jolene and John Callahan to raise us. I missed Dad when he went a couple of years ago, but I miss Mother even more."

"Me, too, but I'm so glad we had that last year with her," Brodie whispered as he made a turned south on a paved road and headed south toward Nocona. "And I'm really glad that y'all came with me up to this area. I can't imagine going through this without you."

"We needed a change after Mother's illness and death," Knox said. "And I can build houses anywhere."

"Same for me. I can put in a leather shop anywhere," Tripp agreed. "But first, I'll have to build one, since there isn't a lot of empty buildings in Spanish Fort for sale."

"You can amend that to no businesses for sale," Brodie said.

Silence filled the cab of the truck for the next fifteen minutes as Brodie drove to Nocona. He figured his brothers were finally feeling the full impact of what just happened.

Like them, he tried to work his mind around such an abrupt change in their lives, but it was an impossible task.

They had grown up in the biggest house in the small town of Bandera, Texas, but their mother would never let them be entitled. She made sure they understood the value of hard work. After graduation, Brodie went into the army. Knox moved out after he finished high school to work for a construction company. Tripp went to college and moved into his own apartment afterward. For the first time in more than a decade, the three were living together in a small three-bedroom house with only one bathroom. Now it was gone, and they were moving back into a big house—the Paradise. He turned on Highway 82, passed the Dairy Queen on the left, and then drove a few more blocks to the Dollar General Store.

"We'll go to the Western wear place and buy a couple of changes of jeans and some shirts after we get done in here," he said.

"Sounds like a plan to me," Knox said and slapped the console between him and Brodie. "My favorite travel luggage is gone! We're going to look like hobos carrying our things into the Paradise in plastic bags."

"I don't imagine Joe Clay or any of the family will kick us out if we aren't carrying expensive suitcases," Tripp smarted off. "But I do hope someone who has the same initials as yours finds your monogrammed suitcases."

"They are probably floating in the Red River," Knox groaned.

"The turtles can crawl up on them and use them like rocks to sun themselves," Brodie said. "We are alive. We are breathing. We aren't dead. Suitcases, houses, even three thick, juicy steaks, do not matter right now." He snagged a parking spot not far from the store.

All three guys got out of the truck at the same time, slammed the doors shut, and headed across the parking lot like three cowboys facing off with the fellers in the black hats in an old Western shoot-out.

We are Texans, born and raised, but not a one of us is a real cowboy, Brodie thought and then looked up to see all of their reflections in the glass storefront. They were slightly out of focus, but it was evident that he towered above them. They had both stopped growing at five feet ten inches. Brodie had kept shooting up until he was well over six feet.

His brothers didn't look or act anything alike even though they were twins. Tripp, the quieter one, had close-cut jet-black hair and deep brown eyes. He was a little thinner than Knox, who had a crop of blond hair that he pulled back into a short ponytail and crystal-clear blue eyes. Before she died after a long battle with cancer, his mother had said that they were her sunshine and storm cloud boys.

"What are you thinking about?" Tripp asked.

"I was just looking at our reflections in the store window," Brodie answered.

"I figured you were about to turn tail and run," Knox said.

"Why would I do that?" Brodie asked. "I'm not too proud to shop at a dollar store."

Tripp chuckled and held the door open for his two brothers. "Because of who's standing over there by the checkout counter."

Brodie closed his eyes, hoping that maybe—just maybe—the woman standing at the checkout counter was not Audrey Tucker, but when he opened them, she was still standing there.

"The Ides of March strikes again," Brodie muttered.

"Yep, and I don't know which storm is the worst," Knox agreed.

Audrey picked up a small bag, turned around to leave, and locked eyes with Brodie. She marched toward him like a soldier on a mission. The sack in her hands swung back and forth like it had a temper of its own that was about to be unleashed upon none other than Brodie Callahan. He could see the top of a bottle of bleach through the thin plastic and hoped that she didn't start swinging it toward his head—or worse yet, lower down on his body.

She didn't stop until she was so close that he got a whiff of her long, dark hair. Coconut with something that reminded him of white sand, hot sun, and cool ocean water. He couldn't tell if her brown eyes were filled with humor or sympathy when she stood toe-to-toe with him.

"I drove past y'all's place. Looks like the tornado wiped out your house," she said.

"It did," Brodie said. "I noticed that your place is still standing."

"It tore up the corner of my cornfield and blew some

debris around. Evidently, the Universe is trying to tell you something." The coldness in her tone and her expression let him know that she had zero sympathy.

"How do you figure that?" Brodie snapped back. "We are all three alive. I'd say that's a blessing from the Universe."

"Tornadoes are an act of God," she whispered and pointed toward the ceiling. "The Almighty is telling you that you Callahans don't belong in my part of Texas. He is saying that you need to sell your land to me and go somewhere else with your stupid ideas about organic farming."

"I'm so glad you've got a hotline to heaven and that God speaks to you. He hasn't told me to sell my land, but if and when He does, I can guarantee you that I will not sell it to you. Besides your Uncle Ira didn't think organic farming was stupid, did he? From what I see in his books, he made a really good living at it." Brodie's eyes locked on her full mouth. She might be the devil's sister, but those lips were made for kissing.

Audrey glared at him. "It doesn't take a genius to read the signs. Why won't you sell to me?"

"Because you are bossy, hateful, and downright mean," Brodie answered. "Why would you want an organic farm anyway? To turn it into a chemically fertilized mess?"

"Your place and mine used to be one farm. I want to reunite the family land," she answered through clenched teeth. "And yes, I would quit the organic crap because I think it's a stupid way to farm."

"Why are you so set on making the two places one?"

Brodie asked with a smile that he knew would make her even more angry.

"My grandfather Frank and Ira were brothers. Because of a woman they both loved they split up their farm." She seemed to remember who she was talking to. "It's really none of your business."

"Sounds like the makings of one of those television movies that chicks watch," Brodie said. "I bought the place from your cousin, and I'm not selling it. But thanks for the history lesson."

"Where are you staying until you can rebuild—if that's what you have in mind?" Audrey asked.

Brodie glanced around and saw that both his brothers had left him on his own. "We are staying at the Paradise, but we'll be on the farm every day. So, don't be getting any of those nasty pesticides that you use on *my* trees and gardens."

She used a forefinger to poke him in the chest. "I guess you have to be screwed, glued, and crying like a baby before you'll sell to me. What's it going to take before you wake up and figure out that organic farming is—"

Brodie picked up her finger, ignored the sparks between them, and dropped it like it was a piece of trash. "Are you blind, or do you just ignore the rows and rows of produce in most grocery stores that have an 'organically grown' sticker on them?"

"It's a phase and won't last, and besides, it's too expensive," she snapped and took a step back. "You have a good time cleaning up your mess, and remember, you can always hop over the barbed-wire fence separating our places and come over to my house. I have a very generous contract all signed and ready for your signature. I won't even lower the price because there's no house on the property anymore. Matter of fact, I'd planned on tearing it down anyway."

"I will never put my name on that paper," Brodie declared, grabbed a cart, and walked away.

"What if your new place burns down?" Audrey called out.

He stopped and turned around. "Then I guess I'll collect the insurance and build it again after I have you investigated for arson."

She stomped her foot on the floor. "You are as stubborn as a cross-eyed mule."

"That would be the pot calling the kettle black," Brodie said with a wide grin.

Audrey shot a look toward him that was probably meant to melt him into a puddle right there in front of the generic aspirin, but he just chuckled. She stormed outside mumbling about men. Too bad the door to the place didn't slam or she would have rocked the whole store. Her attitude and the way she stomped reminded Brodie of the tornado that swept his house away—but his feet were still firmly planted on the tile floor.

Tripp peeked out from behind a stack of men's sweatpants and grinned. "I'm glad I don't own the farm."

"Some brothers you and Knox are, leaving me to deal with her alone," he grumbled as he moved on down the aisle and tossed a toothbrush and deodorant into his cart.

Tripp pushed his full cart toward Brodie. "I'd rather deal

with another tornado as with that bag of pure meanness. She is meaner than a whole den of Texas rattlesnakes."

Knox came from the end of another aisle and put a tube of toothpaste in his cart. "I'd say she's meaner than a class five tornado."

"Combine them and you might have her down to rights," Brodie growled. "We've got to be at the Paradise by supper, so y'all better forget about Audrey Tucker and get busy."

"Hard to forget something that caused enough sparks to set this store on fire," Knox teased. "If she wasn't the enemy, I'd say that there is chemistry between you two."

"Bad sparks, not good ones, and the electricity you saw was anger, not attraction." Brodie continued to fill his cart with toiletries and changed the subject. "They don't have my shaving lotion, so I'm going to grow a beard."

Knox made his way slowly down the aisle, tossing in several more items. "Not me. I'll use the cheaper stuff until we can get to the mall in Wichita Falls. I'm afraid Audrey might like beards and go after me to get to you."

"Hand me a bottle of that stuff you are getting," Brodie barked. "It'll do until I can go to the mall."

"Smart choice," Tripp said. "Can you believe we are going to live in an old brothel? Mother would think that was a hoot."

"It's just until we figure out what we're going to do," Brodie reminded him, "but I agree with you. Mother wouldn't only be glad that we have a place to live but that we have found a big family."

"It'd be a safe place for you to hide from Audrey. All the sisters will gang up on her if she even sets foot on the property. But the flip side is that Aunt Bernie is going to continue to fix you up with dates. How many are you up to now?" Tripp asked.

Brodie groaned and held up five fingers.

"She sets them up, and our brother here knocks them down. He's turning into the heartbreaker of Montague County," Knox said.

"Yeah, right. One date with each woman does not a heartbreaker make," Brodie declared.

Chapter 2

"I WISH THAT THE tornado would have left the Callahans' house standing and pulled up every tree in his orchards and tossed them into the Red River." Audrey growled as she slammed a cabinet door so hard that it rattled the salt and pepper shakers in the middle of the table. "Maybe then, he would sell his place to me."

Hettie made herself a whiskey sour and started across the room. "I sure enough wish the same thing. I want the farms reunited before I die, but then I get to thinking about Walter. He's getting old and talking about retiring. You are working double time while he's on his two-week vacation in Florida. What would you do without him if he moved down there permanently?"

"I don't want to even think about that," Audrey groaned. "Walter was around before the original farm was split, wasn't he?"

Hettie turned around and nodded. "So was I, and we were both younger and stronger in those days."

"I miss Walter, but he deserves a couple of weeks off to visit his family. I don't even want to think about him not working for me. But now, let's talk about your drinking.

Isn't that your second whiskey sour? That stuff is going to kill you."

Hettie set her thin mouth in a firm line and narrowed her eyes. "Everybody has to die for even a chance to get into heaven. I'm past ninety years old, girl. My bones are bad, and my liver is already shot. I'm not good for much other than cooking a pot of beans to put on the supper table. Before my precious Amos went on to heaven, he and I always shared a little nip before bedtime. He said that it made me spicier in the bedroom. You and my whiskey and my friend Bitsy is all I've got left, so don't gripe at me."

Audrey grabbed a beer from the refrigerator and followed Hettie outside. She plopped down in one of the two rocking chairs on the front porch and used her foot to set it in motion. "The family at the Paradise all rallied around them after the tornado passed. Brodie and his brothers are going to live there until they rebuild, and Bernie will probably have them all married off before they finish a new house. Once that's done and they've put down roots, we'll never get that land."

She didn't tell her aunt about the encounter at the dollar store in Nocona or that every time she was around Brodie, she felt more alive than she had in her entire life.

Hettie clenched her teeth together. Her nose wrinkled up like she was smelling what a skunk left behind. "I don't like Bernie. I'm nice to her in church because Jesus wouldn't like for me to speak my mind in a holy place, but if we both go to heaven, the good Lord better put a barbed-wire fence between us."

"Tell me again why just the mention of Bernie makes fire shoot out of your eyes," Audrey said.

"She drove into town draggin' that travel trailer behind her truck and lives behind the Paradise. Any place that starts out as a brothel still has bad juju in it," Hettie said.

Audrey took a long drink of her beer and then argued, "It's been way more than a hundred years since the Paradise was a brothel."

"But it still has a name. If someone talks about this place," she waved her free hand around to take in the whole farm, "they say the Walter Tucker place. But the Paradise sounds like anyone going there is getting a taste of heaven."

"Maybe the men who visited that place thought they were," Audrey chuckled. "But that can't be the only reason you are crossways with Bernie."

"Nope, it's not," Hettie said through clenched teeth. "She owned a bar up in Oklahoma"—she snarled—"and then she comes down here and takes over everything she can in my church, even the jobs I've had for years. She might have lived around these parts at one time years ago, but I've been here my whole life. My precious Amos, four children, and more recently my last living brother, Ira, are all out at the Spanish Fort Cemetery," Hettie snapped. "If anyone should be the queen of Spanish Fort, it's me, not Bernie! Me and Walter are the oldest folks in town. We should have the crowns, and people should be..." she rambled on so long she lost her breath. "She can't think that she's getting a ticket to heaven because she's on the quilting committee and gets to bring the flowers for the foyer every month."

Audrey had heard enough and chose that moment to try to change the subject. "The way your brothers acted with each other makes me wonder how you could be friends with both of them and not take sides."

Hettie took a sip of her whiskey. "There was just the three of us, and I was already married when that woman Clarice came into their lives. I told them how it was going to be and what would happen if they didn't get their heads out of her butt, but would they listen? Oh, hell no! To keep the family intact they both needed to give up Clarice. She didn't like either of them—not really."

"Then why was she—"

Hettie held up a palm. "She had always been what you kids today call a drama queen. She liked the attention, and she was almost past the marryin' age. Back then women who were thirty…" she slid a judging look over at her great-niece.

"Hey, now!" Audrey held up a palm to protest. "Things are different today."

"And not for the better," Hettie said. "Anyway, Frank ended up with her and she made a miserable wife, as you well know since you spent so much time here. I told them I would not choose sides. I would visit with both of them, and I would leave if either started talking hateful about the other one."

Audrey turned up her bottle of beer and drank about a fourth of it before coming up for air. "I guess I got my strength from you. Mama was wishy-washy, and Daddy was out with his long-distance driving more than he was ever home."

"Yep, you did," Hettie finished the last of her drink. "All this talk makes me dry. I might have to make another one."

"Aunt Hettie!" Audrey scolded.

Her bony finger shot up and pointed straight at Audrey's nose. "Don't you scold me. I'm old, and I would have told Jesus to come get me years ago if I didn't want to live long enough to see these two farms put back together before I step off this mortal earth."

"Evidently, you are too sassy for heaven, and the devil don't want you for fear you'll take over his domain. You might live to be as old as Methuselah," Audrey told her.

When she smiled, Hettie's wrinkles deepened, and her eyes disappeared. "Be patient, my child. I've prayed for this to happen, and it will. Never underestimate God's power, and when it happens, if there's any life left in me, I'm going to the retirement village where Bitsy is. I miss her so much."

"Did you ever ask God to send Bernie away?" Audrey asked.

The smile disappeared. "I did, but He said no, that she had been sent to Spanish Fort to test me."

Audrey turned up her beer and took several gulps. "How is God testing you?"

"I'm still trying to figure that out, but if He expects me to learn to love her, it ain't goin' to happen. There's some things I won't do even for God."

"Did you ever learn to love Grandma Clarice?" Audrey asked.

"That woman was always sick with something. That's why you spent more time with me and Amos than you did with her," Hettie answered.

"But your farm was right next door, so I ran back and forth," Audrey reminded her.

"Yes, you did, and I'm tired of talking about those people. While you went to town, I sat right here and enjoyed a lovely sunset and the fact that God sent that storm to take out the house next door. That's the first step in getting what we want." Hettie was quiet for a few seconds and then went on as if she hadn't said she didn't want to talk about her kinfolk anymore. "I remember doing this with Ira and Frank when we were teenagers, back before they let a woman destroy their lives and relationship. The sun has gone down, but it's a blessing that this place is untouched and we can still sit on the porch and visit after the afternoon we just had. It's a sign, I'm telling you."

"Yes, it is," Audrey agreed. "Do you like Bernie even less than you did Clarice for tearing apart your family?"

"Twice as bad as I did that evil woman, or her worthless cousin that married Ira. My husband, your great-uncle Amos, was a wonderful man. Ira and Frank were both smart, kindhearted, and generous, but neither one of them had a lick of sense when he came to women," Hettie answered with pure venom in her tone. "Those two women caused my brothers to stay apart until the end of their lives. When

Clarice died, Ira and Frank might have made up, but Maude kept them apart. Then Ira and Maude both died in the car wreck and the farm went to their granddaughter, Zelda, and you know what happened. We have to be patient. God will answer our prayers in due time."

Audrey finished off her beer and set the empty bottle on the porch.

"I'm going in to make another whiskey sour, and I won't be hearing a word from you. Do you want me to bring you another beer?"

"Yes, please," Audrey answered.

Audrey was tall compared to the rest of her family, but she was still only five feet five inches. Hettie didn't reach five feet, and her two brothers, Ira and Frank, were only slightly taller than she was. Her dark-brown eyes were the exact color as Audrey's, and she wore her long gray hair in two braids that wrapped around her head like a crown.

"Patient, my butt," Audrey muttered. "I want to dance around in the wet grass like a witch and call up another tornado to wipe out the rest of Brodie's place."

That's what you are saying, but why do you really want him to leave Spanish Fort? the pesky voice in her head screamed.

"Yes, I do," Audrey whispered. "He's dating every woman Bernie can drag up, and she's never asked if I'd like her to fix me up with anyone. She won't even nod at me after church services, much less speak to me. Not that I want to go out with any of those Callahan brothers, but..."

"Who are you talking to?" Hettie asked as she backed

out the door with a beer in one hand and what looked like a double whiskey sour in the other.

"Myself," Audrey answered and took the beer from Hettie's hand.

The elderly lady groaned when she sat down in the rocking chair. "Trying to talk yourself out of something or into something?"

"I'm not sure."

"Well, be careful. When you are arguing with yourself, you are about to mess up. If you just sit back and wait, you'll find that things usually work out the way you want."

I don't see that happening, Audrey thought, but she didn't say anything.

———

Brodie took stock of the way everything was laid out in the room that was twice the size of his bedroom in the house that was now scattered over northern Texas and southern Oklahoma. The bed was to his left, with a nightstand on one side and a chest of drawers on the other. His new inexpensive shaving lotion and other toiletries were lined up on a dresser to his right. He stood in the middle of the room and blinked several times. Nothing disappeared so this was real, not a dream.

A very distinctive smell of marinara sauce and chocolate floated up the staircase. His mother always said that everything looked better after a good, solid meal. Thinking about her brought tears to his eyes, but he didn't let them fall. She had been born with not only a silver spoon but a huge trust fund that had been handed down from selling cotton in World War I. Then she married the owner of an oil company, and together they invested well. But down deep, Jolene Callahan was a country girl who didn't care about money or prestige. She was happiest when she was digging in the dirt and had passed that down to Brodie—along with a big inheritance.

He hung his new jeans and shirts in the closet and put away his underwear, then crossed the room to look out the French doors onto the balcony that surrounded three sides of the house. He wondered which lady had lived in this room when the Paradise was a brothel and tried to imagine a time when Spanish Fort was actually a booming town that thrived on the cattle drives.

Tripp startled him when he said, "This is pretty dang nice living quarters."

Brodie whipped around to see both of his brothers standing in the doorway. "Don't get too comfortable. It's not a forever thing."

"Have you seen the rest of the house?" Knox asked. "I could so make this a forever thing."

Tripp said, "Right now, we'd better go to supper. I smell something Italian cooking."

"And chocolate," Knox said with a nod.

"We're acting like we really are homeless," Tripp said.

"Maybe so," Knox answered, "but this is a whole lot better than staying in my travel trailer with y'all two claiming floor space to put down sleeping bags."

"What sleeping bags?" Brodie asked as he led the way out into the hallway and then started downstairs. "The tornado took those, too."

"Then I guess you'd be sleeping on the floor with nothing," Knox said.

"Yep, it's better than that," Tripp agreed. "And we get a hot meal here, too."

Brodie and his brothers had been at the Paradise several times since they'd moved to Spanish Fort. Sunday dinner was a family tradition, and the house was always full. The vibe in the kitchen and dining room wasn't the same as when the whole family was there on Sunday. The noise level alone had dropped from eleven on a scale of one to ten to maybe a three.

Joe Clay came out of the living room and motioned the three of them to follow him to the dining room. "Come on in and have a seat. Tertia and Noah are about to put supper on the table, but Mary Jane has already poured the sweet tea, so have a swallow or two while we wait."

"Thank you again for everything," Brodie said as he took a seat.

"Yes," Tripp and Knox said in unison.

Knox patted Joe Clay on the shoulder. "This is like a luxury hotel."

Mary Jane came through the archway into the dining room with a basket of steaming-hot rolls in her hands. "We're glad you like your rooms. Make yourself at home. You have been in and out, so you know where the laundry is. Kitchen is always open to whoever wants to cook. I'm in my writing cave five days a week, but I do take an hour lunch break, and Joe Clay brings me a cup of coffee at ten thirty if he's free."

"We are very capable of taking care of ourselves, and we all know our way around the kitchen. We'd be glad to cook every morning," Knox told her. "We're just grateful for a place to sleep. Most days we'll be gone right after breakfast unless it rains. There's a lot of clean up to be done at the farm."

Noah brought in a huge pan of lasagna. "We'll pitch in and help when we can."

"Thanks," Brodie said, still in awe of the fact that such a huge, adopted family had come with his biological father.

Tertia, the sister with brown curly hair and aqua eyes, brought a tray with different kinds of cheese and pickles to the table, and Mary Jane followed her with a bowl of salad. When the two women took a chair, Mary Jane nodded toward Joe Clay.

Brodie had been around long enough to know what that meant, so he bowed his head. Joe Clay said a short grace, ending with, "Thank you, Lord, for keeping all our boys safe through the storm. Amen."

"Amen," Brodie muttered under his breath.

"Boys upstairs?" Tertia's tone said she was teasing.

"For the first time," Mary Jane said.

"When the girls were growing up, house rules said that no boys were allowed upstairs," Joe Clay explained.

Bernie pushed open the back door and came inside like a

whirlwind with her little chihuahua, Pepper, straining at his leash. "Am I in time for supper?"

"Yes, you are," Mary Jane answered. "Turn Pepper loose and grab a plate."

Brodie did not roll his eyes, but it took a lot of effort and determination. "Miz Bernie, you come on in and sit down. I'll get another plate," he said.

"Why, thank you, Brodie," she said. "You're the reason I came over tonight, besides the fact that I'm starving and Tertia makes wonderful lasagna. I have set you up with Linda Massey for next Friday night. I just know she's the very woman for you. She'll make a good farmer's wife. She's already a vegan—"

"Well, Brodie is an organic farmer," Knox butted in. "That is very different from vegan. And I'm sorry, Miz Bernie, but we'll be working from daylight to dark out at the farm. We need Brodie every single day for the next few weeks."

"Except Sunday?" Tertia said.

"Well, then, Sunday it is," Bernie cocked her head to one side. "I'll talk to Linda and change the date to a week from this coming Sunday. You can take her to church and dinner afterward. Somewhere nice where they have vegan options on the menu. And she did mention that she only ate organically grown food, so that's what I was talking about."

With her red hair, smart-ass attitude and small build, Bernie reminded Brodie a little of Swoosie Kurtz, the actress who played a sassy, hippie-type lady in a couple of episodes of the television series *Lethal Weapon*.

"Well?" Aunt Bernie said in a no-nonsense tone and narrowed her eyes at Brodie when he stood up and held the chair for her.

"What he's trying to tell you, Aunt Bernie, is that he isn't interested in blind dates," Tertia answered for him.

Bernie sat down and tipped her chin up a notch. "Of course he is. He's too busy to meet women on his own, so I'm helping him. Linda is excited about going out with him. She's a good woman and a perfect fit for Brodie. Everyone knows I'm the matchmaking guru of Montague County. I found all you girls a suitable husband—"

"Thank you for that." Noah's brown eyes lit up when he grinned.

Bernie shot a half-mean look across the table. "I got y'all together with reverse psychology. Tertia never was one to listen to good advice. I forbade her to fall in love with you, and since she always did the opposite of what I said, it worked out beautifully."

"She still doesn't listen," Noah teased and then leaned over and kissed his wife on the cheek.

"You *better* be nice to me after that comment," Tertia said.

Joe Clay passed the basket of bread around the table. "I got to admit that I was glad to have seven sons-in-law and then for you boys to show up at Christmas. For years, I felt like the only rooster at a coyote convention."

Mary Jane patted him on the cheek. "Poor baby. Changing the subject now. Tripp, you've said that you work in leather, making saddles for the most part?"

"Yes, ma'am," Tripp answered. "I worked for an old guy in Bandera when I was growing up. He kind of mentored me in the art, and it's more of a hobby right now. I wanted to take over his business when he sold it, but my mother insisted I get a college degree and go to work for Dad in the oil company."

"The Johnsons are trying to sell their house just east of Luna and Shane's convenience store. It's small. Just two bedrooms and one bath. Probably less than a thousand square feet, and it's got a lot of problems. You could tear it down if remodeling it would be too big a job, but the barn out back would make a wonderful place for you to do your work and sell your products. It's sturdy and has a good roof, but you'd have to do some work to turn it into a workspace and a store."

Knox took out a second helping of lasagna. "You've got a carpenter right here."

"I'd just like to see some kind of business go in that old barn," Noah said. "Along with the old store where Bo and Maverick have their music business, that barn is part of the history of Spanish Fort."

"Ask Mama about this town," Tertia said. "She's written several historical romances about the Paradise when it was a brothel, back in the cattle run days. They stopped here on their way to Dodge City."

"What's the attraction of the old barn?" Tripp asked.

"Justin Boots got its start right here in Spanish Fort," Mary Jane answered. "I couldn't find any absolute details about the barn, but it's been standing there for at least a hundred years. Wouldn't it be something if you carried on the tradition of leather works here."

"And while we're talking about jobs"—Joe Clay grabbed another hot roll and then sent them around the table again—"Knox, you are welcome to use any of my tools out in the barn when you guys start to rebuild."

"Thank you," Knox said.

Brodie took four gulps of tea but didn't get the lump in his throat to go down. His mother had told the boys the stories of their parentage only a few days before she died. Since college, Tripp had been working as the CEO of their father's small oil corporation. Knox had won the battle with their folks about college—opting to go straight into carpentry work. They had all thought that they were orphans until Brodie decided to make a trip to north Texas and find his biological father. He never expected the family would take all three of the Callahan brothers in like they had or that he would find a working organic farm for sale.

"I might not need a room in the new house if I start up a leather goods business," Tripp sounded excited. "I could make a small apartment in the back of the barn. I could not only build saddles, boots, belts, purses, and all kinds of things, but I could also do boot repair."

"You would have a place to live as well as a store to sell your goods," Knox told him. "But after a while you might need or want something bigger than a little apartment. When that time comes, what kind of house would you like?"

"A log cabin," Tripp answered.

"You better make your log cabin big enough for a family, because when I get Brodie to the front of the altar, I will begin looking for a wife for you," Bernie said.

Knox chuckled.

Bernie pointed a bony finger at him. "Don't laugh, young man. I'll be on the lookout for you as soon as we get your brothers married off. I'm only working for one of you at a time, starting with the oldest and working my way down to you!"

"Don't get in a rush, Aunt Bernie," Mary Jane said. "I like these guys being around. We can get to know them a lot better when they live here. Coming around for Sunday dinner when the whole family is here doesn't give us much time."

"Thank you," Brodie mouthed from across the table.

Mary Jane barely nodded.

"Hmmph," Bernie snorted. "There ain't a one of them getting any younger."

The emotions that ran through Brodie's mind when Tripp reached out and snatched him away from the fierce tornado winds replayed through that evening when he shut his eyes. He had gone back into the house to grab the ledgers Ira had left behind and was the last one running toward the shelter. The memory made his hands tremble just like they did when he finally collapsed on one of the two wooden benches lining the sides of the cold concrete shelter.

His eyes snapped open to get away from that clear visual branded in his head. He threw back the covers, got out of bed, and went out onto the balcony. The night air was cool and stars dotted the sky, but even gazing at them brought him no relief. He couldn't stop his hands from shaking or get rid of the tightness in his chest. He stood just outside the doors for several minutes, looking out over the land and listening to the coyotes howling in the distance. Finally, he sat down on one of the chairs and propped his bare feet on the railing.

"Mind if I join you?" Joe Clay opened the door from a couple of rooms down.

"Not at all," Brodie answered. "You having trouble sleeping, too?"

"Yep, and when I do"—Joe Clay answered and held up a bottle of whiskey—"I bring this up here and look out over the land and my life. I didn't bring glasses, but I'll share."

Brodie took it from him, tipped it up, swallowed once, and handed it back to Joe Clay. "That's the good stuff. Smooth." Strangely enough, it stilled his nerves, and breathing was easier.

Joe Clay pulled a chair over and sat down. "Still playing the events over in your mind?"

"Yes, and I've got to admit, fear of closing my eyes won't let me sleep," Brodie admitted, and told him about Tripp saving his life.

"When I saw the funnel was headed for your place, my heart nearly stopped," Joe Clay said.

Brodie tried to imagine what it would be like for a thirty-year-old son to show up on a man's doorstep at Christmas, get to know him a little by mid-March, and then stand by to watch a deadly tornado dropping down out of the sky and going right toward him. Then he thought of his mother Jolene, and what she must have felt when she found out she was pregnant and was about to be a single mother.

"Will you tell me about you and Mother?" Brodie asked.

"There's not a lot to tell," Joe Clay answered. "I was in the military and met her in a bar. She sat down beside me and bought me a drink since I was in uniform. We talked, and I bought the second and third rounds. I introduced myself, and she told me her name was Jolene. That was Friday night, and she had a room in a pretty fancy hotel. We both went our separate ways on Sunday. I can't remember the name of the song we danced to about five times, but it was about a country boy who had a night with a rich lady who was used to diamonds and lace. That was the underlying feeling I had all weekend. She had come to the city looking for a good time, and we had just that."

"Did you ever see her again?" Brodie asked.

Joe Clay shook his head. "We agreed that when we walked out of that room, we'd never look back. But that we wouldn't have regrets either. You look like I did at your age, but there's something about your mannerisms that remind me of her. Had I known that she was pregnant, I would have been a part of your life."

"She married my dad, John Callahan, when I was just

a baby, and he adopted me," Brodie said. "She had a rough time having me and was told she couldn't have any more kids. Dad was a lawyer, and he had some connections somewhere. They adopted Tripp and Knox as newborn babies when I was only two."

"I'm glad that you grew up with siblings," Joe Clay said. "And like I've said before, I'm really happy that you found me, but I'm sorry that y'all lost your parents."

"Me, too, on both issues," Brodie said. "I knew that she'd given birth to me and that my brothers were adopted from the time we could all ask questions. She told us about our biological parents just days before she died, but she didn't tell me anything other than your name and that you had mentioned you were from Nocona, Texas. That's all I knew about you."

They sat in silence as they passed the whiskey back and forth a few more times. "I grew up north of Nocona, went into the military right out of high school, and came home when I retired, but I wasn't happy. I was living in that little hotel east of town and thinking hard about reenlisting when Mary Jane knocked on my door. I'd had a big crush on her in high school," he said with a grin. "She offered me a job remodeling this house and said I could have room and board. Sounded good until I found out she had seven daughters," he chuckled. "I almost quit, but she more or less dared me to stay. I didn't even like kids, but those little girls stole my heart. You want another swig of this before I go?" He held up the whiskey bottle.

"I'm good, but thanks for telling me that much about your past."

Joe Clay stood up. "You aren't going to let the tornado make you sell out and leave, are you? I know that Audrey Tucker has been after you to let her buy the farm, but I don't want you to leave this area. I've still got a lot of making up to you to do."

Brodie shook his head. "I'm not going anywhere, and I don't think Tripp and Knox want to leave either. They aren't farmers, but they've sure been helping me a lot while they get their leather and carpentry businesses lined up."

"I'll help anyway I can," Joe Clay said.

"You already have," Brodie said, and watched him disappear down the balcony and into the room that he'd come out of a few minutes before.

Brodie had sown his wild oats in the military, and there had been more than a few one-night stands in his past. He couldn't help but wonder if sometime in the future a child would show up on his doorstep.

Chapter 3

"I MAY START GOING to church in Nocona," Hettie declared as she got into Audrey's pickup truck. "And that means you'll have to go with me, or else let me drive the old work truck. Or maybe when Walter gets home, he will take me to whatever church he goes to in Nocona."

"You are not driving any vehicle," Audrey declared.

"Then I guess after today, we'll be going to another church," Hettie said.

"Are you going to let Bernie run you out of *your* town?" Audrey asked.

"It's all in how you look at it and how you study it," Hettie answered. "When I go to the church that I've gone to my whole life, I go in with a bad spirit, and I leave with an even uglier one. Sunday services are supposed to make us happy and full of peace when we walk out the doors. I'm not feeling that anymore, so maybe if I go to another place, I won't be grouchy for hours afterward."

Audrey backed out of the driveway and drove to the end of the dirt road, then turned north toward Spanish Fort. "Here all this time I thought you were in a bad mood because you didn't have a whiskey sour to drink during services."

"Who says I don't?" Hettie pulled a flask out of her big, black purse.

"What…when…how…" Audrey stammered.

"If Bernie ain't there, I don't use it. If she is, then I make a trip to the ladies' room about halfway through the sermon. Most of the time, I'm sitting on the pew trying to figure out ways to do justifiable homicide anyway, so all that stuff about loving your neighbor is hittin' a brick wall. Everyone understands that an old woman has a bladder the size of a thimble and doesn't even bat an eye when I shuffle off to the bathroom. But don't worry, darlin', I also keep these," she dug around in her purse and brought out a small bag of hard peppermint candy.

Audrey drove to the end of the road and turned left. The church was only a block down the road and the parking lot had already filled up. She finally found a spot and was busy lining up her truck between the yellow lines when Brodie pulled in beside her. He and his two brothers got out and, without so much as a nod her way, headed toward the church.

"You are welcome to help me get to the ladies' room if things get too rough in there," Hettie whispered. "A little sip of whiskey isn't as big of a sin as—"

Audrey butted in before Hettie could finish. "I might take you up on that."

"Anytime," Hettie grinned. "We'll sit here for a minute. As long as that man's legs are, he'll make it inside in just a minute or two."

"Okay," Audrey said with a nod, and stared at his strut and the way he filled out his jeans. A vision popped into her head of Brodie with only a towel slung around his hips. Her pulse kicked up a notch, and her breath came out in short bursts.

"Too bad Brodie is shirttail kin to Bernie," Hettie said as she opened the truck door. "He's one fine-looking feller."

"Forbidden fruit," Audrey muttered as she got out of the truck and looped her arm in Hettie's.

"What was that?" Hettie asked.

"Nothing," Audrey answered.

"Do you need a little nip before we go inside?" Hettie asked.

Audrey considered the idea seriously but finally shook her head. "Those people are not going to drive either one of us to drinking."

Hettie chuckled and turned up the flask. "Speak for yourself."

A credenza covered most of the wall on the left side of the foyer with an arrangement of pastel-colored silk flowers in a white basket. After Easter, Bernie would likely change the centerpiece to a vase of red roses for Mother's Day. The ladies' room door was beyond that. A coatrack and a blue velvet wingback chair were on the other side of the men's bathroom door.

"I used to be in charge of fixin' them flowers up for the holidays or seasons, and then Bernie told Parker she could take care of them," Hettie growled.

"Why did he do that?" Audrey asked.

"The family out there at the Paradise have lots of silk flowers they've used for weddings and their Christmas event, so it would save the church money," Hettie answered.

"If you wanted the job, you should have offered to buy the flowers yourself," Audrey told her.

Hettie sat down in one of the chairs. "Parker is all about saving money so we can give more to the three missionaries the church supports. Bernie used the flowers to get her toe in the door, and now she's on the cookbook and the quilting committees. I bet she didn't even go to services up there in Oklahoma. I need to rest a minute."

Audrey glanced through the double doors that were open wide into the sanctuary. "We'll have trouble finding a seat if you rest very long. Looks like we've got a full house this morning."

Hettie got up with a long sigh. "Folks ain't here for a spiritual lesson. They're here to be able to talk about the tornado before and after services. Or to give thanks that the tornado didn't tear up their houses, like it did the Callahans'."

"So, you've learned that Brodie's place was the only one that got wiped out?" Audrey asked as she looped her arm into Hettie's and led her down the long center aisle.

"Yep, and he's here to offer up gratitude that his orchards and gardens didn't get hit. Tornadoes are good about just taking whatever they want and leaving the rest behind. One time I saw a convenience store with no outside walls left, but those little lightweight boxes of pudding and full bottles of wine were still sitting on the shelves," Hettie said.

"Sweet Lord!" Audrey gasped.

"What?" Hettie whispered.

"Come right in and have a seat," the preacher said loudly. "Looks like we are a little crowded today, but there's room for two beside the Callahan brothers. I bet they saved them just for you ladies."

Hettie stood to one side and motioned for Audrey to go before her. "I need to sit on the end because I'm definitely going to need to escape," she said out the corner of her mouth, "and I don't want to crawl over you."

"But…" Audrey started to argue.

Hettie nodded toward her left. Audrey saw that they would be sitting right in front of another whole row of the Paradise family, complete with Bernie. And more families were in the two pews behind them. She had a choice—walk out of church when Parker was already behind the lectern or else spend a miserable half hour sitting beside Brodie. The latter won, and she eased down beside her enemy.

She kept her eyes straight ahead, but there was no denying that sparks were dancing around the church like happy little Easter bunnies. Of all the men in the entire state of Texas, why did she have an attraction to Brodie. Life wasn't fair. It was a four-letter word worse than any curse word in the dictionary. And she was definitely taking a bathroom break with her Aunt Hettie in the middle of the sermon.

"You kind of got stuck between a rock and a hard place, didn't you?" Knox whispered at the dinner table that afternoon.

"More like between a boulder and the back forty of hell," Brodie answered.

"Which one was I?" Knox asked with a chuckle.

"You were the boulder because you wouldn't scoot down an inch so I wouldn't have to literally rub shoulders with Audrey," Brodie told him.

"I guess that means she was hell?" Knox continued to chuckle.

"Yep," Brodie agreed.

"Can you believe that Hettie sat with our family?" Bernie said from the other end of the table.

"I can believe that they didn't have a choice unless they wanted to stand at the back or sit on the floor in the center aisle," Mary Jane answered. "I'm sure they didn't want to be recognized when they came into the sanctuary after everyone had sat down and gotten quiet."

"Aunt Bernie, I've got a question. Why haven't you tried to hook Brodie up with Audrey?" Remy asked.

"I'd rather eat dirt," Bernie snapped, and pointed her finger at Remy and then whipped it around to aim it at Brodie. "This is not reverse psychology talking to you. Audrey Tucker is the only woman in the whole state of Texas that I forbid you to get involved with. If you did, I would have to be nice to Hettie, and there will be snow cone stands and air-conditioning in the devil's back forty before I do that." She dropped her hand and glared at Knox and Tripp. "That goes for both of you, too. Audrey is off-limits to all of you."

"Yes, ma'am," Knox said. "She's got too much fire for me anyway."

Brodie shoved a fork full of mashed potatoes in his mouth, so he didn't have to answer Bernie. The devil really would install air-conditioning before Brodie Callahan let anyone tell him who he could or could not date. Aunt Bernie did not hold that privilege in the palm of her bony little hand.

"Hey, all you guys," Remy raised his voice to get everyone's attention. "I thought maybe since it's a nice sunny day and it's supposed to rain tomorrow that all us menfolk could get together this afternoon and clean up Brodie's property."

God bless you, Remy Baxter, Brodie thought.

"That's a great idea," Joe Clay said. "With all of us working, we might get it finished by dark. I'll hitch up the flatbed, and we can dump all the junk we pick up in the landfill on the back side of the Paradise property. There's a deep gully back there that I've been trying to get filled in for a couple of years now."

"I could bring my cattle trailer," Remy offered.

"Thank you all so much," Brodie said.

"And us sisters can have an afternoon with Mama and Aunt Bernie at the mall in Wichita Falls," Ursula said. "We need to shop for Easter dresses."

"And a 'my first Easter' outfit for Clayton," Endora added.

An eight-foot folding table had been set up at the end of the really long dining room table to accommodate all twenty of the family, and with so many conversations going on at once, it was easy for Brodie to block everything out. He finished his dinner and then sat back to think about the next step after his land was cleaned up. A house would have to be built eventually, but taking care of the crops would slow down that process for sure.

"Daddy, y'all guys can go on as soon as you finish eating," Endora said. "We'll take care of cleaning up the kitchen. Be sure to leave the keys to the van. We'll need it if we're all going shopping together."

"The keys are on the hook by the back door." Joe Clay pushed back his chair, stood up, and then bent down and kissed Mary Jane on the forehead. "Looks like we're all done here, so let's get headed out to the farm. And y'all girls have a good time at the mall."

That word, *Daddy*, stuck in Brodie's mind. He had more right to call Joe Clay Daddy or Dad than any of the girls. The seven sisters did not belong to Joe Clay by blood.

You had a Dad that did not share a drop of DNA with you, but he raised you just like Joe Clay has done with these girls, the pesky voice in his head scolded him.

He was still thinking about his little bout with jealousy when he, Joe Clay, and the seven brothers-in-law arrived at the mess the tornado left in its wake. Would Joe Clay even want him to call him Dad? Would things be simpler if they just kept their relationship as good friends? That was more than Brodie had ever thought he could have with Joe Clay when he met the man for the first time. Of course, he would have never believed that he and his two brothers would be accepted by such a large family, either.

"Brodie Callahan!" Knox's voice brought him back to reality. "Where's your mind? Remy just asked if you wanted to save any pieces of the boards."

"Sorry about that," Brodie raised up and wiped sweat from his brow with a bandanna he pulled from his hip pocket. "No, I don't want to keep anything."

"Toss it all!" Knox yelled.

A movement out across the barbed-wire fence caught Brodie's eye. He thought it might be a deer coming around to trample his strawberry field, so he took a couple of steps that way. Then he realized it was a person and picked up the pace and jogged to the barbed-wire fence.

"What are you doing here?" he asked Audrey.

"Aunt Hettie wanted to come out and see what was left of her brother's house," Audrey answered, and tipped up her chin in a defiant gesture. "We didn't expect to see all y'all cleaning up the place this afternoon. But since you are here, my offer to buy the place still stands. Like I told you before, I won't even lower my price because the house is gone."

Brodie looked toward Audrey's house and sure enough saw Hettie slowly walking away and leaning heavily on a cane. "Why do you want it so badly?" he asked.

"I already told you," she answered.

"That's why your aunt wants the place," Brodie said. "Why would you want to deal with an organic farm?"

"Maybe I want to win this battle with you," she answered.

"Keep dreaming," Brodie told her. "I'm more stubborn than you'll be in your entire lifetime."

"We'll see." She turned and walked away without even looking back over her shoulder.

Brodie turned around to see Tripp at his elbow. "I don't need backing up. I can handle Audrey on my own."

"We would have quit cleaning up if we found out that you'd gone and sold out to her," Tripp said at his elbow. Tripp raised an eyebrow. "Well?"

"I'm not selling my place," Brodie declared. "Not now. Not ever. It's what I've dreamed of doing since I was a kid and Mother had that little organic garden in the backyard."

"She loved working in that. No one would have ever believed that she had a trust fund big enough to choke a full-grown Angus bull," Tripp said.

"Mother was her own person," Brodie said past the lump in his throat. "I'm living proof of that."

"Yes, you are, and so are me and Knox," Tripp said with a sigh. "The flatbed, my truck, and Knox's are all loaded, so we're going to the landfill with it all. The guys are finishing up by filling your truck and Remy's with the last of it. With the family's help, we've gotten a week's worth of work done in half a day. And brother, that woman is going to be the death of you."

"Joe Clay says that family is everything, and Tripp, that

woman isn't a match for me when it comes to being stubborn. She might as well get prepared to lose this war," Brodie said as he turned around and headed back toward the empty spot where his house used to be.

Tripp patted him on the back. "Good to hear, and I got to admit that I'm loving this big family. Not just for the help but for the fellowship."

"Me, too," Brodie whispered.

"Done in time for supper and Sunday night services," Parker, Endora's husband, yelled and then threw the very last shingle over into Brodie's truck. "And that finishes the job."

"Does that mean we have to go to church again tonight?" Tripp said out the corner of his mouth.

"Think about all we've gotten done today," Brodie answered. "Sitting on a pew for an hour is a small price to pay, and also shows respect. Plus, it's a way of giving thanks for this family."

"I understand all that, but I didn't sleep too well last night," Tripp said. "I was looking forward to a little nap when we get back to the Paradise."

"Too late for sleep now," Brodie told him. "I promise to kick you in the leg if you snore in church."

"Thank you so much for that," Tripp said in his most sarcastic voice.

"Hey, before everyone splits and runs, I want to thank you again for all this hard work," Brodie yelled out across the yard.

"You are welcome," Parker said. "Will I see you guys at church?"

"You bet," Tripp answered. "Wouldn't miss it."

"You better sit up straight and listen to the sermon after that lie," Brodie whispered.

Tripp patted his brother on the shoulder again. "I will because I'll be watching you and Audrey battle without saying a single word to each other. The looks that you give each other could fry the horns off Lucifer. That'll be so much fun that I'll forget all about taking a nap."

"I'm going to win this war," Brodie declared again. "She'll get tired of messing with me after a while."

Chapter 4

"THE NICE THING ABOUT Sunday night services is that Bernie keeps her butt at home," Hettie said as she slid out of the passenger's seat of Audrey's truck.

Audrey pointed toward the three Callahan brothers walking across the parking lot just like they'd done that morning. "You might get some relief, but I don't."

"They've been in Spanish Fort right at three months, and they haven't ever come on Sunday night, not one time," Hettie said. "Bring my cane around here. I might beat on them with it."

"They're here to aggravate me," Audrey said with a long sigh.

"The parkin' lot is only about half-full. That means there will be lots of empty pews. We will sneak in and sit on the back pew," Hettie said.

Audrey handed the cane to Hettie and walked slowly beside her. "Brodie is so stubborn that I feel like I'm losing the war with him."

"Maybe so, but going down with a slingshot in your hand is better than lying down and giving up," Hettie said as she entered the church. "Well, ain't that the luck!"

"What?" Audrey asked.

"Look who's on the back pew," Hettie hissed.

Audrey glanced around the edge of the double doors, and sure enough Brodie, Tripp, and Knox were sitting side by side just inside. "I'd turn around and go home, but that would mean he would win," she whispered.

Hettie let out a sigh that could have been heard halfway to the Pearly Gates.

"If you want to go back home, I'll bite the bullet and let him win," Audrey said.

Hettie pulled herself up to her full height. "And let that hussy Bernie win? No, I will *not*."

"What's that about Bernie?" Audrey asked.

"See that mop of dyed red hair up there on the third pew? That's Bernie, and Mary Jane and Joe Clay are right beside her. They never come to Sunday night services, but they're here now to test the Jesus in me."

Audrey suppressed a giggle. "Did you bring your flask?"

"Nope, I left it at home because they aren't supposed to be here," Hettie groaned.

"I guess the Jesus in you is really about to get tested," Audrey said.

Hettie shot her a dirty look. "Let's go home."

Before Audrey could answer, she caught Brodie looking over his shoulder right at her. Their eyes locked, and she could feel the chemistry between them. Whatever it was—like, love, or hate—the electricity was hot and fiery. But she was not going to let the sparks that lit up the room get between her and buying his farm. And there was no way she was going to leave the church now that he had seen her. That would be letting him mark up a win. She raised her fingertips to her lips, pasted on a fake smile, and blew him a kiss.

His eyes widened, and he quickly turned around.

"One for me," she whispered.

"What was that?" Hettie asked.

Audrey looped her arm into Hettie's and led her down the center aisle. "That was firing round one of the cannon. I feel confident that I rattled Brodie. We're not letting the Callahans, or Bernie, or any of their other shirttail kinfolks run us off."

"I'll need a couple of whiskey sours when I get home," Hettie said in a low voice.

"Me, too." Audrey could feel Brodie's eyes on her as she and her great-aunt walked down the center aisle, so she put a little extra swing in her hips.

———

Brodie couldn't take his eyes off Audrey, not even when she sat down on the end of a pew about halfway up the aisle. He had always been attracted to brunettes with brown eyes, but there was no way he could ever let whatever it was between them get in the way of him hanging on to his land. Not even a tornado had the power to wipe his dream away, and Audrey Tucker was surely not that mean or dangerous.

"Don't let her get to you," Knox whispered.

"I'm doing my best," Brodie said.

Silence filled the sanctuary when Parker took his place behind the lectern. "Let's all turn to page six in our hymnal and sing, 'Love Lifted Me.'"

Knox elbowed Brodie. "Maybe this is a warning. If she can't get the land any other way, she'll marry you."

"When tractors fly," Brodie snapped.

When the song ended, Parker read the parable of the Good Samaritan from the book of Luke. Then he closed the Bible and looked out over the congregation. "Loving our neighbors isn't always an easy job, but Jesus said we need to do it."

Brodie tried to listen, but pretty soon all he heard was the buzz of Parker's deep voice and a few amens from up close to the front pews. He could easily love all the Paradise families—all seven of his half sisters had accepted him better than he'd ever hoped they would. Credit for that could be given to Mary Jane, who was the fairest person he had ever met. But to love Hettie Morris and Audrey Tucker? He would rather be like the chief priests in the parable who left the poor man by the side of the road to die.

Knox poked him on the arm when services ended.

When Brodie realized that Parker was closing with prayer, he bowed his head, but his mind was still on the idea of how much eternal trouble he would be in if he couldn't love all of his neighbors. Parker's amen at the end was followed with a hearty echo from the congregation, and people began to stand up all around him. He had barely made it to his feet when Linda Massey appeared in front of him. She was a tall blond with crystal-clear blue eyes. The kind of trophy woman that most men would have loved to have hanging on their arm, but there was no electricity between the two of them—not even when she put on her best flirty smile.

"I'm so excited about our date next Sunday," she said. "Where are we going?"

"I've got two places in mind, but I want it to be a surprise," Brodie said.

"I love surprises," she almost squealed.

"Great," Brodie said. "See you then."

She patted him on the cheek. "I'll look forward to it all week."

"So, you've got a date with Brodie?" Audrey's voice cut through all the noise.

Linda whipped around, crossed her arms over her chest, and narrowed her eyes at Audrey, who was right behind her. "Yes, I do. Were you eavesdropping on our conversation?"

"Nope," Audrey answered with half a shrug. "I could care less who you date. I hope you like long conversations about organic farming."

"Oh, honey…" Linda flipped her hair over her shoulder and glared at Audrey. "I could listen to his deep drawl read the dictionary." She turned back to Brodie. "Miz Bernie has my number if you want to call and talk anytime this week." Her high-heeled shoes on the wood floor sounded like the rat-a-tat-tat of a snare drum as she headed outside.

"Good luck," Audrey said. "She's a clinger. She made a trip to Wichita Falls to try on wedding dresses after the second date with the last guy she went out with. He works for me, and I'll be glad to share his phone number if you want to verify that."

"Why would you do that?" Brodie asked.

"If I don't get your farm, I don't want her to be my neighbor. After tonight's sermon, I might not get past the front gates of heaven if I have to love that woman," Audrey answered.

Bernie wedged her way through the crowd until she was standing between Audrey and Brodie. "Don't listen to her. Linda is a sweet woman and holds several positions on church committees."

"Why are you letting Bernie fix you up with dates?" Hettie growled. "Seems to me that with your good looks, you could find your own women."

Bernie's expression looked like she could fry Hettie on the spot, leaving nothing but a couple of long braids left on the church floor. She was only a few inches from Hettie's nose when she turned around. "You stay out of this, Hettie."

"If you keep up this pushy attitude with them, they'll head for the hills before summer is done, which would suit me just fine," Hettie said, and pushed Bernie to one side so she could pass her.

Bernie bowed up to the woman, put her hands on Hettie's shoulders, and shoved her against the end of the pew. Hettie regained her balance and hit Bernie on the shoulder with her cane.

"That's enough," Ursula got between the elderly women.

"You are both in church. If you want to duke it out, take it out in the parking lot."

Audrey took Hettie by the arm. "Let's go home."

"And don't come back," Bernie hissed.

Hettie whipped around and raised her cane. "The likes of you will never run me out of *my* church. I was here long before you left your bar and came to my town with your dyed red hair."

Ursula draped an arm around Bernie's shoulders. "Let it go. Take the higher ground."

"Not today," Bernie snapped and glared at Hettie. "I'm a scrapper. If you ever hit me again, I will take you down on the spot. God might even put an extra star in my crown for doing it."

"You might get a surprise," Hettie said as Audrey hustled her outside.

Brodie felt like he was driving past a train wreck. He couldn't look away from the fight between the two old ladies, and yet, Knox was pushing him out into the aisle.

Brodie turned to say something, but Knox pulled him toward the far end of the aisle. The space was narrow, so they had to leave by single file, but they were away from the cat fight between Hettie and Bernie. Tripp opened a side door leading out into the parking lot.

When they were all three outside, Tripp wiped imaginary sweat from his brow. "Can you believe that just happened?"

"I can, but what's our brother going to do about his date on Sunday?" Knox answered. "Looks like Linda will be looking for the white dress, a wedding cake, and a gold ring on her finger by Monday morning."

"You want to take her out in his place?" Tripp asked as he got into the passenger's seat of Brodie's truck.

"Absolutely not!" Knox answered. "I want a woman with some spunk, not one that will make me listen to church stuff every evening."

"So do I," Brodie said under his breath.

"Don't give me those looks," Hettie told Audrey as she poured a little whiskey in her coffee on Monday morning.

"You let Bernie get the best of you, and now you are drinking before sunrise," Audrey said through clenched teeth. "You deserve any looks I want to give you."

"She riled me up," Hettie said and then took a sip of her coffee. "I'll be fine by tomorrow and will only need a single whiskey sour at night to help my arthritis pain. So quit fussing at me. At my age, I intend to eat what I want, drink when I want, and die when I'm supposed to. I just hope that we have the farms back together soon, so I can tell Bitsy I'm coming to join her in the retirement center."

Audrey set a platter with fried eggs, bacon, biscuits, and hash browns on the table. "I've got a crew to keep busy today. I don't have time to watch over you."

Hettie took her regular place across the table from Audrey and loaded her plate. "Don't need no babysitter. I could run a tractor and fertilize apple and peach trees better than you or any one of your so-called crew. What I need is to be able to kick Bernie across the Red River. When she landed, she could pick herself up and go on back to whatever bar she ran up in Oklahoma."

"That isn't going to happen," Audrey said as she slathered a steaming-hot biscuit with butter. "Not any more than Brodie is going to show up on my doorstep and ask to sign a bill of sale. We might as well get used to the idea."

"You can," Hettie barked. "It ain't over 'til it's over, and I've still got faith. I heard that Tripp is looking at the old Johnson place. He's thinking of putting a saddle and boot shop in the barn. I liked Spanish Fort better when it was almost a ghost town. Now we've got a convenience store, a winery, a music store going into the old store, and a restaurant. And the sheriff of the county lives here, too. Mary Jane's family is going to take the town right off the ghost town list for sure. I won't live to see it, but this place could run Dallas some competition before too many years."

Audrey laughed out loud. "Ain't danged likely."

Hettie buttered a second biscuit and shook her head. "Stranger things have happened."

Audrey had never liked change, and everything around her wasn't the same as it had been when she was a child. "Maybe so, and we'll have to accept that, but we still don't have to like it."

"Amen!" Hettie raised her coffee cup.

Brodie woke up Tuesday morning feeling like he was in a state of limbo. He had spent Monday at the farm, mostly just walking through acres and acres of fruit trees and then checking on his strawberries. The grocery chain that had bought his crop this year would be sending pickers out to gather the spring harvest on Friday. From the books Ira had left for him, he was looking forward to a profitable year. But that morning, he felt like he was just in a waiting mode.

"Hey," Tripp poked his head in the door. "The real estate agent out of Nocona that's handling the house and barn will be here at ten. Will you and Knox go with me to look at the house and barn?"

"I thought he wasn't coming until tomorrow," Brodie said.

"Looks like they had a cancelation for today, and it's a woman that we will be talking to," Tripp told him.

"I'm going to run out to the farm and check on the strawberries, but I'll be there for sure," Brodie answered.

"Great! I'll go with you to the farm. I'm too excited to sit still for three hours and wait," Tripp told him.

Knox peeked in the other side of the open door. "What's got you so happy this early?"

"He's going to see the house and barn today," Brodie answered.

Knox covered a yawn with his hand. "How did that happen? I thought it was tomorrow."

"Nope, we're looking at it today, and I'm buying it, no matter what the asking price is," Tripp said. "A barn store will be amazing for a leather goods and boot repair shop. I lay awake half the night planning how we'd set it all up."

"What's this *we* business," Brodie asked as he got out of bed. "You got a mouse in your pocket?"

"No, and don't tease me," Tripp answered, and stepped out into the hallway. "Me and Knox have helped you on the farm for weeks. Now it's my turn."

Brodie walked out of the room and headed toward the bathroom. "I'll give you every waking hour that I can spare, little brother. I'm excited for you, and I agree that the barn will make a great store. You'll have people coming from all over the state to get at a pair of your custom-made boots or a saddle."

Knox raised a foot. "And I will show them this pair that you made for me when I graduated from high school. That way everyone will know that you make quality that lasts."

"Thanks," Tripp said. "I'm sure the smell of coffee is coming from the kitchen, so I'm going to follow my nose."

"See you there." Brodie closed the bathroom door behind him.

At nine thirty, the brothers left the farm and drove north until the road ended and Brodie made a right turn. Shane waved as he drove past them, evidently heading to the Paradise or maybe into Nocona. Brodie stuck his hand out the window, waved back, and checked the gas gauge on his truck. He made a mental note to buy fuel when they finished looking at the property.

"Brother, that house might have been livable at one time, but unless you want a shower every time it rains or a broken leg or arm when you step up on the porch, I'd say that we better build you a place before we put a new house on the farm," Brodie said.

"I guess Noah hasn't been down here to look at it in the last little while, but truth is, I don't care about the house. I want to see the barn," Tripp groaned.

Knox reached over the back seat and patted his brother on the shoulder. "If I can hire some help, we can have you in your own home by the end of summer."

Brodie opened the truck door and stepped out. "I hear a vehicle coming this way. That could very easily be the woman from the real estate company."

A bright-red truck pulled up, and Linda Massey got out with a big smile on her face. "I wasn't expecting you to be here, too, Brodie. This is a wonderful surprise. We might even count this as our first date, and Sunday can be the second one." She crossed the unkempt yard and looped her arm in his. "Let's look at the house first. It's a fixer-upper for sure. The roof needs repair, but the foundation is solid. You might have to strip it down to bare bones, but at the price they're asking, you'll have no trouble getting a loan from the bank for the property."

Brodie was surprised that the porch held up under their weight, and even more so when Linda didn't even use a key to open the door. "I understand Knox is a carpenter. I bet he has all kinds of ideas about this place."

"Just one," Knox said as he scanned the living room. "Raze it."

Linda hugged up closer to Brodie. "Oh, come on now.

You can work this little place over to be a cute little cottage for you and Tripp to live in."

After the second date, she was looking at wedding dresses. Audrey's words played over and over through Brodie's mind. Was she angling for Knox and Tripp to leave the farm, so she could take over? Would she want doilies and lace curtains in a house that she would insist on designing?

A rat the size of a possum ran out of a hole in the wall and ambled across the toes of Linda's high-heeled shoes. She squealed, jumped straight up, and wrapped her long legs around Brodie's waist.

Brodie wasn't sure what to do so he took two steps back, and a roach every bit as big as a hummingbird fell onto Linda's shoulder. She swiped at it and squealed. When she nearly knocked Brodie backward, he finally had the good sense to take her outside, disentangle her from his body, and set her down on the grass.

She leaned into him, put her palms on his chest, and looked up at him with tears in her eyes. "Oh, Brodie, you saved me. You are my knight in shining armor. We were meant to be together."

He removed her hands and took a step back. "Let's don't get ahead of ourselves."

She took a deep breath, let it out slowly, and whispered seductively. "The heart knows what it wants, and my poor little heart wants you."

"Can we look at the barn, and would you show me the property lines?" Knox asked.

"Thank you," Brodie mouthed.

"Of course, but it's just a dusty old barn," Linda said.

"I'm interested in seeing it anyway," Knox said.

She glanced at her watch. "I really don't have time, but feel free to look around all you want. The property line starts at the road and goes all the way back to the river." She swung her forefinger around to point at the barbed-wire fences on either side. "That's where it all ends. The Johnson family is eager to sell and have said they will negotiate. I'm not supposed to tell you that, but since you are Brodie's brother, I'm making an exception. Here's my card with the asking price on the back. Call me when you've had time to scope everything out. And Brodie, I will see you Sunday. I'll save you a place beside me in church." She got into her truck and drove away.

"Hettie won't have to kill Bernie," Brodie muttered. "I may do it for her."

Chapter 5

"So, how do I get out of this date?" Brodie groaned out loud to himself on his way to the farm on Friday morning. Joe Clay, Knox, and Tripp were at the barn taking measurements and estimates on how much it would cost to get the barn in shape to be a leather goods store. Mary Jane was in her writing cave, so there was no one to answer his question. He had seven sisters and that many brothers-in-law and yet had no help from any of them either.

"Looks like Joe Clay or Mary Jane could step up to the plate and stop Aunt Bernie when it came to her matchmaking business," he grumbled as he turned into the driveway and looked over at the pitiful wall still standing with all the bathroom fixtures. He parked his truck, got out, and looked up. "Lord, can't you send me something?"

No answers came floating down from the clear blue sky, either, so God, Fate, and the Universe must all be busy with something more important than helping him figure out a way to gracefully and gentlemanly get out of going out with Linda. Being downright rude would hurt Aunt Bernie's feelings, and he had been brought up to respect the elderly.

She would shoot you and drag your carcass out in the woods if she heard you call her elderly. Joe Clay's voice laughed in his ear.

Brodie was so lost in his thoughts that he had completely forgotten why he was going to the farm that day. Seeing two big trucks at the end of the strawberry field and a dozen or more men already harvesting berries jerked him right back into reality. He reminded himself that he still had a little time for someone to help him out of the jam Aunt Bernie had slapped him right in the middle of, but for now he needed to put on a smile and be a businessman.

"Good morning," he called out.

A tall, lanky man waved and then crossed the yard to meet Brodie. He stuck out his hand and said, "Pete Riley, supervisor of this operation. We've talked on the phone. Glad you let us harvest for you again this year. We didn't know how things would go after Ira's sudden death. Looks like someone already picked the lower end of the field."

Brodie shook with him. "I'm Brodie Callahan, and I'm glad that Ira left a written notebook of all his harvesters. And yes, my sister and her husband own and operate a winery, and they took part of the crop to make strawberry wine."

"Pleased to meet you. It's good to put a face with a name," Pete said and dropped Brodie's hand. "And no worries about your kinfolks harvesting part of the crop. With all these spring rains, there's a bumper crop this year."

"How long do you think it will take you to get them all picked?" Brodie asked.

"We'll be done today unless a storm blows up. Speaking

of that, I'm real sorry about your house. That back wall still standing with the bathroom fixtures intact looks kind of pitiful. You going to build back right where the place was?"

"We haven't made up our mind yet, but it does make sense since the plumbing is all in the ground right there," Brodie answered.

"Glad you made it out safe. You are a lucky man that the tornado didn't destroy your orchards and that the trees protected the gardens. Ira was smart to lay out things the way he did."

"I understand you've been buying his produce for years," Brodie said.

"We have, and we're glad you are continuing to sell to us. Folks do love their organic food," Pete said. "We left a few feet on this end for you to pick for personal use like you asked."

"I want to pick a sack full or two to take to the Paradise to make shortcakes for tonight's supper," Brodie told him.

"Too bad we'll be gone by that time, or I'd beg an invitation," Pete chuckled. "But to be honest, I plan on taking some home to my wife so she can make some of her famous strawberry tarts. You go ahead and pick what you want, and I'll get back to work. We'll send a check as soon as we weigh the trucks. And we look forward to a call when the watermelons and cantaloupe are ready." Pete waved over his shoulder as he turned and walked back to the strawberry field.

"You can expect it, for sure," Brodie called out.

"Hey!" Audrey called out from the barbed-wire fence.

The last thing Brodie wanted to do that morning was face off with Audrey again. He would have trouble choosing which was worse—a blind date with an annoying woman or an encounter with a frustrating neighbor. The answer came when his heart tossed in an extra beat as he watched Audrey put a foot on the bottom string of barbed wire and pull the next one up with her hand. Then she expertly crawled through the two without getting a single hair tangled up in the barbs. He couldn't imagine what was so important that she would come onto his property. He created all kinds of scenarios in his mind. The one that stuck was that Audrey needed help taking Hettie to the hospital in Nocona. Bernie would be ecstatic if the old girl didn't show up in church for a few weeks.

That scene vanished when he heard another voice yelling to his right. He whipped around to see Linda with a big smile on her face and waving.

"Yahoo!" Her high whiny voice pierced through the air.

Brodie did not feel like he was between a rock and a hard place. No, sir! He could almost feel a nine-point earthquake causing the ground to shake beneath his feet, and the gentle spring breeze felt like a class five tornado coming from the other way. To get to his truck, he would have to run between the hurricane named Linda and the tornado labeled Audrey.

Men don't run. They face their enemies head-on and plow through them. This time his drill sergeant's voice was in his head.

Brodie really had no choice but to stand and fight

because the gap was closing between the two women. Linda continued to smile and wave as she carefully picked her way around the mud puddles to avoid getting her high-heeled shoes dirty. Audrey's boots stormed across the distance as if she was running on dry ground.

"Good Lord!" Brodie gasped, and jerked his head around from one woman to the other. An old George Jones song, "The Race Is On," played through his mind so loud that it wiped out whatever Linda was saying. The lyrics of the song said that pride was coming up the backside and heartaches were going to the inside. He wasn't real sure which woman was pride and which was heartaches, but if his sense of judgment hadn't failed, they were going to reach him at the same time.

Audrey pushed ahead at the last minute and ran toward him with open arms. Just before she reached him, she gave a running leap and jumped. He caught her, but she knocked the wind right out of him when she hit him in the chest with her body and wrapped her legs around his waist. She cupped his cheeks in her hands, looked him in the eyes, and kissed him—long, hard, and lingering.

"What was that?" he gasped when the kiss ended.

"You can thank me later," she whispered.

"You two-timin' son of a bitch!" Linda screamed from a few feet away. "I wouldn't go out with you if you were the last man on earth. Our relationship is over."

The heat from Audrey's body and the steaming kiss had wiped out the whole world around him, so that for a split second Brodie wondered who was yelling so loudly. He wished whoever it was would leave so he could stay in the bubble with Audrey. He didn't know that a forbidden kiss could make a man forget about everything until that very moment.

"You are welcome," Audrey hopped down and landed on her feet.

"For what?"

Linda popped her hands on her waist. "Don't you have anything to say to me? An apology at the very least would be nice. You've probably been seeing this hussy for days while you led me on."

Audrey handed Brodie her phone, took a few steps, and leaned toward Linda. With their noses only a few feet apart, she said, "You did not have a relationship. You've never even been out with him, so scoot along home"—she motioned with her hand toward Linda's car—"and call Bernie to set you up with someone else."

Linda narrowed her eyes, reached out with her palms, and pushed Audrey. "I'm willing to fight for my man."

"I'm not your man, and both of you need to leave," Brodie hollered above the thick tension filling the air.

Audrey smiled, drew back a fist, but opened it at the last minute and slapped Linda across the cheek. "Go home and lick your wounds."

Linda charged like a bull with a red flag in front of his eyes, and both women hit the ground in a thud. Linda was on top, pulling Audrey's hair and screaming cuss words that all blended together. Brodie took a couple of steps forward but then stopped. If lightning bolts zigzagged out of the clear blue sky, he didn't want to be anywhere near Linda Massey.

With one hard shove, Audrey pushed the woman to the side, sat on her chest, and pinned both her arms. "You need to grow up and stop acting like a high school sophomore. Why would Brodie kiss me or"—she paused long enough to wink at Brodie—"or sleep with me if he wanted to go out with you?"

Linda freed one hand and threw a fist full of mud at Audrey's face. Audrey let go of her other arm so she could wipe the mess from her eyes, and Linda took that opportunity to push her off her chest. Audrey landed in another puddle and came up slinging both fists.

Pete came running and shook his head. "I'll get the brunette. You take care of the blond. Looks like all the rain we've had this past week hasn't helped matters."

"No, thanks," Brodie said. "I'm not going near either one of them."

"Okay, then," Pete nodded. "I wasn't lookin' forward to getting dirty anyway. Want to put a bet on who calls uncle first?"

Brodie folded his arms over his chest and didn't take his eyes off the mud wrestling in front of him. "The blond is loud and bossy, but the brunette is meaner than a crocogator, so I'll put my money on her."

"What is a crocogator?" Pete asked.

"That's an animal with a crocodile head on one end and an alligator head on the other," Brodie answered.

Pete scratched his head for a couple of seconds. "How does a critter like that go to the bathroom?"

"It don't," Brodie said with a chuckle. "That's what makes it so mean."

Pete laughed out loud. "That's funny, but if that brunette is that mean, I'll just go back to work."

"Thanks for the offer," Brodie said. "They'll get tired after a while."

"Hope the brunette wins," Pete said. "I think she likes you."

Brodie didn't even try to explain the situation but watched the two women rolling around in the mud like a couple of puppies. Linda's blond hair was now brown. The slippery mud had caused both her high-heeled shoes to come off. Her skirt tail had flown up over her head and made a cape around her shoulders. The only thing left that wasn't covered in mud was a tiny, lacy swatch at the top of her red bikini underpants.

The whole fight seemed to be playing in slow motion, and then it went right into warp speed when Audrey put Linda face down to the ground, slapped the ground three times, and stood up with her hands over her head.

"And the winner is Audrey Tucker." She picked up Linda's high-heeled shoes and hurled them toward her car. One bounced off the hood, and another landed on the trunk with a loud pop. Then she fished Linda's blinged-out pink phone from the mud and tossed it in the same direction.

Linda sat up and shook a fist at Audrey. "Those were my most expensive high heels, and my phone is probably ruined." She turned her glare toward Brodie. "I'm calling Bernie, and I hate both of you."

"Feeling is mutual from this area, and let that be a lesson to you to never cross me again," Audrey said, and stomped across the distance to Brodie. She wrapped him up in a bear hug and whispered. "I'll take strawberries instead of a winner's trophy for saving your sorry ass." Then she kissed him again.

"Why did you do that?" He panted when she took a step back, leaving mud all over his shirt and his face.

"I told you before, in case you don't sell to me, I don't want her for a neighbor," Audrey answered, and turned around and walked away. "You can leave the strawberries on my front porch. Until you sign a bill of sale, you aren't welcome inside."

―――――――

"What in the hell happened to you?" Walter said from the back porch.

"It's a long story that I'll tell you later when I get cleaned up," she answered, and left her manager/supervisor/surrogate uncle shaking his head as he walked away.

"You better not track mud onto Hettie's clean kitchen floor," Walter said.

"I told her not to mop," Audrey snapped. "She's going to fall and break a hip one of these days."

"Been tellin' her that for a long time, but she's even more stubborn now than she was back when she was younger," Walter waved over his shoulder as he walked away.

Hettie gasped when Audrey came in the back door and stripped out of dirty jeans and T-shirt right there. "What happened to you, and where have you been? Walter came looking for you to say that he was back from his trip. Did you roll in the mud? You get in the shower out there in the mudroom before you come on inside the house. I just cleaned the floor."

"Yep, I did roll in the mud, and I haven't had so much fun in years," Audrey answered. "We'll talk after I get cleaned up."

"Be sure the drain cleaner is handy because half of the dirt in Texas is stuck in your hair right now," Hettie scolded. "Then we're going to have cookies and hot chocolate, and you're goin' to tell me what happened. Me and Amos tried a lot of things, but we never had sex in the mud, so if that's what happened, I want the details."

Audrey dropped her bra and panties on the floor, turned on the water, and stepped into the shower. "For the first time, I understand why they call this a mudroom," she said.

After washing and rinsing three times, the water from Audrey's hair still ran in a dirty streak, so she went through the process twice more. Then she noticed the mud between her toes and groaned. She slapped the side of the shower and moaned, "If the mud got all the way to my feet, then my boots are messed up beyond repair, and it's all your fault, Linda Massey."

"Are you all right in there?" Hettie hollered.

"I'm fine. I'm just mad as a wet hen," Audrey said as she

turned off the water and stepped out onto the bathroom mat in front of the shower. "My boots are ruined."

"Well, you are as wet as an old settin' hen right now. There's a major difference in a plain old hen who doesn't want to be wet and one that is trying to keep her baby chicks safe. I'm waiting to see what you are protecting, so hurry up in there," Hettie giggled from the kitchen. "I've cleaned up a lot of Amos's messy boots, both inside and out a few times, so I'll take care of yours. Get dried off and dressed, and don't keep me waiting. I'm an old woman who might not live long enough to hear the story."

Audrey wrapped a towel around her head and one around her body. She grabbed a snickerdoodle cookie from the middle of the kitchen table as she passed by on the way to her bedroom.

"Those are for storytelling," Hettie growled.

"I need one for enough energy to get dressed. Fighting over a man I don't even want takes a lot of energy," Audrey yelled before she closed her door.

"Sounds like a very good story unless that man was Brodie Callahan. You better not have been fighting with or for him," Hettie got in the last word.

Audrey pulled on a pair of underwear and a T-shirt with a faded picture of Chris Stapleton on the front. She padded back to the kitchen with the towel turban still wrapped tightly around her head. Her hands trembled, and her knees felt like rubber. She wasn't sure if it was a drop after the adrenaline rush from the fight or if the kisses had set off a flood of desire.

Hettie set two cups of hot chocolate on the table and motioned for her to sit down. "You've had one cookie. You can have another one when you start talking. Sex?"

"Lord, no!" Audrey took a sip of the chocolate and sputtered. "This is…"

"It has a little nip of Irish whiskey to give it some kick. The way your whole body is humming you need it, so drink it and don't fuss. Besides, it goes well with the snickerdoodles," Hettie said. "I'll be disappointed if the story is too bland for it."

"It's not," Audrey promised, and told her about taking a walk out to the fence to see if the harvesters would sell her a basket of strawberries. Then she picked up a cookie and took a bite. "Then I saw Linda Massey's car coming down the road, and Lord help me, but I hate that woman, and I don't want her for a neighbor. As pushy as she is, she could have had Brodie dragged to the church and married before he can blink."

"That's a good beginning," Hettie said. "But what's it got to do with all that mud? Please don't tell me that he threw you down and had his way with you right there in front of Ira's harvest crew? The only thing worse than having him live next door to us is if he got you pregnant."

"He did not!" Audrey's whole body tingled at the idea of a romp anywhere with Brodie.

"Whew!" Hettie wiped her brow. "Now that I know I don't have to load my sawed-off shotgun and go after Brodie, I want to hear the rest of the story."

By the time she finished, Hettie was laughing so hard that she could hardly breathe. "The only way that could have been better is if it had been me and Bernie. I know I could whip her skinny ass, and rolling her in the mud would be icing on the cake."

Audrey didn't tell Hettie that kissing Brodie made her feel like stripping off his clothes and dragging him down into the ground to have wild, passionate sex. A hard knock on the front door erased the visual from her mind.

"It's probably something from the post office that's too big to put in the mailbox out by the road," Audrey said.

"You be sure about that before you open the door. No one needs to see you in that garb you are wearing," Hettie told her.

"Yes, ma'am," Audrey snapped.

She left the kitchen, walked down the short foyer, and cracked the door open. She peeked outside and saw Brodie walking toward the road where his poor old, beat-up truck was parked. She felt sorrier for the vehicle than she did the man. When she remembered the way those kisses and the hardness of his body pressed against hers had made her feel, another delicious little shiver of desire danced through her body. She watched him slide in behind the steering wheel and drive away before she opened the door and found a paper sack sitting on the porch.

"Who is it?" Hettie yelled.

"Brodie Callahan, paying his bill," she answered as she picked up the bag of strawberries and carried it to the kitchen.

Brodie groaned and slapped the steering wheel when he parked in front of the Paradise that afternoon. Tripp and Knox waved from the porch steps and held up their beers. He had hoped to sneak in and get cleaned up before anyone could see the mess he was in—dried mud covered the front of his shirt and pants. His boots were in a frightful mess from all that wading through the wet ground to get to the strawberry beds. He let out a heavy sigh, picked up a bag of berries, and opened the truck door.

"What do you have there?" Tripp asked.

"Strawberries for Mary Jane," Brodie answered.

"Did you roll around in the garden?" Knox asked.

"Nope." He set the sack down and nodded toward his brother's beer. "Got another one of those?"

Tripp handed him a beer. "You're the one making supper tonight, so I guess the strawberries are for you."

Knox reached inside the bag and brought out a handful. "I'll have these for a snack while we wait for supper. What are you making?"

"Meat loaf," Brodie answered, and took a long gulp of the beer.

"Now, tell us what got you so dirty," Tripp said.

"You go first and tell me about the barn." Brodie hoped that if he changed the subject enough he could bypass the story altogether.

"We measured and drew up a rough draft to divide the barn into a back workroom, a front room for the store, and a little shotgun apartment over to the side," Knox told him.

"When the realtor arrived, who by the way was not Linda today, I made an offer, and he was sure the sellers would take it," Tripp added.

Brodie stood up. "That's great. I'm excited for you, Tripp. This has been your dream like the farm has been mine. Who would have thought we'd both find it in this little place?"

"Not me," Knox answered. "Now, it's your turn. In addition to the front of your shirt looking like you wrestled with an alligator, there are a couple of dirty handprints on the back. What happened? Damsel in distress?"

"Nope, more like organic farmer in trouble," Brodie laughed, and sat back down on the step. If he hadn't lived through it, he wouldn't have believed it, so most likely his brothers would think he was weaving a tall tale. "The truth is stranger than fiction. Audrey doesn't want Linda to be her neighbor, so…" he went on to tell them what had happened.

"I'll go pack up my bags," Tripp said when the story ended and he had stopped laughing long enough to catch his breath.

"Why?" Brodie asked.

Knox wiped his eyes with the back of his hand. "Linda is going to call Bernie, and she's going to come in here with a pot of tar and a rail to run us out of town. We need to make a hasty exit before she gets here."

"Hey, guys," Joe Clay came from around the end of the house.

Tripp handed him a beer. "I made a bid on the barn, and we're celebrating."

"Before we light a shuck out of here," Knox teased.

Joe Clay took the can and pulled the tab from the top. "I'm glad that you are going to put in a leather shop, but y'all don't have to be in a hurry to leave the Paradise. We love having you guys with us."

"Thanks, but Brodie has done gone and wore out our welcome," Knox chuckled.

"Why would you say that? There's no way you guys can—" Joe Clay declared.

"Don't be so quick to judge," Brodie butted in, and then told him what had happened.

When Joe Clay stopped laughing, he said, "Bernie has a trailer. If she don't want to be around you guys, she can stay in it. There'll be no running you off, and if she comes out here with a bucket of tar, I reckon the four of us can take it away from her."

"Thanks, Dad." The word slipped out as easily as if he'd used it all his life. He cut his eyes around to find Joe Clay beaming.

———

Brodie had just put a bowl of mashed potatoes on the table when a flash of lightning lit up the sky that evening, and rain mixed with hail pelted against the windows. The lights flickered a couple of times, then finally went completely out. "Thank goodness everything is done and that the strawberries were harvested today instead of next week. This hail would have destroyed them," he said.

Joe Clay fumbled around in the kitchen and brought a couple of jar candles. "Looks like we'll be eating by artificial light, with bursts of lightning flashes. And while you are thanking goodness, whoever or whatever that is, we can also be grateful that the orchard trees aren't in full bloom. A hailstorm could have destroyed your crop."

Mary Jane brought another candle from her office. "I heard what you just said, Joe Clay. And I've always felt like blessings come in all forms." She sat down and smiled. "This all looks wonderful. I didn't know I was getting cooks as well as sons, and eating by candlelight makes everything taste better."

"Our mother made sure we knew how to take care of ourselves before she kicked us out of the nest," Knox said, "but Brodie is better in the kitchen than me and Tripp."

"Speak for yourself," Tripp disagreed. "I can outbake both of you."

The back door flew open, and Pepper ran into the dining room, stopped long enough to shake water off his whole body, and then headed for the living room.

"Does she have a bucket of tar?" Brodie leaned over and whispered to Joe Clay.

His father leaned back in his chair and shook his head. "Nope, but the look on her face would melt the barbed wire in Hades."

"Come in, Aunt Bernie," Mary Jane called out in a sweet

voice. "We haven't even said the prayer yet, so grab a plate on your way."

Brodie heard dishes rattling around and then another loud clap of thunder. Bernie stepped into the dining room, and lightning flashed through the window, lighting her up. Her eyes seemed to glow with anger, and Brodie dreaded the next few minutes. It was too late to run, so his only option was to take his medicine like a man and hope that she didn't throw her plate at him.

She sat down and held her tongue until Joe Clay finished a short prayer. Then she turned her glare on Brodie. "Are you in love with Audrey Tucker?"

He passed the mashed potatoes to her. "No, ma'am, I am not," he sputtered.

She put two big scoops on her plate and exploded. "Well, that much is good news. I don't like that woman and despise her aunt, so I forbid you to get mixed up with her. I never figured Linda for a fool. I'd heard that in the past she tended to get serious way too quick, but I gave her the benefit of a doubt when I fixed her up with my kin. She called me whining about what happened out there. I know there's two sides to every story, and I want to hear yours before I completely take her off my matchmaking list."

"What happened?" Mary Jane asked.

Brodie glanced over at Joe Clay.

"Don't look at me, son. It's your story," Joe Clay chuckled.

"I've already told it twice," Brodie groaned.

"The third time is the charm," Bernie said.

"Okay, here goes. I was about to go pick some strawberries for tonight's supper, when…" he went on to tell how everything went down.

Knox raised a palm. "And she's been stalking him all week."

"She's a disgrace to my service," Bernie said through clenched teeth. "She needs to grow up and act her age. I'll find you another woman, Brodie, and this time I'll pay more attention to the rumors."

"I really—" he started.

Bernie held up a hand and cut him off. "But Audrey Tucker is off-limits. I will not be related to Hettie—not even through shirttail kin. Why would Audrey do such a foolhardy thing anyway? A decent woman don't throw herself at a man and kiss him. I ran a bar in Ratliff City, Oklahoma, and I thought I'd seen everything, but this takes the cake."

"She said that she didn't want Linda to be her neighbor," Brodie answered, glad that Linda and Audrey were taking the brunt of Aunt Bernie's anger.

The electricity blinked again and then came back on.

"Let there be light," Mary Jane said. "Aunt Bernie, I tried to tell you that Linda had some issues. I guess next time around you'll listen to me."

"Yes, I will, and I've got another lady already lined up for Brodie. You will be going to Tertia and Noah's restaurant with her tomorrow night for dessert and coffee. Just a little getting to know each other evening. She'll meet you there at six o'clock. You are welcome. Now I want to hear the part about the mud fight again. God, I wish that had been me and Hettie going at it. I would have won the fight for sure."

"Is everyone ready for dessert?" Tripp asked. "Brodie picked fresh strawberries and made shortcakes from scratch."

"Yes!" Joe Clay said. "Knox and I will bring them in."

Brodie told the part about the mud wrestling one more time, but he hadn't told anyone, not even his brothers, about the strawberries that he'd left on Audrey's porch for payment.

Chapter 6

"Why am I doing this?" Brodie asked his reflection in the mirror above the dresser.

"Probably because you feel beholden to Bernie for not shooting you over the Linda deal."

Brodie whipped around to find Knox leaning against the doorjamb. "You are right, but at least it's only for dessert and coffee."

"Blackberry cobbler is the Saturday night dessert at Tertia and Noah's place," Knox said.

"Just my luck," Brodie groaned. "My favorite pie, and I have to carry on a conversation rather than enjoy it."

"Maybe Audrey will storm in and kiss you again," Knox teased.

Brodie shook his head slowly. "Not if she wouldn't mind having this Wanette woman for a neighbor. She'll leave me hanging out to dry if she likes the lady. But if she's going to create a scene, I hope she does it before Tertia brings out my cobbler."

"The way your love life is running, that probably won't happen," Knox said.

"Don't I know it," he said and patted his brother on the

shoulder. "Want to take my place? The woman has never seen me."

"Nope," Knox answered with a grin. "I like peach cobbler better than blackberry."

Brodie felt like his boots had fifty-pound weights attached to them as he slowly made his way down the stairs, across the foyer, and out on the porch. He told himself that this woman *could* make him feel like Audrey did when she kissed him, but the little voice in his head laughed.

He checked the time on his phone, and whether the situation was win, lose again, or maybe a draw this time, he had to go. He crossed the yard, slid behind the wheel of his beat-up truck, and hoped that Wanette only liked men who drove fancy cars. "That silly thought was something a teenage boy would come up with," he scolded himself. "I'll just tell her that I'm not interested in dating right now."

Driving down the lane and across the road to the café seemed ridiculous since he could have walked in less time than it took to get in the truck and start the engine. But after the recent spring rains, all the grounds were saturated. If he hadn't driven, he would have arrived with muddy boots and quite possibly splotches of dirty water halfway to the knees of his jeans. His mother taught him that a gentleman left his boots at the door if they were in a mess, but if his jeans had dirty water spots halfway to the knees he couldn't leave them very well. He checked the clock on the dashboard—five fifty-five. According to Bernie, six o'clock on the dot was the magic hour when he was supposed to walk through the doors.

He had seen a picture, albeit not a good likeness, of the first five women that Bernie had set him up with. Linda was the sixth one, and she went to the same church, so he knew what she looked like. He hadn't even seen a picture of the woman he was to *get to know* that evening, but he knew her name and he could scan the place for a yellow rose lying on the table.

"Seven isn't even my lucky number," he muttered as he parked close to the door, got out of the truck, and went inside. "And speaking of luck?"

Evidently, dear old Aunt Bernie had not done her homework. A bouquet of yellow flowers in a pint jar sat in the middle of every single table. Brodie wasn't up on his flowers enough to know if they were roses or tulips.

Tertia came from the kitchen and whispered, "Back table in the corner."

"Thank you," Brodie said with a nod and started that way. Had he known that meeting his biological father came with a long rope with a noose already tied to hang unmarried men, he might have thought twice about coming to north central Texas.

"No, I wouldn't," he whispered.

"You must be Brodie Callahan." A red-haired woman slid out of the booth, stood up, and said in an accent that left no doubt that she was from the Deep South, "I'm Wanette Richards."

Brodie held out a hand. "Yes, I'm Brodie, and I'm pleased to meet you."

"Likewise," Wanette said and shook his hand. "Shall we

sit and get to know each other? I took the liberty of ordering black coffee and blackberry cobbler for you and a cup of green tea for me."

"Thank you," Brodie said, and waited for her to sit before he slid into the booth on the opposite side. "So, no dessert for you?"

And no sparks or feelings like I have with Audrey, he thought.

"I avoid sugar, red meat, and carbs," she answered. "I'm not diabetic or a vegan, but I do take care of my body. I own a gym in Gainesville, so I have to set an example for my clients."

"I'm an organic farmer," Brodie said.

She didn't stare at him, but through him. "That means you play in the dirt?"

"I do," he answered.

"Well, then this date is a bust," Wanette said. "But since I drove all the way up here to meet you, I'll still have my tea before I leave."

Brodie stopped himself from rolling his eyes toward the ceiling, but he did give a silent *thank you* for whatever reason Wanette didn't like farmers.

Tertia brought out a mug of tea, one of black coffee, and a bowl of cobbler with ice cream on the top. "Y'all enjoy."

"Thank you," Brodie said, and was glad the date didn't have to last long. Maybe she would drink her tea fast, and he could at least enjoy part of his cobbler without her staring at him from across the table.

This date may be a complete bust, but you will be the

gentleman I taught you to be. His mother's voice was loud and clear in his head.

"So, you're from the South?" he asked.

"Born and raised in New Orleans but spent ten years in Los Angeles trying to get a toe in the movie business. I thought my Southern accent and well-toned body would get me somewhere, but it didn't," she answered. "I'll explain why I was so blunt about this date. I'm thirty-six years old, and I'm looking for a husband. You are a fine specimen of a man, but you are a farmer. I'm ready to have kids, and time could be running out for me. I like the city life. Gainesville is the smallest town I've ever lived in, and I really don't like it. As soon as I sell my gym, I'm heading back to California to put in a surf shop on the beach. With the right man, I can have my career and a family both."

"O…kay," Brodie said. "Didn't Bernie tell you that I was a farmer?"

"Yes, but you're sexy and the age I want, so I thought I'd meet you and see if you are definitely into the farming business before I wrote you off," she answered. "Can I persuade you to date me with a serious relationship in mind with a move to the sunny West Coast at the end?"

Brodie dug into his cobbler and took a bite to give himself some time to think. Audrey would not like this woman for a neighbor either. When he swallowed and sipped on his coffee, he finally asked, "I don't think that's in the cards. Did you honestly just drive up here to meet me to see if I'd make pretty babies? That's pretty brazen."

"That's the story. No use in wasting time on what won't be," she answered and scanned as much of his body as she could see from across the booth. "I could use someone like you to work in my surf shop if you are willing to change your mind about living up here in the boonies. We might have a good partnership."

He looked at the huge helping of cobbler and shook his head. Could he finish it off in three bites? "I guess you made a trip for nothing."

"And you got dressed all for nothing," Wanette said, "but we can talk for a few more minutes until you finish your pie. How many of these blind dates have you been on?"

"The last one canceled, but you are the seventh," Brodie answered. "How about you?"

She took a sip of her tea. "Third. I'm probably going to do better on the West Coast, where there are lots of hard-bodied surfers. Bernie told me that you hadn't been here long, and she didn't really expect you to put down roots. I thought I'd take a chance on you."

"Sorry to disappoint," Brodie said.

Before either of them could say another word, the door opened and Audrey yelled, "Brodie Callahan, where are you?"

Everyone in the café, including Wanette and Brodie, turned around to look at her. Brodie blinked half a dozen times, but the pot-bellied pig she carried in her arms did not disappear. She marched to the back of the café and glared at him.

"You are insufferable," she declared in a loud voice. "This thing has rooted up Aunt Hettie's tulips, and…"

"That's not mine," Brodie raised his voice above hers.

"Oh, yes it is," Audrey said. "I called all the neighbors, and no one claimed it, and when I chased it out of the flower bed, it ran straight over to your place and hid under the travel trailer."

A faint vision surfaced of a pig flying through the air just before Tripp jerked Brodie into the cellar. He'd thought it was a full-grown hog, but the critter could have been smaller. Still, where had it been and why did it show up at his place this long after the storm had passed?

"Well?" Audrey asked.

"The tornado must have blown it in from somewhere. Since you found it, it's all yours." He hadn't felt so alive in years as he did when he looked up into Audrey's angry face.

"Oh, no! Your trailer. Your land. Your pig!" she said and set the muddy pig down in the middle of the table.

The animal immediately slurped up some of Wanette's green tea and then nudged the half-empty cup into her lap, leaving wet streaks all down her light-green silk blouse. Before Brodie could grab it, the pig finished off his cobbler and kicked the bowl with lots of juice onto his white shirt.

He turned to say something to Audrey, but she had already left, leaving only a trail of dirty boot prints on the tile floor. Wanette sat there with a frozen horrified look on her face. "I cannot believe this!" she finally squealed.

The pig must have felt sorry for her because it turned around, scattering salt and pepper shakers in its wake, and put its front feet up on her shoulders.

"I think she likes you," Brodie said.

"Get this nasty thing off me," Wanette's voice went even higher and squeakier.

For a split second, Brodie wasn't sure if it was coming from her or from the pig, but one of them definitely was not enjoying the experience. Brodie slid out of the booth, wrapped his arms around the animal's round belly, and stood up with it.

"Are you sure that you don't want a pet?" he asked. "I hear you can train them to a litter box, and the kids you are going to have would love it."

"This is the worst date I've ever been on," she hissed as she picked up her purse and marched out of the café.

"Me, too," Brodie whispered.

Tertia came out of the kitchen with a mop in her hands and a smile on her face. "Looks like the tornado took your house and left you a pot-bellied pig. What are you going to do with it?"

"I don't know, but I'll figure something out," he said. "Think one of the sisters would want her?"

"Don't even ask," Tertia giggled. "That's your new pet, and I'm telling you right now, Mama will not let it live at the Paradise. She barely tolerates the cat and Pepper."

"Okay then," Brodie said. "Sorry about the mess."

"How was the date going?" Tertia asked as she mopped up the mess.

"Badly. The lady wants a boy toy to father her babies, and one who is willing to live on the beach in California," Brodie answered.

Tertia had trouble containing the next giggle. "Aunt Bernie is losing her touch."

Brodie started across the room. "Maybe only with me, but this is my last blind date."

"Don't be so sure," Tertia said. "Bernie is one persistent old gal."

———

Brodie had no place to go with his newly acquired pet other than the trailer. He set the pig in the back seat of his truck and drove to the farm. Before he got out, he sent a text to his brothers: Come to the farm. Emergency.

He opened the back door, tucked the pig under his arm, and carried it to the trailer. When they were inside, he set the critter on the floor. Like a nosy cat, it sniffed out the place and finally curled up on a blanket that had fallen on the floor and went to sleep.

"What's the emergency?" Knox burst through the door.

Brodie pointed to the corner. "That is the problem. I can't take it to the Paradise. Asking Mary Jane to let me keep it would be too much. I didn't know what else to do other than bring it here. Y'all got any ideas?"

Tripp followed his brother into the house. "What the... Is that a real pig?"

The animal raised its head, grunted, and then plopped right back down.

"That should answer your question," Brodie replied.

Knox wedged in beside Brodie on the seats around the

table. "You want to explain, and while you are at it, tell us what happened to your new shirt?"

"A blind date, a pig, and Audrey Tucker walk into a café." Brodie said.

Tripp sank down into the seat next to Brodie. "Are you serious?"

"Audrey again? Where'd she get the pig?" Knox asked.

"Says that it came out from under this trailer and rooted up Hettie's tulips. She set it down in the middle of the table, and it proceeded to make a big mess." He pointed to his shirt.

"Good grief!" Knox gasped. "Did Tertia run all of you out of the café?"

"No, she was calm about it, but the whole evening was a big waste of time. If I had a Bible in this place, I would lay my hand on it and swear that I'm done with blind dates," Brodie answered.

"What're you going to do?" Tripp asked.

"Think an animal shelter would take it?" Knox whispered.

The animal raised her head and gave him a dose of pot-bellied pig evil eye.

"I'd say that she was probably someone's pet, and they'll be looking for her," Brodie answered.

Tripp glanced over at Knox. "From the way she's acting, it's pretty evident that she's been a pet, so we need a pen for her, or else someone is going to have to live in this trailer."

"Why are you looking at me?" Knox covered a yawn with his hand.

"You are the carpenter, and this is your trailer," Tripp answered. "You can make a small outside pen for her and—"

"I can do that," Knox butted in, "but it's Brodie's pig so he gets to stay in the trailer the next couple of nights until I get it done."

Thoughts went through Brodie's mind faster than the wheel of a hamster on steroids. Even though Tertia said that none of the sisters would take the pig, maybe Ursula and Remy would adopt the animal to live on their ranch?

They have dogs, the aggravating voice in his head reminded him.

He went through the whole list of sisters and quickly decided that none of them would even consider taking in a pot-bellied pig.

"You used to beg Mother for a pet," Knox chuckled. "Looks like she's finally granted your wish. Now that we've decided everything, I'm going home to a nice soft bed."

"Me, too," Tripp said.

Knox stood up, took two steps, and opened the door. "There's breakfast bars, bottled water, and coffee in the cabinet above the sink and plenty of water in the tank right now to last a couple of days, and remember not to flush the potty any more than you have to or else we'll have to drag the trailer to a dump site. Or you could go out to what's left of the house and take an open-air shower."

Brodie looked down at his ruined shirt. "This is not the time for jokes. I'll be home tomorrow morning in time to get ready for church. Maybe if I put a note on the church bulletin board, someone will either claim her or else adopt her." He rolled his eyes toward the ceiling. "I wanted a puppy or a hamster, not a pig."

"Mother always did have a sense of humor," Knox laughed out loud. "See you tomorrow. There might be one of my shirts still hanging in the closet if the new baby keeps you up half the night and you don't have time to come by the Paradise."

Brodie hurled a pillow at him, and it hit Tripp in the back as he ran outside right behind Knox. Brodie could hear them both laughing all the way to the driveway, and then the sound of a truck's engine drowned them out.

"Okay, Pansy. That's your new name because you were tearing up Hettie's flower garden." Brodie glanced over at the sleeping pig. "Looks like it's just you and me for the night. I don't even know what your kind of critter eats or if you are housebroken. I'll try to find out what I can on the internet when it comes to your food, but if you make a mess in the trailer, I really will take you to a shelter." He slipped his phone out of his hip pocket and googled the information.

"Looks like you need special pellets or else roots from untreated ground. I hope there's a store open on Sunday in Wichita Falls where we can buy such things and that whatever roots you ate over at Audrey's place didn't have all those nasty pesticides on them," he said. "You just sleep for now. I'm going outside for a breath of fresh air."

He peeled off his shirt and tossed it in the tiny kitchen sink. Tomorrow he would ask the sisters if any of them had a magic trick to take the stain out. He grabbed a bottle of water and eased out the door. The night air would have been perfect if he hadn't been naked from the waist up. But with a bare chest, it was more than a little cool. A few dark clouds to the southwest covered the moon, but stars dotted the rest of the sky. The smell of rain was in the air, but according to the weatherman, that wouldn't arrive until later in the night.

Pansy was either snoring or grunting, neither of which made him want to jump up and go see if she was alright. Then the door hinges squeaked, and the pig was on the porch with him. He made a grab for her and missed. She squealed like she'd been kicked and tore out across the yard, ran under the bottom string of the barbed-wire fence, and stopped dead on the other side.

"That's right"—Brodie ran along behind her but stopped when he reached the fence—"you know you're not welcome on that property, so get your sorry little butt back here."

Pansy seemed to think about it for a minute, but then she took off like a shot and headed straight for Hettie's flower bed in the front yard. Brodie put a hand on one of the ancient wood posts with full intentions of leaping over the fence like he was back to running hurdles in high school. He was in the air when the post gave way, and he landed on the other side with a length of barbed wire stuck firmly in his chest. Four thin lines of blood ran down his chest. He swiped at it with his hand, and the wire fell to the ground, but that didn't stop the flow.

He was winded when he reached Hettie's flower bed and

grabbed the pig, but it wiggled free and headed around the house. He was sure that Audrey and Hettie both heard all the squealing Pansy made every time he almost had her in his arms. Evidently she was afraid that he was going to throw her in a hot pit and serve her up with an apple in her mouth, because she zigzagged across the backyard like streaks of lightning.

"Whole new meaning to a greased pig," Brodie grumbled as he ran along behind her.

———

Audrey had taken a long shower, but she imagined that she could still smell that fat little critter on her body. Brodie had brought a semi load of trouble with him when he moved in next door with his stubborn attitude. First, he wouldn't sell her his farm. Second, he made her heart thump around in her chest every time she was around him. And third, he had a stupid pot-bellied pig.

She wrapped a towel around her body and stomped barefoot into the kitchen. "He's not just the most stubborn man on earth but in the whole damn Universe. I hate pigs, even those little pot-bellied ones."

One look at Hettie said that she was still steaming mad over her tulip bed. "Me, too. I wouldn't let Amos bring one of those animals to our ranch. I told him I would buy bacon and ham at the store." She set about making herself a third whiskey sour and carried it to the table. "Them Callahans have sure brought a truckload of trouble to our little town.

You'd think we were going back in time to the cattle run days and everything was wild and woolly around here."

"I agree," Audrey said. "I'm going to get into my night shirt. Leave out the whiskey. I need a drink, too."

If you didn't feel something for Brodie, he wouldn't upset you so much, the voice in her head whispered.

"I'd feel more for a baby kitten, and I don't even like cats," she declared as she got dressed and went back to the kitchen.

"The only good thing about tonight is that I bet Bernie is fit to be tied since she's failing to get Brodie Callahan hooked up with a wife," Hettie said. "I made you a good stiff drink. Sit down and let it settle your nerves."

"I hope she's so mad that the anger blows the top of her head off," Audrey agreed, but she didn't tell her aunt that her reasons were far different. She might not want to date Brodie, but she sure didn't want him to go out with anyone else.

"God don't like her anymore. I'm back in the favorite seat," Hettie said. "I'm taking my drink and going to my room. I'll watch one of them reruns of *Lethal Weapon* and try to forget about Bernie and *your* next-door neighbor."

"He's your neighbor, too," Audrey told her.

"I don't own this land," Hettie yelled as she closed her bedroom door.

Audrey closed her eyes, shook her head, and whispered, "God does not have the time or patience for two feuding old women, and I do not have the patience for Brodie Callahan."

She finished off her drink and paced the floor for a few

minutes. The walls began to feel like they were closing in on her, so she shoved her feet down into a pair of rubber boots and went outside. She intended to take a short walk out to the barbed-wire fence and back. But she only made it to the end of the back porch when a squealing blur that looked a lot like that pig she had parked on the café table raced past her. Brodie was right behind it—bare chested, bruised, and bleeding.

"What the hell?" she screeched and started chasing him. "If that critter tears up my cornfield, I'm going to shoot it and you."

"If she eats anything on this place, she'll die from pesticide poisoning anyway," Brodie hollered over his shoulder.

"So, you've got an organic hog?" Audrey's boots got stuck in the mud. Her feet came out of them, and she kept running in her bare feet.

Brodie stooped and got a firm grip on Pansy and took a step, but he stepped in a hole and fell flat on his back. The pig got loose and ran right into acres and acres of corn plants that were about a foot high.

Audrey bent at the waist and put her hands on her knees. When she could catch her breath, she took a good look at Brodie. "We've got to catch that thing before it roots up the corn." She panted and then straightened up. "You look like hell. Did number seven work you over with her fists and fingernails? I hope she did. You deserve it."

"How did you know Wanette was number seven?" he asked.

"Everyone in town"—she panted—"keeps track. Aunt Hettie and her Sunday school friends are betting against Bernie. This will be her first fail if she don't get you married. Aunt Hettie will probably dance a jig in her underwear in the church parking lot if she wins that pot."

"That's a picture I don't want in my head, but I can't unsee it." Brodie shivered.

Pansy had made a wide circle and ran back toward him. He reached for her, but she shimmied out of his hands and ran between Audrey's legs. It startled Audrey so badly that she tumbled backward and fell on her back on the muddy ground. Brodie offered her a helping hand. She took it but slipped when she tried to get enough traction to get up and pulled him down on top of her. She pushed him off to the side, wiggled free of his arms and legs, and sat up.

"Was that as good for you as it was for me?" he teased.

"That is *not* funny," she snapped. "I wish that woman would have shot you rather than just beat the hell out of you."

"Sorry to disappoint, darlin'," Brodie chuckled. "But this is blackberry cobbler stain, and the blood is from barbed wire. I knocked down a post when I tried to jump the fence. The rest is mud. It will all wash off."

"If it wasn't for bad luck..." she started.

"So, I'm bad luck?" he asked.

"Absolutely, and also a pain in my ass," she told him as she carefully stood up. "Now I have to take a second shower."

"You aren't getting any pity from me. I have to turn on the garden hose and clean up outside in cold water," he said.

"Why?" she asked.

"Can't take Pansy to the Paradise, so I'm living in the trailer until we can get a pen built for her," he said as he got to his feet.

"Why do you call that thing Pansy?" Audrey asked.

"Because she tore up Hettie's flower beds," Brodie answered.

"Tulips, not pansies," she snapped.

Brodie started walking away. "Pansy fits her better."

Audrey caught up to him and rattled off a string of numbers. "That's my number. If your new best friend isn't at the trailer and has circled back around into my corn, you better run, not walk, back over here and find it or else. And fix my fence before the sun sets tomorrow."

He pulled his phone from his hip pocket, wiped the messy screen well enough that he could see it, and said, "Tell me that number again."

She said it slowly, and he typed it in.

"And honey, that fence could be mine rather than yours, depending on which brother put it up, so I will fix it when I damn well please," he told her in a low voice.

She stomped her bare foot in a puddle and sent more mud flying up onto his jeans. Not even that brought her a bit of peace.

Chapter 7

BRODIE STARED AT THE garden hose and then at the open-air bathroom that the tornado had left behind. The electricity had been cut off. That meant no hot water. But the shower would still be better than what came out of the well, which would make an Eskimo shiver. As crazy as it was, the tornado had left the shower curtain draped around the bathtub still, so he would have a little bit of privacy.

"I hear that cold showers are a good thing," he muttered, and then remembered that he was supposed to call Audrey about Pansy. Instead of calling, he texted: Pig is in the house.

He got an immediate response: Keep it there.

Pansy raised her head up from the corner and grunted at him when he peeked inside the trailer. He pointed at her. "Don't you dare make a run for the door when I open it."

He stepped outside, made sure the door was firmly latched, and sat down on the porch step. "Cold shower or really cold garden hose?"

Or you could forget either one and just curl up in all your filthy clothes, the pesky voice in his head chuckled.

"It's not funny." He stood up and crossed the yard to the bathroom.

He stepped up over the splintered floorboards and into the tub. He pulled the curtain and stripped out of his dirty jeans, boots, socks, and underwear. He put his phone in one of his boots and then tossed everything out onto what was left of the bathroom floor. He would have made his mother proud for not throwing swear words out into the open air when the water hit his body. Truth was that the stream coming from the showerhead was so cold that he couldn't utter a single word. He had to clench his jaw shut to keep his teeth from chattering.

He washed his hair and rinsed but there was no repeating. He turned off the water, threw back the curtain, and threw one foot out onto the floor. Before he could pick up the other one, what felt like an earthquake jerked his feet out from under him. Splintering wood and pipes being jerked away from the tub made for a deafening noise. Then in an instant was total silence, followed by cold water spraying everywhere. For what seemed like an hour, but in reality couldn't have been more than a few seconds, he tried to collect his bearings. Finally, he figured out he was sitting down with one leg hanging over the edge of the old green tub and the other stretched out to the end, and the busted pipes were shooting a jet of water straight up into the air. He eased up and bent at the knees—nothing was broken. The tub was sitting flat on the ground, so he didn't have to step out on the rotted boards.

Naked, shivering, his pulse racing, he grabbed his boots and made a beeline for his truck. He grabbed his toolbox from the back floorboard and found a crescent wrench. Then he hurried out to the road and turned off the water at the meter. He had just settled the cover back and started jogging toward the trailer when the dark clouds above him opened up and raindrops the size of silver dollars poured down on him. He slung open the trailer door and stopped just inside the trailer. Pansy waddled across the floor, smelled his feet, and went back to her corner. Brodie grabbed a fluffy throw from the bench that circled the table, wrapped it around his body, and sat down with a thud.

When his teeth stopped chattering and his body quit shivering, he dried himself off with the throw and padded back to the other end of the place. He found a T-shirt hanging in the closet and jerked it over his head. He opened all the drawers under the twin bed before he found a single pair of clean underwear and the beach shorts that Knox wore on their last vacation with their mother. That was it as far as clothing went, but at least he wouldn't be stark naked when his brothers arrived the next day.

Brodie sighed when he crawled into the bed and drew the covers up around his neck; he closed his eyes and let the warmth lull him into a deep sleep. He dreamed of Audrey running toward him with her arms outstretched, the skirt of her sundress and her dark hair flowing in the wind. When she reached him, she jumped and wrapped her legs around his waist. Their lips found each other in a fiery-hot kiss. He backed up and sat down under the apple trees that were filled with pink blossoms, which told him that everything in his dream was happening in the spring.

He awoke with a start, his eyes darting around the room to see if Audrey had come home with him after the make-out session in the orchard, but the only thing he found was Pansy rooting around the room looking for food.

"No truffles here," he said as he sat up, "but I will see if we can find a store that's open so we can buy you some food." He slung his legs out over the side of the bed, stood up, and retrieved his phone from his boot that was still parked beside the door.

"Good grief, Pansy!" he said when he checked the phone and realized that it was past noon. "I missed church because of you."

The pig just grunted and kept searching around the small trailer for something to eat. Brodie opened the dorm-sized refrigerator and found two withered carrots, a six-pack of warm beer, and a jar of dill pickles. He tossed the carrots on the floor and Pansy gobbled them up, then went back to her bed in the corner.

"You sleep right there, and do not use any part of this trailer for a bathroom. When I get back, you will have a collar and leash, food, and a dog bed to sleep in if I can find one," he said as he shoved his feet down into the dirty boots. "I hope my wallet is still in my jeans and that my money and credit cards aren't ruined. If so, you might have to starve."

He caught his reflection in the long mirror on the back door of the tiny bathroom. His T-shirt used to be red, but now it was something between orange and pink. With all the white splotches, Brodie figured it had lost a battle with a good amount of bleach. The shorts were bright blue with pink flamingos all over them. Dirty boots added enough to definitely give him the homeless look.

He opened the medicine cabinet and was relieved to find toothpaste and a couple of brand-new toothbrushes. There was no comb or brush, and his dark hair was beyond what could be called bedroom hair.

He made sure the door was closed tightly, straightened his back, and walked out to the place where the old tub was still sitting on the ground. His jeans had landed in a way that folded several times over the back pocket, so his wallet was only slightly damp.

With the way his luck was running, he sent up a silent prayer of thanksgiving that his truck even started. He had full intentions of driving all the way to Bowie to the Walmart store and hoped that the folks there had seen enough strange people coming in and out that they wouldn't call the police. But when he passed the feedstore in Nocona, he noticed that the front door was wide open. He whipped into a parking spot and crawled out of the vehicle.

"Well, look what the cats dragged in, or should I say the pot-bellied pig," Audrey said as soon as he walked inside.

Why didn't I go on to Bowie? I do not need this today! he groaned to himself.

"What are *you* doing here?" Brodie growled. Was there no place in the whole of Montague County where she wasn't there, or was she stalking him?

Hettie stepped out from behind her. "Buying more

plants for my flower bed that your pig rooted up and made a terrible mess of."

Both women looked as if they had just come from church. Audrey's hair was twisted up in a knot on top of her head. Her denim skirt accentuated her waist and rounded hips, and just looking at her made Brodie's mouth go dry. Not a single hair escaped Hettie's braids, but that didn't surprise Brodie. Nothing, not even a strand of hair, would defy her or Aunt Bernie—not if they didn't want to wither up and melt into nothing more than a spot on the floor.

"Well, you ladies have a good day," he said and grabbed an empty cart. When he found the right aisle, he tossed a bag of pot-bellied pig food into the cart, along with a harness and leash and a fluffy bed that looked like it might be the right size. He was on his way out when he saw that Hettie and Audrey were right ahead of him in the only open checkout lane. The lady rang up two flats of flowers and a rose bush.

"I'll pay for those," Brodie called out.

The disgusted look the woman gave him left no doubt that she didn't think he could afford one of the candy bars beside the counter, but she simply nodded.

"You should since it was your pig that tore up my tulips," Hettie declared.

"Yes, ma'am, I agree, and I will," Brodie agreed and pushed his cart ahead when they moved away.

Hettie had almost reached the door when she turned around and shook her fist at him. "And you better get that fence fixed today, or else I'm going to sue you for destruction of property."

"Now, Miz Hettie, judging from the fact that the barbed wire is on my side of the property, I'm sure that Ira put the fence up. That means it's mine and not yours to sue anyone over. I'll fix it when I'm ready to do so, or I might just tear it down. It's an eyesore, and I don't have any cattle to keep inside my place, so I don't need it."

She narrowed her eyes so much that they disappeared into the rest of her wrinkles, and she shook both fists toward him. "Fix it!"

Afraid that he would give her a heart attack if he argued any more, he just smiled and tipped an imaginary hat toward her. "Can I take you ladies to dinner at the Dairy Queen?"

"I'd scoot around the chicken yard on my scrawny butt and pick off the white tops of their doodah for my dinner before I'd eat with you," she declared, and marched out of the store.

"She's a pistol," the lady behind the counter giggled. "Always has been, and probably won't ever change."

"I'm learning that," he said, and handed her his credit card to pay for everything.

———

"Can you believe that man came to town dressed like a hobo?" Hettie grumbled as she got into Audrey's truck.

"Nope," Audrey said, but she did not say that in her eyes he was still sexy even in the mismatched ugly garb he wore to the feedstore or that she figured that was the only clothing he had to wear after ruining his shirt and jeans the night before.

"I'll fix that fence myself tomorrow," Hettie muttered. "I still know how to stretch wire and set a fence post."

"Let's talk about something else." Audrey drove down the street toward the Dairy Queen. "You wanted nachos and a burger for dinner. Let's enjoy those and forget about Brodie Callahan, pot-bellied pigs, and the fence."

Hettie crossed her arms over her chest. "I'll talk about whatever I want."

"Okay, remember what you always told me. She who stirs the pile of manure has to lick the spoon."

"Don't you be turning my words around to argue with me," Hettie growled.

"Then stop stirring." Audrey drove the short distance to the DQ and found a parking spot close to the front. "I bet your blood pressure is over the moon."

"Probably, but when we get home, I'll make a double whiskey sour and that will bring it down." Hettie got out of the truck and beat Audrey inside.

"Hey, Miz Hettie," the young girl behind the order counter waved. "What'll it be? Nachos and a burger with everything on it?"

"Yep, and a double order of fries and a pineapple milk shake." Hettie claimed a booth by the window.

"I'll have a steak finger basket and a large sweet tea," Audrey added, and took out her wallet to pay the bill when she realized that Brodie was in front of her.

He took a while to decide what he wanted and then turned around slowly. "Fancy meeting you again so soon."

"Seems like the Universe hates us." Her chilly tone did not match the hot little sparks dancing around in her insides.

"Yep," he said with a smile and went to the back side of the place.

Audrey took a couple of bills from her wallet and handed them to the girl, but she shook her head and said, "Brodie paid for your order."

"Order up!" the cook yelled from the kitchen.

"Brodie Callahan!" the girl hollered. "Your takeout order is ready."

He appeared at Audrey's elbow, and she tried to hand him the money still in her hand. "You are not buying our dinner."

He brushed her hand away. "Darlin', I had to buy y'all's dinner to wipe that visual of Miz Hettie scootin' around a chicken pen searching for white tops on doodah. Now, the picture is all gone from my head because I know she's having a good Sunday dinner. Y'all have a nice day now."

Before she could say another word, he had left the restaurant. How on earth he had managed to get there before them was a complete mystery. Then she realized that Hettie had shuffled across the feedstore parking lot slower than usual. Every few steps she stopped to breathe and cuss out Brodie some more. That plus the fact they had had to stop at both traffic lights in town had put them behind.

"What was that all about?" Hettie asked when Audrey slid into the booth on the opposite side from her.

"Brodie paid for our food. I tried to repay him, but he refused to take it," she answered, and went on to tell Hettie what he had said. "So, don't go gettin' mad at him. You caused this."

"I didn't cause that fence to get knocked down or the pig to tear up my flowers. Don't tell me I can't be mad. That man is arrogant, and who does he think he is, going around in public looking like..." Hettie was on a real rampage until the waitress brought a tray with their food and set it in the middle of the table.

"I wish I'd come to whatever church y'all go to," the lady said.

"Why's that?" Hettie asked.

"You must have had some kind of program this morning. Was Brodie playing the part of Jonah in the story about the whale? That man is so sexy, I could just fall over backward and pull him down on top of me," she sighed and hurried back to the counter to wait on a big family coming inside.

"Is that any way for a young girl to talk?" Hettie fussed as she unwrapped her burger. "I swear this old world is going to hell in a handbasket."

"That's not any worse than you threatening to have chicken doodah for dinner," Audrey reminded her. "Or asking me if I had sex with someone in a mud lolly."

"Hmmph," Hettie snorted. "Eat your dinner and take me home so I can get the taste of this morning out of my mouth with a good whiskey sour."

"After we go by the cemetery to see Uncle Amos?" Audrey asked.

"We are not going today, and don't give me no sass," Hettie told her. "Amos will understand that I need a good stiff drink after the morning I've had."

"Yes, ma'am, if that's what you want," Audrey said.

"What are you going to do all afternoon?" Hettie asked.

"I am going to take the book I've been reading out to the hammock in the backyard and read a while, nap a while, and repeat the process until it gets dark," Audrey answered. "I bet you are going to call Bitsy and gossip about Brodie, right?"

"That's not a bit of your business, but yes, I am," Hettie said, and then stuffed her mouth with a french fry. "Ain't no one in the world can make a burger and fries like this place."

"You mean like Dairy Queen does?" Audrey asked.

"Nope, I mean like this very one," she said and reached for a nacho. "Amos brought me here every Sunday after services. He said it was biblical because the scripture says, 'Blessed is he who hungers and thirsts after righteousness.' We had listened to the preacher teach us about being right with the Lord, and we were hungry, so it was right and proper."

Audrey chuckled and took a long drink of her sweet tea. "Does the Good Book also say that it's alright to go home after being fed and have a whiskey sour?"

"There's a lot of verses in there, but remember that Jesus himself turned water to wine, so you can't condemn me. Are you going to have a beer when we get home?" Hettie asked.

"Probably," Audrey said, and felt the corners of her

mouth turn up in a grin. "I might even ask Brodie if he'd like for me to bring him one."

Hettie grabbed her heart and groaned. "Don't you ever tease me about something that serious. I hate that man, and you will not ever have anything to do with him. Is that understood?"

"So, the feud between two parcels of land is still going full strength," Audrey said. "It used to be between Grandpa and Uncle Ira. Now it's between us and the Callahans."

"You got it, if you toss Bernie in there with it," Hettie answered with a nod.

Chapter 8

BRODIE'S THOUGHTS WENT FROM figuring out what to do with Pansy in the long term to helping remodel the old barn for Tripp. Then it jumped the tracks like a train wreck and settled on all the times that God, Fate, or the Universe—folks could take their pick—had put Audrey in his path.

What do you expect? Your houses might be separated by a barbed-wire fence, but they're less than a hundred yards apart, his mother's voice fussed at him.

He was surprised to see both his brothers tearing down the last wall of the house when he parked beside their trucks in the driveway. "Hey, are y'all hungry?" he asked as he got out of his truck. "I brought a sack of burgers from the Dairy Queen."

"We had Sunday dinner at the Paradise, but I can always eat a burger," Knox answered and laid down his hammer.

"We're supposed to be building a pen for Pansy, and besides, y'all don't have to work on Sunday," Brodie said.

"We heard this morning that Jesus ate corn on the sabbath because he was hungry," Tripp told him. "I reckon if God didn't zap him for that, we can build a pen for a miniature hog. I'll take one of those burgers, too."

Knox took three lawn chairs from the back of his truck and popped them open. "Might as well take a little break while we have a snack."

Brodie sat down in one and passed out three of the six burgers. "Again, why are you tearing down the rest of the house?"

"The boards will make a good hog pen," Tripp explained. "What happened here to make the bathtub fall in?"

"Long story," Brodie said.

"Does it have something to do with the fact that your jeans are lying back there in a muddy mess?" Knox asked.

"Yep," Brodie answered.

"And that you look downright pitiful in that garb you are wearing?" Tripp asked.

"Hey, don't be dissing *my* beach shorts," Knox said.

Brodie finished swallowing a bite of burger and washed it down with a sip of his root beer. "I'm just lucky that I found a shirt and shorts in the trailer, or I would have had to run around with a throw wrapped around me like one of those things that island folks wear."

"What you are lucky about is that the tornado bypassed the trailer and that I forgot all about having a couple of things stored away when we moved to the Paradise," Knox told him. "But your blessings ran out when that pig showed up. Since you seem determined to keep the critter, we'll be good brothers and build the thing a pen. Think you'll be able to leave her all alone tonight?"

Brodie finished off his burger, wadded up the paper, and

tossed it into the sack. "To sleep in my bed at the Paradise and have a whole day and night when I don't have to see or fight with Audrey, I would leave her alone for a week."

"Plus having decent clothes to put on your body," Knox chuckled.

"Two weeks," Brodie growled. "Let's get busy. We've got to start fertilizing the orchard and putting down straw around each tree tomorrow. Glad that we are promised some good sunny days for most of the week. I'll be at the feedstore when it opens in the morning to get the supplies. But right now, I've got to let Pansy out of the trailer, harness her up and put her on a short leash, and give her some food and water."

"Do you think that maybe having a pot-bellied pig will make it harder for Bernie to find eligible women for you?" Tripp asked.

"That's the plan," Brodie grinned.

"Whoa!" Knox put up a hand. "You didn't tell us how the bathtub fell or why you shucked out of your jeans out here."

"Like I said, it's a long story," Brodie answered.

"Daylight savings started a couple of weeks ago," Knox told him.

"What's that got to do with a bathtub?" Brodie asked.

Knox reached over and patted him on the knee. "It won't get dark for quite a while, so we have time to hear the story. Does it have to do with that broken-down fence and with Audrey? Did y'all have wild mud sex in the old bathtub? Is that the reason it fell through the floor?"

"Yes, no, and no," Brodie answered.

"Explain all those please," Tripp said with a wide grin.

Brodie told them the whole story, barring none of the details, and ended with the fence being on his side of the land. "I'll be so glad to get back to the Paradise so that our paths will be less likely to cross. She's nothing but bad luck."

"Amen to that."

"And speaking of that..." Knox pointed to the truck passing by very slowly. "What do you say we build the pigpen on the far end of the trailer so neither she nor Hettie can fuss about the smell?"

"Sounds great to me," Brodie agreed. "Do I need to drive back to Nocona and get some wire?"

"Nope," Knox answered. "Joe Clay donated that and all the nails and screws we need, plus he loaned us a couple of battery-operated drills and hand tools. We should have this job done before the day is done."

"He had lots of scrap wood, but Knox said we could use the boards from what's left of the house and kill two birds with one stone," Tripp added.

Two birds. One stone.

Brodie didn't want to kill Audrey and Hettie, but if he had a virtual stone or two in his pocket, he might throw them.

You already did! His mother was back in his head. *You paid for their flowers and for their food. Stones thrown.*

Audrey tried to analyze her emotions as she changed into a pair of loose-fitting athletic shorts and a comfortable T-shirt. She could absolutely wring Brodie's neck for getting the upper hand when he bought the flowers and paid for dinner. But before she could muster up enough anger to hate him, she remembered the way he made her feel when they were chasing that stupid pig, and even more so when she had kissed him.

No amount of trying to study how or why she was sitting on the fence when it came to the love or hate situation between them seemed to have answers. She left her bedroom, grabbed a bottle of sweet tea from the refrigerator, and carried it out to the front porch.

"About time you got here," Hettie said. "I changed into my muumuu in five minutes and made my first drink of the day."

"Congratulations. You get a gold star," Audrey snapped, and pointed at the drink in her aunt's hand. "You are working your way right into those anonymous meetings."

"Honey, I'm not an alcoholic, and I will not go to any of those meetings. These little drinks are for medicinal purposes. They keep my arthritis from hurting so bad. They also are my mood enhancers and take away part of the anger that would make me get my gun and shoot those Callahan brothers and then go take care of Bernie before the law comes to carry me away to jail. If I ever run out of whiskey, will you sneak some into the prison when you come to visit?"

"Nope, so you better control your anger," Audrey answered. "What do you think they're doing over there?"

Hettie took a sip of her whiskey. "Making a lot of noise on the Lord's Day. Maybe I won't have to do a thing but just wait for Him to zap them for not taking a day of rest."

Audrey twisted the top off her bottle. "Looks like they might be tearing down what's left of the house to build a pen for that pig."

Hettie sucked in long breath and let it out in a snort. "Why would he keep such an animal? Hogs are terrible about rooting up everything."

"Maybe he wants to use its *doodah* for fertilizer since he's all into the organic stuff," Audrey said with a chuckle.

"Just like Ira," Hettie grumbled. "Me and Amos could never figure out why he switched from perfectly fine fertilizer to that natural stuff."

"Why did he take the orchards and gardens instead of the cash crop fields?" Audrey asked.

Hettie finished off her drink in one gulp. "He and Frank divided the land right down the middle. Ira had been looking into all that natural stuff, hoping to help heal Clarice's imaginary illnesses. I guess he figured he would show her that she made the wrong choice when he decided to go all organic with his gardens and the orchards. Looks like they've got the boards torn away from what is left of that last wall, and they're stacking them up on the far end of the trailer."

"Yep, do you want to borrow my binoculars so you can see better?" Audrey teased. "Or maybe we can get them to put up a big-screen television and film what they're doing so you can watch it better."

"Don't be sassy with me," Hettie snapped. "I thought you were going to lay up in the hammock all afternoon and read a book, and yet, here you are being just as nosy as I am."

"I'm protecting my interests," Audrey argued. "I might want to lower my bidding price for his farm if it's got a tacky hog pen tacked on to the end of that travel trailer."

"To get these two places put back together, I'll take the trailer and the hog pen. They can both be burned to the ground or hauled to the dump, along with that pig," Hettie declared. "My Sunday afternoon nap is calling my name." She stood up and went into the house without another word.

A butterfly caught Audrey's attention when it landed on a red tulip. She forgot all about the romance book she had planned to read that afternoon. She made a quick trip inside for her gloves and a gardening trowel. She could easily get all the flowers planted and watch what was going on next door at the same time while Aunt Hettie was sleeping.

"And I won't have to listen to her bossiness while I do it," she muttered.

That evening, Brodie stripped out of Knox's beach shorts and T-shirt and stepped into a steamy, hot shower. As the water beat down on his back, he vowed that he would never take such a luxury for granted again. What had happened in the café with Wanette and poor little Pansy seemed like a month ago, but in reality it had only been twenty-four hours. He looked down at the stain and the four puncture marks the wire had made. He'd been able to wash away some of the blueberry stain, but his chest still looked like he had lost a battle with a rattlesnake.

He finished his shower, brushed his teeth, and got dressed in a pair of pajama pants and a sleep shirt. When he got to his bedroom, he opened the balcony doors and stepped outside. The air was still warm even though it was fully dark, and there were no dark clouds in sight. Maybe tomorrow, with the help of his brothers, he could get a lot of the fertilizing done and the straw around the base of the trees. He sat down in a chair. The waning crescent moon seemed to be holding court for all the twinkling stars around it, and that made him think of his mother. She loved to sit on the front porch and look up at the sky. Even during those last weeks of her life, he would carry her outside, wrap her in a quilt, and sit with her. That's where they were the night she told him about Joe Clay. The next morning, she told the twins about their parents, and then she died that night right after midnight. She'd always said that she wanted to pass away on her birthday to make it a full circle, and she did.

Joe Clay came out from a doorway with two beers in his hand. "I thought maybe you might could use one of these after what all you've been through. Mind if I join you?"

"Not a bit." Brodie reached out and took a beer from him. "And you are so right. I could really use a good cold one."

"Tripp and Knox told me and Mary Jane what all happened. Mary Jane says that she would use the story about

Audrey and Linda in one of her books, but her readers would call her out for going too far out there," Joe Clay chuckled.

"The truth is stranger than fiction," Brodie smiled. "Did I ever tell you that my whole name is Brodie Carter Callahan? I never knew until just before Mother died that my middle name came from you. She said that it made me a part of a wonderful memory."

Joe Clay swiped a tear from his cheek with the back of his hand. "Thank you for sharing that with me. It means a lot."

"I should have told you before now," Brodie said. "And back to Audrey. That woman is like a major thorn—no, that's not right—she's more like a whole tree limb in my…" he paused and took a long gulp of the icy cold beer.

"In your butt or your heart?" Joe Clay asked.

"Can it be both?" Brodie asked. "I wouldn't admit that to anyone else, especially to Bernie, but Audrey makes me so mad that…"

Joe Clay chuckled again. "You don't have to explain. I felt the same way about Mary Jane at the first, but I didn't have to contend with a feud going between two old ladies, and I had to live right here in the house with her."

"For real?" Brodie was amazed that there could ever have been a cross word between his father and stepmother.

"Yep," Joe Clay answered. "I was going out the door and planning to go straight to the recruiting office to reenlist when she called me a chicken."

"Why would she do that?"

"I didn't like kids, especially seven little sassy girls," Joe

Clay admitted. "She made me so mad that I stayed just to prove her wrong. My heart kept telling me that she was the one, but my mind didn't want to accept it. Is Audrey the one?"

"I hope not," Brodie answered.

They sat in silence and listened to the sounds of a spring night—crickets, tree frogs, cows mooing over in Remy and Ursula's pasture. Brodie kept going back over the events of the last few days and wondering if he was fighting against something that was supposed to be. Could Audrey be the one? If she was, what kind of stink would that cause?

Finally, he put the questions to the side and asked, "The barbed wire on the fence between my place and Audrey's is on my side. Am I right in assuming that it belongs to me and not her?"

"Yep, you are right," Joe Clay answered. "Why?"

"Well, the part that Tripp and Knox might have left out is this." He told his dad about the post falling when he tried to jump over the fence.

"And now Hettie and Audrey are insisting that you fix their fence?" Joe Clay laughed out loud.

Brodie nodded and sipped on his beer. "That's right, and thanks again for this beer. I would have traded my new pig for anything cold last night. Other than icy water out of the shower, I might add. Matter of fact, I would have traded that pig for a bucket full of dirt before the night was done."

"So, are you going to keep her?"

"Probably," Brodie answered. "Mother supported a local

animal shelter and got me a weekend job there when I was in middle school. Her theory was that parents fail their children when they don't teach them to work. Someday I hope to have a family, and the farm will be a perfect place for them to learn responsibility."

"That's a good goal," Joe Clay agreed. "And your mother was right in teaching you to work and respect animals. What kind of pen did you build?"

"We attached a framework to the west end of the trailer and boarded underneath the other three sides to give her a good shelter. Then we stretched wire—thank you for that— all around the frame and covered all the other boards with wire for extra protection. That way Pansy can lie in the sun or get under the trailer for protection when it rains. Knox came up with the idea."

Joe Clay chuckled under his breath. "And nosy Hettie can't see what's going on, right?"

"I hope it drives her crazy," Brodie laughed with him. "Maybe having a mess like that right next door will make her hush about me fixing my fence."

"Don't bet on it," Joe Clay said. "My beer is gone, so I'm going back down to get a piece of the chocolate cake that Tertia brought over this evening. Want to join me?"

"Thanks, but I think I'll sit right here and enjoy the view while I finish my beer, and then I'll go in and appreciate a bed that's longer and wider than the one I slept on last night," Brodie answered.

Joe Clay stood up and gave Brodie's shoulder a gentle

squeeze. "Here's hoping tomorrow treats you better than yesterday and today."

"Amen!" Brodie agreed.

He replayed the conversation he'd just had with Joe Clay over again a couple of times in his mind and wondered if, after all was said and done, he and Audrey would find common ground in the future. If they did, would Bernie and Hettie burn down the whole town of Spanish Fort, or would they simply disown Brodie and Audrey?

"Maybe that wouldn't be so bad," Brodie whispered.

Finally, he gave up trying to figure out anything and went inside. He removed his socks and crawled between the sheets. "This feels so good," he whispered as he closed his eyes.

He dreamed again of Audrey. This time she held a little dark-haired girl up to pick a low-hanging peach. The bright sunshine lit up the child's green eyes, and when she'd chosen the peach from all the dozens making the limb droop, she ran over to Brodie and handed it to him.

"Here, Daddy, you get the first one," she said, and then wrapped her arms around his leg and squeezed tightly. "Now I'll get one for Mommie and then one for me."

He awoke the next morning with a smile on his face. "It was only a dream," he told himself, "and it could never happen. We'll be fighting until we are old and gray. There's no way we would ever have children together."

Chapter 9

THE DREAM HAUNTED BRODIE all day on Monday as he and his brothers fertilized all the apple, peach, and pear trees, then covered the ground under them with a bed of straw. When they finished, all three of them sunk down in the lawn chairs in the front yard.

Knox passed out the last three beers in the cooler and groaned. "This farming business is more tiring than framing out a five-thousand-square-foot house."

"Or tooling an entire saddle," Tripp added. "I'm almost too tired to enjoy the lovely sunset."

"All I want to do is take a shower and fall into bed," Brodie said, but he wondered if Audrey was sitting on her porch enjoying the lovely sunset that splashed the sky with brilliant colors that evening.

Tripp took a long drink of his beer. "Have you been bored today?"

"Were you ready for a little peace and quiet?" Knox asked.

Brodie had trouble following their trains of thought. "Why are you asking me those questions?"

"We haven't seen Audrey all day. After all the excitement

you've had recently, fertilizing and laying straw would seem a little boring, right?" Knox answered the question with another one.

Brodie glanced across the fence that was still broken down. "Been a wonderful day. Got a lot done with y'all's help, and I was not bored. I love this farm, and tomorrow we sign all the papers to buy the barn for Tripp." He changed the subject in hopes that they didn't talk about Audrey anymore since, if he was truthful with himself, he missed the excitement of seeing her that day.

"Yep, and then I'm calling all the favors for helping you with the farm the last three months," Tripp said.

Brodie stretched his long legs out in front of him and leaned his head back. "I'll be there to help all I can, and I'll bring Pansy with me."

"If you do, you will keep her on the leash," Tripp said with a nod. "Maybe she and Aunt Bernie's yappy little mutt will be friends."

"What makes you think those two will ever meet?" Brodie asked.

"Bernie takes Pepper for a walk every day," Knox answered. "Usually, it's down to Luna and Shane's beer, bait, and bologna store. Since the barn is on her way back to the Paradise, chances are she'll use the excuse to come see how the work is going so she can pester you about the next blind date."

"I'm done with that," Brodie declared. "If she sets me up with more, I simply will not show up. It's your turn, Tripp."

"I'll pass. Knox can have it," Tripp said without a hint of a smile.

"Thank you so much, brother." Knox's voice was dripping with sarcasm. "But I'll let the next eligible bachelor step right up to the plate."

Brodie chuckled. "How many bachelors, other than us three, have you seen in this part of the state? Bernie is running out of product to sell."

"Yuk!" Knox said. "The notion of being a commodity for her matchmaking mill makes me need a shower."

Tripp laughed out loud. "Brother, after the way we've sweated all day, we all *need* a shower. When it comes to Bernie, I'm going to swear that I'm too busy to date because I'm working on my new store, and then I'll be too busy producing product." He air quoted the last word. "Then I'm going to hire a pretty lady to help me out, and one of the prerequisites to her working with and/or for me is that she has to pretend to be my girlfriend."

"Dang it," Knox groaned. "Why didn't I think of that?"

"I called it first," Tripp said.

"Or you could both say *N-O*, like I'm going to do," Brodie told them.

Tripp shook his head. "*N-O* reads *Y-E-S* in Bernie's head. Let's get on home to the Paradise. I put a big pot of chili on to simmer all day before we left this morning. I'm hoping there's enough left to feed us tonight."

"If it's all gone, I'll whip up breakfast for supper," Brodie offered. A picture flashed in his head of him and Audrey making pancakes together in a small kitchen and bumping into each other at every turn. A warm feeling rushed through his body, and he was glad that his brothers had walked on ahead of him so they couldn't see the smile on his face.

———

"Think that Callahan feller will ever sell his place to you?" Walter asked as he wiped sweat from his brow with a red bandanna.

Audrey shrugged. "I'm trying, but the news isn't good."

"Well, whether he does or not, I'm retiring, so get ready for it," Walter said. "I went to work right here back when Frank and Ira were teenagers, and their daddy was still alive. I want to have a few years to relax before I die, and besides, trying to supervise all the work on both places would be too much for this old man. Heck, this farm alone is too much, and you can count this as my notice to quit after the fall harvest is in."

"No!" Audrey gasped. "You're the backbone of the place, Walter. You've been like a grandpa to me all my life."

He removed his worn straw hat and fanned his face. "I know, baby girl, but the time that I spent down on the coast with my sister and her family got me to thinking real hard about retiring anyway. She owns one of them tiny houses right next door to her place, and she's offered to let me move into it. But don't you worry none; I ain't planning to leave until after fall harvest."

"Fair enough," Audrey said, but down deep she hoped she could talk him into another year before he went south.

Walter was eighty years old. That crazy pot-bellied pig of Brodie's could have hidden in the deep wrinkles in his long face. His tall, lanky frame looked like a gentle spring breeze could blow him all the way across the Red River and into Oklahoma. He would make a perfect actor to play the scarecrow in *The Wizard of Oz*, but when folks got to know him, they looked right past his age and body build and saw only his big heart.

"Now, let's put that conversation on the back burner and talk about that fence that's down. Want me to have one of the hired help fix it?" Walter asked.

"Nope," Audrey answered. "Brodie says since the barbed wire is on his side of the posts that the fence belongs to him."

"That's right. Ira put it up when he and Frank divided the land. He had the place surveyed and them little flags put up in a row, so he'd know what was his property. Frank told him that he'd better not take an inch of what belonged to him, so Ira set his fence back one foot from the edge," Walter explained. "Them fightin' over a woman like they did broke me from suckin' eggs."

Audrey slapped a hand over her mouth. "Is that the reason you never married?"

"Yep," Walter answered. "Love 'em and leave 'em with a smile on their faces has been my motto ever since that fence was put up."

"And you're saying that if I walk right up to that fence, then I'm actually on Brodie's property."

Walter looked down at her feet. "I reckon with a shoe size as small as you wear, the answer would be yes."

"Well, dang it all!" Audrey said.

─────

Brodie was more than a little nervous the next morning when he walked into the real estate office with his two brothers. He scanned the office and then breathed a long sigh of relief when Linda Massey was nowhere in sight.

"Little spooked, were you?" Knox asked under his breath.

"No, not a little—a lot," Brodie admitted.

"Hello!" A short lady with gray hair came out of a door at the end of the short hallway. "You must be the Callahan brothers. Jody will be with you in a minute. He's just finishing up with another client. Please have a seat. Can I get you a cup of coffee, a cold soda, or water?"

"I'm fine," Tripp said with a smile.

"Me, too," Brodie and Knox said at the same time.

"Are we really doing this?" Knox asked. "We can always run out the door if you aren't sure that you want to sink so much money into renovations. We can start fresh and build a spanking brand-new place for your business."

Brodie chuckled. "That sounds like the speech you would give a groom just before he walks down the aisle."

A smile tickled the corners of Tripp's mouth. "I'm not marrying the barn, but I am sure about buying it."

An older man came out of the first office. A younger one, not much older than the Callahan brothers, shook his hand and then motioned for them. "Y'all come on in. I'm sorry that my meeting went a little longer and apologize that you had to wait. I'm Jody Thompson, and I'll handle all the paperwork on this deal. Y'all have a seat." He opened up a thick folder and riffled through some papers. "My Uncle Walter told me that you guys own the farm next to Audrey's place. If you're interested in selling it, he says that Audrey would give you top dollar for it."

"Thanks, but I'm not interested," Brodie said. "Actually, I own the place, and Tripp will be the only one on the deed for what we're buying today."

"But we help each other out," Knox said.

"So, you are putting a leather store in the old barn?" Jody asked.

"That's right," Tripp answered.

Jody looked over at Knox. "What about you? There's a couple of parcels of land just east of Spanish Fort going up for sale soon. Keep me in mind if you decide to buy something to build on."

"Thank you, and when I get ready to build or buy, I'll give you a call," Knox said with a nod. "But today, Tripp needs to sign whatever papers you have and write you a check."

"Uncle Walter?" Brodie asked.

"Small world, isn't it?" Jody said and whipped a stack of papers around and handed Tripp a pen. "Sign on all the yellow highlighted lines. Walter has been the foreman, or supervisor as he likes to be called, at Audrey's for years. He worked for her great-grandfather and then for Frank until he died. He's talking about retiring, but he's threatened to do that so long that no one believes him. He'll probably drop dead out in the cornfield one of these days. He's been down in Florida visiting one of his sisters for the past couple of weeks, but I believe he came home yesterday. I haven't seen him yet to see how his vacation went," Jody explained.

Tripp signed every one of the papers and turned them back around to Jody. "Is that all?"

"No," Knox said with a straight face. "You have to raise your right hand and stand on your head."

Tripp shot him a dirty look and took out his checkbook. "Do you need to verify that my check is good?"

"If you don't mind. That's a lot of money," Jody answered.

"Go ahead," Tripp said. "If I need to tell them it's okay, just hand me the phone."

In less than five minutes, the brothers were finished and headed toward Brodie's truck. Brodie patted Tripp on the shoulder and said, "Congratulations. An antique barn now owns you."

"Hey, that was my line when you signed the papers for the farm, and I was right," Knox said. "You don't own that farm. It owns you and all your time."

"Yep, and we are a match made in heaven," Brodie laughed. "Now, let's go take that list that's in your pocket to the lumberyard."

Knox rubbed his hands together as he got into the back seat. "I can't wait to get started. Joe Clay said I can move his saws and other equipment on-site, and he also offered to help us. I'm not sure if it's because he's got spring fever or if he wants some time away from Bernie."

"I understand he remodeled the Paradise, so I bet he'll be really good help," Tripp said.

"Changing the subject here," Knox said, "but what are we going to do about our trucks? I like mine so well that as soon as the insurance money comes in, I'm going to take it to a body shop."

"Me, too," Brodie agreed, and then let his thoughts wander to the third dream he had had about Audrey. In that one they were both older folks with gray sprinkled through their hair and crow's feet around their eyes. The picture was still in his mind when Tripp started the playlist on his phone. Alan Jackson was singing, "Livin' on Love." Brodie kept time to the fiddle music by tapping his thumbs on the steering wheel.

"What are you thinking about?" Tripp asked.

"Why?" Brodie asked.

"You've got a weird look on your face," he answered.

"I was wondering if any of us would ever find a love that could really walk through fire without blinking like the song says toward the end," Brodie answered.

"Not with Bernie around with her never-ending supply of women to set us up with," Knox chuckled.

The next song that played was "Bigger Houses" by Dan and Shay.

Every word in it seemed to be thrown right at Brodie

and made him think of his mother. The lyrics were basically what she had preached to him all his life. "We live in a big, fancy house," she had said, "but happiness isn't this house. It's what's in our hearts, so strive to fill every day with joy, not with material things."

Yes, ma'am, and thanks for the reminder, he thought as he parked in front of the lumberyard. "If y'all don't need me, I'll just hold down the fort here in the truck until y'all get through, and then we'll go have banana splits at the Dairy Queen to celebrate buying a barn."

"We won't be long," Knox said. "We just basically give them the list and ask them when they can deliver the first load. We'll start on the roof tomorrow."

Brodie leaned his head back and closed his eyes and listened to Luke Combs singing, "Beer Never Broke My Heart."

"Amen!" he agreed with the words. "But I've got a feeling Audrey Tucker would not only break a heart. She would throw it down on the ground and stomp it to mush with her boots."

He was singing along when someone tapped on the window right by his ear. Startled, he jumped and paused the playlist. His eyes widened so much that they hurt when he saw Hettie standing there with Audrey and a tall, lanky man right behind her. He hit the button to roll down the window.

"Miz Hettie," he said with a nod.

She set her narrow mouth in a firm line and narrowed her eyes at him. "You haven't fixed Audrey's fence yet, and I can smell that pig, so you need to get rid of it."

"Who built the fence?" Brodie asked.

"Ira did, but—"

"No buts, ma'am. I bought the land, so the fence is mine, and I don't care if it all falls down. If you or Audrey touch it, then you'll be damaging my property," he said in a respectable tone.

The elderly man behind her chuckled. "I told you that was Ira's fence and one foot over on your side belonged to him, too."

Hettie whipped around and shook her fist at the man. "Walter, this is not your fight."

"You're right," Walter grinned. "But there's no way you can win this battle, so let these boys alone."

Hettie whipped around and stormed toward the lumberyard. "Men! Ain't a dozen in the whole state that's worth the poison to kill 'em."

Brodie's heart pounded, and he couldn't have wiped the grin off his face if he'd sucked on a green persimmon. He not only owned the fence but a foot on the other side of it. That might prove to be an ace in the hole when he and Audrey had their next big fight.

Audrey gave him a dirty look and followed Hettie across the parking lot.

"I'm Walter," the guy said. "Hettie refuses to kick the bucket until the two farms are back together that her brothers divided. The way you and Audrey are looking at each other, I think there's something between y'all."

"You do know that I'm an organic farmer?" Brodie asked. "And Audrey hates me."

"So was Ira, and son, hate is just a line in the dirt with love on the other side," he said, and then turned around and headed toward the store.

"That sounds like something Mother would say," Brodie whispered, "but the line in the dirt between me and Audrey is as deep as the Grand Canyon."

He hit the button to start the playlist and laughed out loud when he heard the Pistol Annies singing "Hell on Heels."

"I wonder if Miranda Lambert knew Audrey Tucker," he muttered.

Chapter 10

BRODIE HAD TO MAKE a quick run out to the farm to feed and water Pansy that morning, so he was the last one to arrive at the barn site. He had expected to see Joe Clay's flatbed trailer loaded with equipment, since he and his brothers had helped load it the evening before. But he was surprised to see several other trucks lined up between the old house and the barn. Remy and Shane were already on top of the roof, and Parker and Maverick were organizing things on the ground.

"Hey!" Knox waved. "Look who all showed up to help."

"Noah would be here, but he has to work at the café," Remy said. "He said he'll take a break as soon as the lunch rush is done and bring us some burgers."

"And Luna is going to bring over some cold tea and cookies that she baked last night," Shane said.

"Well, thank you all," Brodie called out so they could all hear.

"That's what family does," Parker said. "Some of us can't be here every day, but we'll all come around every chance we get. I've done a fair amount of carpentry. I've been up on the roof, and we can probably throw some four-by-eight sheets of plywood on what's already there and then lay the sheet metal roofing on top of that. That will put it in the dry so we can work on the inside no matter what the weather is like."

"Exactly what I was thinking," Knox said with a nod.

"Then let's get on with it," Joe Clay said. "Man, I'm glad to have a job today. Mary Jane is working on a deadline, and Bernie is all wound up looking for another woman for Brodie."

Brodie jogged over to help Shane bring a sheet of plywood out of the barn, where the folks from the lumberyard had unloaded supplies the evening before. "Bernie might as well save her energy. I'm not going out on any more blind dates," he said.

"Bo and I will sell tickets to see the show when you tell her," Maverick said in a serious tone. "She fussed the whole time me and Bo were seeing each other. When we moved into the trailer together and started getting the old store in shape to sell musical instruments and teach piano lessons, she really threw a fit. It's only been since y'all arrived on the scene that she took a step back and declared that she was using reverse psychology on us. So, thank you."

"You are welcome, I guess," Brodie said.

"She liked me from the beginning. I guess being a preacher helped," Parker said.

"I'm the golden boy," Remy chuckled. "Bernie did everything she could to get me and Ursula together."

Brodie would bet dollars to cow patties that not a one of the brothers-in-law had a problem like he would have if he asked Audrey out on a date.

Audrey shoved the MP3 player down into the bibbed pocket of her faded jeans and got her earbuds situated. She started her playlist and listened to the Pistol Annies sing "Hell on Heels" as she affixed the seeder to the back of her smallest tractor. She crawled up into the seat of the tractor and set a cooler with several bottles of water on the seat beside her and a brown paper bag holding a couple of sandwiches and a bag of chips on the floor.

She settled into the seat, put the tractor in gear, and sang along with the songs on her playlist. Every song reminded her of Brodie—his walk, the way his eyes twinkled when they argued, but most of all the heat when she kissed him.

The sun was out and not a single cloud dotted the sky, but she could feel the sparks of an internal storm going on between her and Brodie when Miranda Lambert sang "Storms Never Last." She was like a wild Texas tornado, and he was the worst hurricane possible. Nothing but disaster could possibly survive when the two of them collided. The south wind kicked up a few dirt devils in front of her. She wondered if the song was right when the words said that bad times would pass with the wind.

"There's my answer," she whispered. "The wind never stops blowing in Texas, so why would I expect an easy relationship of any kind with Brodie Callahan? In this case, the storms will most likely last until we are both knocking on heaven's door—just like they did with Uncle Ira and Grandpa."

As if on cue, "Holes in the Floor of Heaven" was next on the playlist. The lyrics didn't exactly fit her situation, but as she listened, she wondered if the Tucker brothers had settled their differences in the afterlife.

At noon she pulled off to the side of the field and slid off the seat for a fifteen-minute break. She rolled her neck to get the kinks out and did some stretches to relieve the stiff muscles in her body. Then she picked up the sack lunch and got a bottle of water from the cooler.

"Hey!" Walter called from the end of the field.

"What are you doing out here?" Audrey asked.

"Hettie has been trying to get a hold of you all morning. She said to tell you to come to the house. She wants you to drive her to the convenience store in town to get some milk. Seems she's got a mind to make chocolate pies this afternoon," Walter answered.

"Guess I had the music turned up too high to hear my phone," Audrey said.

"I would have taken her, but you know how she likes to talk to whoever will listen when she gets out and about. We'd be gone for a couple of hours, and I get antsy waiting that long for her," Walter said. "I'll finish up this job while the crew works on the corn."

Audrey handed the paper bag to Walter. "And besides, you're tired of listening to her gripe about the Callahans and their fence. You might as well have my lunch. There's water and tea in the cooler."

"Thanks. I had a package of crackers and an apple at

break time, but I wouldn't want a couple of good sandwiches to go to waste," he said, and sat down on the running board. "I hear the Callahans have started work on the old barn, so that should fuel Hettie's temper."

"Sweet Lord!" Audrey groaned. "We have to drive right past the barn to get to the store. Are you sure you don't want to take a break and drive her to the store?"

"I'd rather face off with a hungry grizzly bear," Walter laughed. "But I will come by the house on my way home and pick up a pie. She's making an extra one for me. I'm sure she's being nice to try to entice me to stay another year."

"I'd make you a pie a week if you'd promise me another five years," Audrey said. "I still have a lot to learn."

Walter patted her on the shoulder. "Baby girl, you learn by doin', and you were ready to take over six months after you arrived."

She wrapped her arms around him and hugged him tightly. "I'll miss you so much."

"You don't need to worry about me leaving. Not until we see these sunflowers and the corn harvested, and we won't even say the words on my last day. We'll just say, 'See you later,' and I'll walk away," Walter told her. "Now get on home before Hettie gets mad at me for keeping you."

Audrey took a step back. "We couldn't have her mad, now could we? She has such a sweet, kind temperament that getting upset might give her a stroke."

Walter laughed out loud and shooed her away with a flick of his bony wrist.

She started up her music again as she crossed the field. She could visualize the video she'd seen on YouTube as Deana Carter sang "Strawberry Wine." She remembered a time when she was about seventeen and had come to spend the summer on her grandpa's farm. A young man with dark hair and brown eyes had come along with the harvest crew, and she had gotten her first taste of love down by the river on a hot July night—just like the lyrics in the song said. That was the story of her life—every relationship ended in a loss, whether it was a relative like her mother and father or a boyfriend who had stuck around for a while and then left like her first love had done.

"Why do I even want…" she said out loud as she left her boots by the door and went inside.

"Want what?" Hettie asked. "And why didn't you answer your phone? I could've already had the pies made, and you could have had a piece for lunch if you'd come home and taken me to the store."

Audrey pulled her earbuds out and wrapped the cord around the tiny machine. "Aunt Hettie, I've got a farm to run. I can't drop everything and drive you to town on a whim. You know what it's like to try to get the seed in the ground so we can have a harvest."

"Don't you preach at me about a harvest. Me and Amos ranched, and some years we had a rough time making the bank note," Hettie snapped. "I want to make chocolate pie, and *someone* drank all the milk. Besides, you inherited *me* with this farm. Frank made you promise you wouldn't throw me in a nursing home and that I could live here as long as I was alive, so there, young lady. You can take time to eat a bowl of soup before we go to the store. I'll get my sweater and put on my good shoes while you have lunch."

Audrey dipped up a bowl of soup and carried it to the table. "I would never put you in a nursing home."

But if you knew how much I've thought of Brodie all morning, you might put me in a convent, Audrey thought.

She had only taken a couple of bites when Hettie came back, wearing her best shoes and sweater. She'd even put on her fancy black funeral hat.

"Did someone die?" Audrey asked.

"While I was waiting on you to finally come to the house, I heard that them Callahans have started working on the old barn this morning. I'm wearing the hat that I usually wear when a friend dies."

"Who passed away?"

"Nobody yet, but it might bring me some pre-type of luck with them Callahans," she said.

"Aunt Hettie!" Audrey almost choked on a mouthful of soup.

Hettie tipped up her chin. "A woman has to do what she can do. I haven't got years to wait to get these two farms put back together. What did you do to your cousin Zelda, anyway, to make her so angry she wouldn't sell to you?"

"I didn't do a single thing, and you know it. I've told you at least a dozen times what she said at her grandpa's funeral. Uncle Ira left her a bunch of money, but there were strings.

She was not allowed to sell to me or you, and if the lawyers found out she had gone through a third party, then her trust fund would be revoked," Audrey answered. "Are you getting dementia?"

Hettie removed her hat and slapped Audrey on the shoulder with it. "My mind will be as good as it is right now the day that I go to meet my precious Amos. People in our family do not get the forgetting disease."

"Amen," Audrey whispered.

Hettie settled her hat back on her head. "What's that supposed to mean?"

"Did your two brothers ever forget their argument? Are you ever going to forget this feud you've got going with Bernie?" Audrey asked.

"No and no," Hettie replied, "and when I get to heaven I'm going to have another long talk with Ira and Frank if they are still acting ugly with each other."

"And Bernie?"

"She ain't goin' to heaven," Hettie snapped.

"So, you've got a deal with God about who gets past the Pearly Gates and who doesn't?"

"If you don't stop fussin' at me, I'll give Walter both of the pies I'm making this afternoon. I'll be in the truck when you finish eating." Hettie turned around and left the house.

You should know better than to bait her, the pesky voice in her head scolded.

"Don't gripe at me. A good argument is like vitamins to her," Audrey muttered, and finished off the last of her soup.

She didn't bother to change her dusty jeans and shirt, or even brush her hair, but simply walked out the back door and got into her vehicle. Before she even started the engine, Hettie air slapped her on the arm.

"What did I do?" Audrey asked.

"For your information," Hettie said, "I read my Bible, and it says that evil people can't go to heaven. Bernie is a wolf in sheep's clothing, and her heart is black. She owned a bar, for God's sake. What went on in that place would be an abomination unto the Lord, for sure."

"Love thy neighbor as thyself," Audrey quoted scripture.

Hettie crossed her arms over her chest. "Bernie lives three miles from me, so she's not my neighbor."

"How about we get an ice cream sandwich and eat it on the way home?" Audrey attempted to change the subject.

"Yes!" Hettie clapped her hands. "You know what we should do? We should get us one of them little trailer things and sell snow cones in the summertime."

"You said that you aren't getting dementia," Audrey reminded her.

"What are you diggin' up that old bone for?" Hettie asked.

"Think, Aunt Hettie," Audrey groaned, "when would we have time to take care of a snow cone stand, and how many do you think you'd sell in a town with less than two hundred people? Half of the town's population is attached in some way to the Paradise. Bernie wouldn't let any of them buy anything from us for fear we'd put poison in the cherry juice."

"You've got a point there," Hettie agreed. "Drive on past the store. I want to see what they're doing to the barn. Look at them fools up on that roof." She removed her hat and tossed it in the back seat, and then leaned forward so she could see better.

"Why did you take off your hat?"

"I don't want to hurt Parker. God might not take too kindly to me puttin' a minister in the ground," she said. "What is Bernie doing here?"

"Probably the same thing you are," Audrey replied. "You want me to offer her a ride back to the Paradise?"

"If you do, I'll get out and hitchhike into Nocona and check myself into the nursing home. Frank will haunt you all the days of your life," Hettie answered. "I've seen enough. Take me to the store."

Audrey turned the truck around, drove back, and parked in front of the convenience store. She hurried out, jogged around the backside of the vehicle, and helped Hettie to the ground. Then she looped her arm into her aunt's, and together they went inside.

"Hey, what can I do for y'all today?" Luna asked from behind the counter.

Luna was one of the youngest of the sisters who grew up at the Paradise. She was Endora's identical twin—blond hair, blue eyes, and just an inch or two over five feet. Unless Audrey saw her in the store or with Shane, or saw Endora with Parker, she couldn't tell them apart.

"You can shoot Bernie," Hettie muttered.

"What was that, Miz Hettie?" Luna asked.

"She said that we need a gallon of milk and a couple of ice cream sandwiches," Audrey answered. "She's making chocolate pies this afternoon, and we are treating ourselves to ice cream first."

"I remember your pies from when I was a little girl. You always brought a couple to the church potluck dinners," Luna said, and turned her focus toward Audrey. "You used to come with her in the summers, didn't you?"

"Yes, I did," Audrey answered. "As soon as school was out, Mama would go with my dad on the long-distance truck route, and I got to stay with Grandpa and Granny."

Hettie ignored both of them and brought a gallon of milk and a couple of ice cream sandwiches from the back of the store. "We ain't got time to think about the old days. We need to get back to the house. The pies will need a couple of hours to cool."

Audrey could have sworn that the temperature in the store dropped at least twenty degrees when the bell above the door rang and Bernie came inside. She stopped in front of the checkout counter and glared at Hettie. They both bristled up like a couple of hound dogs with a ham bone between them.

"What are you doing here?" Hettie hissed.

"This is my niece's store, and I can come here anytime I want," Bernie said. "Not that it's any of your business, but I'm going to mind the store for her while she takes some cookies and tea down to the guys working on the barn."

Hettie straightened up to her full height, narrowed her eyes, set her mouth in a firm line, and shot daggers at Bernie. "Come on, Audrey, we'll drive down to Nocona for milk."

Audrey laid a bill on the counter. "Don't be silly. I don't have time to go to Nocona. I need to get back and relieve Walter out in the sunflower field."

"Then I just won't make pies." Hettie's shoulder bumped Bernie on the way to the door.

"My mama taught me not to hit an *old* hussy," Bernie said through gritted teeth, "but if you touch me again, I will lay you out, old woman."

"Aunt Bernie!" Luna raised her voice.

"You stay out of this, Luna," Bernie said, and kept her eyes trained on Hettie.

"Don't let my age stop you," Hettie said. "I'll gladly whip your skinny ass right here."

Brodie came into the store and stopped in his tracks when he saw the two old women. His eyes darted back and forth from one to the other. "What's going on?"

Hettie glared at him. "I need my hat from the truck. Audrey, go get it."

"We are leaving right now," Audrey told her. "And I'm not going to get that silly hat. No one is dying today."

Hettie popped her hands on her hips. "I'll stage one of them sit-in things if you don't bring me my hat."

"Why do you want a hat?" Brodie asked.

"It's my funeral hat," Hettie said, "and when I get through with Bernie, there will be a funeral."

Audrey tried to loop her arm in her aunt's, but Hettie shrugged her away.

"Okay then," Luna finally said, and pointed toward the door. "If you two want to dust it up, get to it, but not in my store where you might destroy something. If you are going to act like a couple of grade school kids, get on outside to do your hair pullin' and screamin' at each other."

"Let's take care of this feud right now," Brodie said and focused on Audrey.

Her pulse jacked up a few notches when he flashed a brilliant smile in spite of the situation growing hotter every minute. "How do you plan to do that, Brodie? Are you going to sell your farm to me?"

"No, ma'am," Brodie said. "I'm asking you to go out on a date with me. I know it's April Fool's Day, but I'm dead serious."

"No!" Hettie and Bernie screeched at the same time.

"I'll say yes if you two don't settle down," Audrey said.

"I don't have to put up with this. I'll be in the truck." Hettie's tone was icy cold.

"I'm here to give Luna a ride to the barn," Brodie said. "But you two better be civil, or I will call Audrey, and we will go to the café right here in town for dinner. I might even kiss her good night when I take her home."

"I...refuse...you will not..." Bernie sputtered.

"I'll be civil, but I won't like it." Hettie threw over her shoulder as she left.

"Me, neither," Bernie yelled.

Audrey picked up the milk, ice cream, and her change and followed Hettie to the truck. "I can't believe you just did that," she said and helped her aunt into the passenger seat.

"Bernie started it," Hettie said in a hateful tone. "You wouldn't really go out with that man, would you?"

"You want to test me to find out?" Audrey asked.

Hettie clamped her mouth shut and looked out the side window the rest of the way home.

Chapter 11

"This could be your last time to stretch your short legs for a couple or three days," Brodie said as he led the pig down the row separating the peach and apple trees. "For the next little while you'll have to stay under the trailer. The weatherman said that a cool front is blowing in, not enough to cause issues with the crops or the orchards, but it will bring another rain with it."

He slowed his pace to match Pansy's short little legs, and they walked all the way to the end of his property. A barbed-wire fence separated his place from forty acres of undeveloped land with nothing but weeds growing on it. "I should buy that land and plant organic corn on it. I bet I could outsell Audrey. What do you think, Pansy?" he asked.

The pig flopped down on her belly and closed her eyes.

"Don't care one way or the other, do you?" Brodie sat down on the dry straw under an apple tree to rest. He had just spent two days roofing a barn and another two starting the framework inside the building to divide it into three sections—store, workroom, and apartment.

Tripp might very well never come out of the barn, especially if he found a place to ship good quality leather to him.

"He's a hermit at heart even though he did have to deal with people every day in the oil business," he said.

Pansy didn't even open one eye to acknowledge that he was talking.

"I'm glad that he and Knox stuck around home when I left. Mother would have been so lonely if we'd all flown the nest," he whispered.

The pig grunted but still didn't look up.

Thinking of his brothers staying home while he looked for adventures took his thoughts to the time he spent on his first six-month deployment in the Middle East. He had lived in Bandera, Texas, his whole life and couldn't wait to see the world, but after a couple of weeks he was homesick for his mother's cooking, his brothers' arguing, and his father's advice. After his time in the sand, he had thought he would never get enough of family again. But he was wrong. He had had enough of Knox's joking and Tripp's bickering that very day to make him appreciate the peace and quiet of his farm.

When they are both in their own places, and you have a house here, you are going to miss them. His mother's voice was back in his head.

"Yep, but tonight, I'm glad to be alone with my own thoughts," Brodie whispered.

Pansy stood up and tugged on the leash. Brodie got to his feet and followed behind her. She took him east toward Audrey's place and down the edge of the fence until they reached the part that was still broken down. Then she flopped down again and closed her eyes.

He pulled on the leash, but she wouldn't budge. "Come on, girl. We are only a few yards from the trailer. I don't want to carry you, but I will."

She opened one beady little eye and then closed it again. Brodie reached down to pick her up, but she wiggled free and snuggled up to the fallen fence post. "Stubborn, just like the whole female race," he grumbled.

"Poor piggy." Audrey appeared out of the darkness and sat down on the other side of the tangled barbed wire still lying on the ground from the broken-down fence. "She might not like to be compared to the ladies in the human race."

"You are on my property," Brodie said.

"I am not," Audrey argued. "I'm on my side of the fence."

"I believe that my land extends to one foot beyond the fence," Brodie informed her.

"Well, pardon me," she said with a head wiggle and moved back a few inches. "Do I need to get a tape measure?"

"Nope," Brodie answered and eased down beside Pansy. "I reckon you are on your land now. What are you doing out this late?"

"Trying to find some peace and quiet," Audrey answered. "Aunt Hettie's either been in a pout or in a tantrum all week."

"I understand completely," Brodie said with half a chuckle. "Bernie has stormed around for days saying that I have ruined her reputation as a matchmaker."

"You'd think that two old women who have lived as long as they have would have better sense than to waste what time they have left hating each other," she said with a sigh.

"Maybe hate is the fuel that keeps them alive," Brodie suggested.

"I've heard Aunt Hettie's side of this feud, but I don't think that's the whole story," Audrey said. "Want to compare notes?"

"You go first," Brodie replied.

"The story coming from this side of the fence is that Bernie swept into town and took over Aunt Hettie's place in the church. She used to take care of the flowers in the foyer and was the head honcho for organizing funeral dinners as well as the quilting club," Audrey said.

"From this side, Bernie told too many stories about her bar in the senior Sunday school class, and she flirted with the old widowers. Hettie called her down, so Bernie retaliated by threatening to put a bar in one of the old empty houses in town and hiring Walter away from the farm to work in it," Brodie told her.

"That's the story I got, too, but then Bernie set about to steal *all* of Aunt Hettie's church privileges away from her," Audrey said with a sigh. "They're acting worse than Uncle Ira and Grandpa."

"We did manage to put a stop to them fighting in public," Brodie said.

"For the time being," she said. "One tornado coming through Spanish Fort does not mean there won't be more to come. They still might start pulling hair and throwing punches in the future."

"Never thought of it that way." Brodie couldn't take his eyes off her.

The night breeze blew her hair across her face. She took something from her pocket and whipped a ponytail up on top of her head in just a few seconds. He had a desire to cross the barbed wire and start a long line of kisses from her slender neck to her lips. That would definitely cause a war to rival the one between Hettie and Bernie. After a long silence, she started to stand up.

"Why did you come here to this spot? You could have found peace in your backyard," Brodie asked in an attempt to keep her from leaving.

Audrey settled back down and seemed to be studying him for a long moment before she spoke. "It's hard to explain, but when something is bothering me, I always come here. It's the one place you wouldn't catch my grandparents, or Uncle Ira and his wife. The fence was more than just barbed wire separating two farms. It set down a line that couldn't be crossed in their hearts. The only person who was allowed to visit both places was Hettie, and yet when she moved in with Grandpa, Uncle Ira told her never to set foot on his property again."

"So, this is no-man's-land, where you could get away from it all?"

"Something like that," she said with a nod.

Brodie nodded. "I can't imagine the tension that you lived with. My brothers and I argued, but our home was a place of refuge and happiness. Did you ever, in all your life, find another person here?"

There was another long silence before she spoke again.

Brodie wondered if maybe she was trying to decide whether to trust him with something personal about her life, or to go back to her house and leave him sitting there alone.

"My cousin Zelda and I were about eleven years old the year we found out we were related. Someone at church mentioned how much we looked alike, and an elderly woman said that it was the Tucker genes. I asked Aunt Hettie about it, and she told me to ask Grandpa. He told me to never, ever speak that girl's name again."

"That seems harsh," Brodie said.

"Yep, and it just made me more curious about her," Audrey said. "I would sneak out of my bedroom at night, sit here in the darkness and look over at Uncle Ira's house, and wonder about my only cousin. I didn't have siblings. Mama was an only child, and so was my dad. Mama's parents died when she was still in high school. Zelda was all I had, and I wondered what she was like."

Brodie shook his head slowly. "I can't imagine anything like that. My mama's side of the family and my dad's side always met up for a big double family reunion on Independence Day. Everyone brought campers or tents, and we spent a few days at a lakeside park. We fought with our cousins or laughed with them and usually bawled like babies when we had to leave."

"Sounds like heaven," Audrey said. "All I had was Zelda and now Aunt Hettie."

In his wildest dreams, Brodie would never have believed that he and Audrey would be sitting only a few feet apart and having a conversation that didn't involve yelling or drama. "Did you ever get to talk to her before you were both grown?"

"She found me right here one night that summer that we figured out we were kin to each other. She sat down on the other side of the fence, and we just stared at each other. It was almost like looking in a mirror, only she was taller and thinner than me. We talked after a while and met here several times during the next few weeks. Then Uncle Ira caught us, and that was the end of our visits. She never came back to Spanish Fort after that year, and I didn't talk to her until Uncle Ira and Aunt Maude's funeral," Audrey said and then paused for a breath. "We sat across the table from each other at the family dinner. I offered to buy the farm, but she told me there was a contingency in the will. She couldn't sell it outright to me or to anyone knowing that they would turn around and sell it to me."

"So, you waited until I bought it, and now..."

Audrey stood up. "You've got the whole story now. When will you let me buy this place and reunite the farms?"

"Why don't you sell me your place, and then it will be put back together?" Brodie asked.

"Not in a million years," Audrey's tone went from warm to downright chilly.

"Then I guess we'll each stay on our side of the fence until eternity dawns," Brodie said.

"I guess we will, but this has been nice." She stood up and disappeared into the darkness.

His phone rang and woke Pansy. She got to her feet and started toward the house.

"Hello, Knox," Brodie said as he walked behind the pig. The faint, faraway sound of thunder rolled in the distance, and Pansy stopped in her tracks when they reached the porch. She quickly climbed the steps and stared at the door.

"Just checkin' on you," his brother said. "Everything all right out there? It's past midnight. I was afraid Audrey or Hettie might have shot you."

"I'm fine," Brodie said. "But Pansy seems to be afraid of storms, so I think I'll just spend the night out here."

"There's no extra clothes out there," Knox reminded him. "And the water tank is probably getting low."

"If I don't have enough water to make coffee in the morning, I'll refill the tank. I keep a packed bag in my truck these days with a couple of changes of clothes," Brodie told him.

"Guess you learned a lesson from last time, when you had to go out in public looking like a hobo," Knox said.

"Yep, I have and from having to run down to the water meter in nothing but my birthday suit," Brodie told him and shivered at the memory of that night.

"Well, then," Knox said with a chuckle. "You and Pansy have a good night. If you'd told me three months ago that you'd be giving up a good bed for the one in the trailer because of a pig, I would have laughed my head off."

"So would I," Brodie agreed. "The weatherman says we'll have rain all weekend, but Tripp's barn is in the dry now, so we can work tomorrow. I'll be there bright and early."

"I'll expect to see you at breakfast," Knox said, and ended the call just as another clap of thunder testified that the storm was approaching fast.

"Okay, girl, let's get inside before we get wet," Brodie said, and opened the door.

Pansy headed straight for her bed in the corner. He kicked off his boots, and in a couple of long strides he was in the bedroom end of the trailer. He carefully hung his jeans and shirt up and slipped between the sheets, but his eyes would not stay shut. He flipped from one side to the other, hitting the wall on his right and almost tumbling out onto the floor on his left. He'd slept in bunks that were more comfortable. Finally, the raindrops pummeling the metal roof lulled him into sleep.

He dreamed of Audrey again, only this time, she was older and standing on her side of the fence with a little dark-haired girl, and he was playing pitch in his yard with a little boy. He awoke with a start and realized that he and Audrey were at a fork in the road. Neither of them seemed able to take a single step either to the east or the west, and yet that very step would decide their future.

Audrey eased into the house through the back door, hoping to make it all the way into the house without waking Hettie, but she failed.

"Where have you been?" Hettie asked from the kitchen table, where she was sitting with a cup of coffee in her hands.

"What if I'd had a stroke like my precious Amos did and I couldn't call you? Or if you'd gotten bitten by a rattlesnake? There's a storm brewing out there. You could have been struck by lightning."

Audrey flipped the switch and turned on the light. "I took a walk to clear my mind. I had my phone with me. If you needed me, all you had to do was call. I didn't see a rattlesnake or even a green garden snake, so I'm okay. The storm could very well go around us. Why are you sitting in the dark?"

"My eyes are every bit as good as a night owl's. I don't have to have light to see," Hettie grouched. "Were you sneaking out to see that rotten Callahan boy?"

"Which one? There are three of them. I'm not sure which one I see on Friday nights. I kind of share the weeknights, but I save Saturdays for Brodie," she teased.

"I want an answer, not a lie," Hettie demanded.

"I wasn't sneaking around with Brodie. I walked right up to his trailer and knocked on the door. I didn't want to have wild sex with a pig watching, so we went out to the orchard. Do you want details about how he—"

Hettie glared at her. "I won't listen to you tell me lies and give me a heart attack. Where were you really?"

Audrey kicked off her work boots and poured herself a glass of milk. "I was taking a walk and thinking about the fit Grandpa threw when he found out I was talking to Zelda through the fence."

That was the truth—maybe not the whole truth and

nothing but the truth—but Audrey didn't see a Bible on the table, and Hettie didn't ask her to raise her right hand.

"I told my brothers that they were being ridiculous, keeping you girls from each other, but would they listen? Hell, no! Their two wives were as conniving and mean as Bernie, and neither of them would back me up," Hettie fumed. "Now that I know you are home and safe, I'm going to bed. Don't wake me for breakfast. As late as it is, I might sleep until noon."

"Yes, ma'am," Audrey said, but she had no doubt that her aunt would be up rustling around in the kitchen long before daylight.

She went to her bedroom, closed the door, and dropped her clothing on the floor. When she had gotten into bed, she closed her eyes, but sleep would not come. She replayed the first conversation she had just had with Brodie over and over in her mind. Finally, out of sheer exhaustion, she drifted off and dreamed of playing hide-and-seek with a little girl in Brodie's orchard.

Rattling pots and pans the next morning woke her up. She opened her eyes and clamped her jaw shut in anger because she had to leave the dream behind. She kicked off the covers and padded barefoot to the kitchen, where Hettie was making biscuits and gravy for breakfast. She covered a yawn as she poured herself a cup of coffee. "I thought you were sleeping until noon."

"Too set in my ways to do that, and I couldn't sleep for the good Lord convicting me," Hettie said.

"God spoke right to you?" Audrey asked.

"Yes, he did, and he made me see things clearly," Hettie answered.

"About the Callahan boys?" Audrey ventured cautiously.

"He ain't got a thing to say about them or any of them people at the Paradise," Hettie declared.

"Then what did he convict you about?" Audrey took a sip of her coffee, set the mug on the table, and then took plates down from the cabinet.

Hettie poured gravy into a crock bowl. "This land is what God talked to me about. My brothers split this land apart, so why should I try to put it back together after they are gone? My father left it to the boys, and I'm sure he didn't fret up in heaven because they were too boneheaded to keep it together." She paused and took a cast-iron skillet of biscuits from the oven. "And all over a stupid woman who wasn't worth a plug nickel. I'm tired of what you are going through to try to please me. This place is already more than you can handle on your own. I'm too broke down to be able to help you with anything other than making food and doing a little cleaning. Walter is about to retire, and you're going to have enough to do once he's gone. You don't need that farm next door, and besides…"

"Maybe I want to buy the Callahan farm just to win the battle," Audrey argued.

Hettie scowled at her as she put the biscuits into a basket. "I'm serious as I'll be on Judgment Day. Girl, you don't know a dang thing about all that organic business. That orchard might just up and die if you put decent fertilizer on the trees." She set the bowl of gravy on the table . "Don't just sit there starin' at me. Say something."

"Does that mean—" Audrey started.

Hettie stopped her with a wave of her hand. "It means I don't care if these two places are ever put back together. It means that God talked to me last night when I was worryin' about you, and I listen when he speaks. He said, 'Hettie, you can't take none of this with you, not even the joy of having the farm all in one piece, so let it go.' Maybe it wasn't in them words, but it was plain."

"So, I can stop pestering Brodie to sell this place to me and date him?" Audrey asked.

"Yes, you can forget about buying that farm. But as far as dating that man or either of his brothers, that's not a no. That is a *hell, no!*" Hettie raised her voice so loud that it scared a sparrow sitting on the windowsill outside. "God didn't tell me to like Bernie, and He didn't tell me that you could make me shirttail kin to the folks that live in a brothel."

Audrey suppressed a giggle. "What if God talks to me and says that I can go out with Brodie?"

"Now, you're just being sassy and teasing me," Hettie said. "Eat your breakfast and then get on out there to help Walter with whatever y'all have to do today. Noon will be here before you know it. Do you have the paychecks ready for the hired help?"

"I gave them to Walter last night," she answered.

"That's good, and don't go askin' me if I'm ever going

to make things right with Bernie, neither. I already told you that she was brazen enough to talk about things in Sunday school class that shouldn't even be mentioned when there's no men around. Raunchy things that shouldn't be whispered in secret, much less in church. And she's a big flirt, wearin' them clothes that make her look like a floozy and dyin' her hair red."

Audrey tried to keep the laughter inside, but it escaped. She grabbed a paper napkin from the middle of the table and wiped her eyes. "I've heard that story before."

Hettie slapped the table hard enough to make the salt and pepper shakers rattle together. "Walter don't need to be spreadin' rumors."

"It's not gossip if it's true," Audrey said. "You know I love you more than my corn crop, Aunt Hettie, and I'm always on your side. I'm glad that you have given up on the idea of putting the two properties back together, but I've got a feeling you would rather give up on reuniting the land than have me fall in love with Brodie Callahan."

Hettie reached over and laid her hand on Audrey's. "I've loved you as much, sometimes more, than I did those four ornery boys me and Amos produced together. When the last one passed away, I thought I would die with him. But you filled the void he left behind, since not a one of them boys gave me grandchildren."

"I don't like to fight with you, either," Audrey said, knowing from experience that Hettie was apologizing for being so hateful all week.

Hettie removed her hand and stared right into Audrey's eyes. "But there will be a war if you even look at any of those Callahan men with longing in your eyes. You can write that down and paste it on the refrigerator door."

Audrey just smiled, split open a biscuit, and covered it with gravy. This wasn't the time to tell Hettie that that ship had already sailed.

Chapter 12

THE WALMART PARKING LOT only had a handful of vehicles in it on Saturday night, but then it was getting near to closing time when Brodie arrived. He grabbed a cart sitting between two cars and pushed it into the store. Tonight, he was shopping for one of those igloo type of dog houses for Pansy, because he was not going to sleep in that twin-size bed again. The new house would protect her from all kinds of weather. He would still take her for a nice long walk each evening, but he would be going home to the Paradise to sleep at night.

The way his luck was going, he figured he would crash carts with Audrey before he left the store. So, he peeked around each corner on the way back to the pet supplies. He loaded the igloo onto his cart and headed toward the checkout counter.

"Hey, Brodie!" someone called out behind him.

He turned around and saw Aunt Bernie waving from only a few feet behind him. She pushed her cart toward him and pointed at the huge box teetering on top of his cart. "Fancy meeting you here at this time of night. What is that?"

"A house for my pig," he answered. Was this the right

time to tell her that he wasn't going on any more blind dates, or should he wait for reinforcement—like his brothers—to be around him to deliver the news?

"You're sure going to a lot of expense for a pig," Bernie said in a disapproving tone. "It'll be a hard sell to get a woman to go out with you if I say you have a pot-bellied pig for a pet."

The door is open wide. You might as well go on through it and hope for the best, the voice in his head said.

Brodie took a deep breath and let it out slowly before he spoke. "I appreciate all you have done and are trying to do, but I do not want to go on any more blind dates."

Bernie drew her brows down and pursed her lips together. "I do not fail, so I'm not considering this a lost battle. I'm layin' all the blame on you. I would have found a good woman for you eventually, but that pig got in my way."

"You just put all the blame on my shoulders," Brodie said, glad that the battle had gone so smoothly. "What are *you* doing out this late?"

"I'm out of wine and like the kind I can get here." She pointed down at a dozen bottles in her cart and then moved her finger to her lips. "Don't tell Ophelia and Jake. I wouldn't hurt their feelings for anything in this world, but the truth is I like cheap wine. I buy from their winery when I want the fancy stuff. I've already been by the liquor store and picked up my Irish whiskey."

"Are you being sneaky?" Brodie whispered.

"Yes, I am." She grinned. "And I promise not to set you

up with another woman if you won't tell that I sneak out late at night to do my shopping."

He stuck out his hand. "Deal."

She shook with him. "Looks like we're both about done. How about we go by the Dairy Queen and have one of them Peanut Buster Parfait sundaes? They stay open until midnight, so we've got time."

"I'd like that." Brodie almost crossed his fingers behind his back. He didn't really want to go anywhere but out to the farm to set the igloo in Pansy's pen and then get on home to get a decent night's sleep in a bed that was big enough that he didn't feel like he was back in the army and trying to sleep on a cot.

Having ice cream with Bernie is a small price to pay since she agreed not to send you or me and Tripp on any more blind dates, Knox's voice whispered in his ear.

"Good," Bernie said. "I'll meet you there, and I'll even treat."

Brodie went through the self-checkout station, toted his pig house out to the truck, and set the GPS on his phone to take him to the Dairy Queen. So far, so good, as far as luck went when it came to running into Audrey. But he still checked out the whole dining area when he walked inside. Only a couple of young folks, maybe even out on their first date, were sitting side by side and making a big deal out of feeding each other a chocolate sundae.

He wondered what it would be like to have the freedom to sit beside Audrey in a booth and feed her ice cream. If he even asked her out, would she say yes or give him an ultimatum like selling his place to her for a date? Would the barbed-wire fence always be between them, both literally and figuratively?

"No, it will not," he muttered.

"What was that?" Bernie asked as she sat down across the booth from him.

"I was talking to myself," he said.

"I do that a lot, or else I talk to Pepper. He's a real good listener and never disagrees with me," she said with a wide smile. "Now what do you want? Is a peanut parfait all right with you?"

"Yes, ma'am, but my mama would haunt me if I let a lady pay for anything when I'm out with her," Brodie said as he slid out of the booth. "You sit right there, and I'll go put in our order."

He stood up at the same time the young couple did and let them pass by him. "Y'all have a good evening," he said.

"Got to have Cinderella home by midnight," the young man said and drew his girlfriend to his side so tightly that air couldn't get between them.

"Drive safe," Bernie said.

"Yes, ma'am," the girl said.

They disappeared outside, and Brodie went up to the counter, made his order, and then went back to sit with Bernie. "I know you had a bar in southern Oklahoma. What made you leave it and come to Spanish Fort?"

"It's a long story, but I'll give you the short version. I

have a twin sister who disowned me years ago. She married right out of high school and got a job as a cashier in a bank. She was and still is deeply religious, goes to church every time the doors are open, and volunteers for everything that has to do with Jesus. I'm not throwing shade, as you kids say today, at my sister. What she believes is between her and God, and that's none of my business. I wish she felt the same about me," Bernie said.

Brodie wished maybe he'd asked a simpler question, like did she like the nice day they had just had?

The lady who had taken his order brought their sundaes to the table, along with two cups of coffee, and set the tray in the middle of the table. "Coffee is on the house. We'll be closing soon, and we'd just have to pour it out."

"Thank you," Bernie said, and ate the cherry on top of the sundae. "Now, to get on with my story. My sister married the bank president, and they had three children: a boy, Joshua, and two girls, Mary Jane and Rachel. One of the girls and the boy took their mama's side against me. But Mary Jane, bless her heart, did not. I never got to be around my nieces and nephew since I might be a bad influence on them, but when Mary Jane grew up, she kept in touch and didn't judge me. She let me visit her and the girls whenever I wanted. After she moved up here close to the border, she and I became even closer. I crossed the river and came down here even more often to visit her. The rest of her family snubbed her for buying an old brothel and for writing what they called trashy books, but not me. I always told her to follow her heart and not worry about what other people think."

"I bet she makes more money and has more joy doing what she loves than any of her family," Brodie said.

"No doubt about that!" Bernie took a bite of her ice cream and then a sip of coffee before she went on. "She still tries to keep in touch with them—calls her mama every week and tries to keep in touch with her sister, but most of the time all she gets there is Rachel's voicemail telling her to leave a message. Rachel has a couple of daughters, Joy and Clara, and they've always been as self-righteous as their mother. But, anyway, that's the reason I came to Spanish Fort. I don't have children, and Mary Jane is the only relative that was sweet enough to offer to let me live on the Paradise property. She begged me for at least two years to retire and come down here before circumstances finally talked me into doing just that."

"What circumstances?" Brodie asked and finished off the last bite of his ice cream. He took a sip of his coffee and set it back down. "That is some stout coffee. It tastes like it's been sitting in the pot all day."

Bernie pulled a flask from her purse and poured a little into each cup. "That ought to cut the bitter. The story about me selling my bar is that a good-lookin' feller, an old lover carrying Pepper and a dead goldfish, and my least favorite niece, Clara, walked into my bar one evening."

"That sounds like the beginning of a joke," Brodie said.

"It does, but it was the beginning of the circumstances

that let me retire," Bernie said. "This has been fun, though, but now it's my turn to ask a question. Are you planning to live here in Spanish Fort forever, or is this whole organic farming business just a passing whim?"

"It's a forever thing," Brodie answered, and took another small sip of the coffee. Be danged if Bernie wasn't right. Whatever liquor she poured in the cup made it taste much, much better. "I never thought I'd be able to buy a farm, but my mother and father left all of us boys pretty well fixed. I didn't think my brothers would stay here, but it looks like they love the area as much as I do."

"Even Knox?" Bernie asked.

"Joe Clay has told him that he can easily find enough construction work to keep him busy. The sisters have already been talking about getting him to design either additions to their houses or remodel what they have. That will keep him going for months, maybe years when you consider that he needs to help Joe Clay build a parsonage and also design and build a house for me," Brodie answered.

"Okay, then, I'll back off trying to fix y'all up for a little while," Bernie said. "I was in a hurry to get roots put down for you. Joe Clay would be sad if you left, and I'd do anything for that man. I thought if I could just get you settled, then your brothers wouldn't leave either."

"Thank you," Brodie said with a nod. "I should be going. Pansy, that's my pot-bellied pig, is waiting on her new house. She can get up under the trailer, but when it rains the water runs under there. She needs a dry place to sleep."

"Joe Clay said y'all boxed the trailer in real good and built a pen for that silly pig. How are you going to empty the sewer tank now that you can't hook the trailer up and pull it into a dump site?" Bernie asked.

"We're going to tie into the sewer line that's already out there, and we can fill the water tanks with the well water we use for the crops," he answered.

"Joe Clay fixed my trailer up the same way, only he made it so all I have to do is reposition a couple of lines, and I'm ready to go." Bernie finished off the last sip of her coffee and slid out of the booth. "Thanks for the date. If you were this good at listening when you went out with the women I set you up with, then there's something wrong with them."

"Thank you. See you around," Brodie said as he stood up.

"Yep," Bernie said, and left while he was clearing off the table.

Brodie crossed the parking lot and got into his truck. If it hadn't been so late, he would have called both his brothers to tell them that an ice cream sundae was all it took to get them all off the matchmaking hook.

"You are going to have to fight to stay awake in church tomorrow if you don't get some sleep," Audrey whispered to herself as she beat on her pillow for the dozenth time that night. She worried about Walter leaving in the fall and about the feud between her aunt and Bernie, but most of all she couldn't get the previous evening out of her mind. She had really enjoyed talking to Brodie and wished that she had not listened to her family when they bad-mouthed all the folks at the Paradise. Those women could have been friends that she could call when she was having a bad day or a good one—but oh, no, the Tuckers did not associate with people who lived in a former brothel.

"And it hasn't been a brothel in way over a hundred years." She sat up in bed and decided that maybe a walk in the night air would clear her head enough that she could sleep a few hours.

She walked to the end of the cornfield, made a left and followed the back fence to the corner, and then walked down to the broken barbed wire. She defiantly stepped over the tangled mess and sat down on his property. The headlights of a pickup truck lit her up like a Christmas tree. She could either run or stand her ground and dare him to file trespassing charges against her. She decided on the latter. A rousting good argument might be just what she needed to fall asleep.

"Hey, what are you doing"—Brodie yelled as he got out of the truck—"on my side of the fence?"

"I don't see a single *No Trespassing* sign," she said.

He crossed the distance between them and sat down beside her. "I bet Ira had several strung down the fence years ago."

"Probably so, but they're all gone now, so you cannot call the police." She covered a yawn with the back of her hand.

"I wouldn't do that anyway, but what brings you out at this time of night?" he asked.

"For a walk because I couldn't sleep," she answered. "What are you doing here so late anyway?"

Brodie nodded toward the truck. "There's one of those igloo doghouses in the back. I bought it for Pansy. These spring rains could cause a mud lolly under the trailer. The new little house will keep her dry as well as cool in the summer and warm on cold nights. Want to go over to the trailer and see how well she likes it?"

"Yes," Audrey answered.

He stared at her as if she had an extra eye right in the middle of her forehead.

"Did you hear me?" she asked.

"I did, but would you say it one more time so I'm sure?" he asked.

"I said yes," she answered.

He stood up and offered her a hand. "Sure that you want to take a chance that Miz Hettie will find out that—"

"I love my aunt, but I'm thirty years old, and she is not my boss." Audrey put her hand in Brodie's. Like always, her pulse kicked into third gear at his touch.

Every single time, she groaned to herself.

When she was on her feet, he let go of her hand. "I'm thirty also," he said. "When is your birthday?"

"I should have said I will be thirty in June, but I'm close enough to it that I wasn't stretching it very far," she said.

"I was thirty last November," Brodie said.

Audrey filed away that little bit of information and then changed the subject abruptly. "I've only actually been on this property one time, and that was after Uncle Ira passed away. I came over here to talk to Zelda one last time to ask about selling the place to me."

Brodie removed the big box from the back of the truck and hoisted it up on his shoulder. "For real?"

"I told you how Uncle Ira and Grandpa felt about the family," she said. "The fear of God was put in me about coming over here. I could walk up to the fence, but I'd better not take one step any further."

"I can't see you obeying rules," Brodie chuckled.

"Well," Audrey said, "I did stick my feet under the barbed wire one time."

Brodie set the box down beside the porch and pulled out a pocketknife. With a few long cuts, he opened it up and removed the igloo from the inside. "How did it make *you* feel when you defied orders?" he asked.

"Exhilarated and scared at the same time," she said. "A vehicle came by about the time that I did it and lit me up somewhat like you did tonight. I worried the rest of that summer that someone saw me and would tell Grandpa. Back then, bright-orange signs really were up and down both sides of the fence that warned folks not to trespass. I never did it again until tonight."

"Why not?"

"I wasn't welcome here," Audrey answered.

"Well, you are now, but it might be a good idea not to

let your aunt or Bernie find out," he said. "I'm just now getting on her good side. We had ice cream tonight, and she's promised to stop fixing me up on blind dates."

"Two miracles in one evening," she teased. "That has to be a record for sure."

"What's the second one?" he asked as he set the little house over the fence. Pansy came out from under the trailer and smelled all around it before she went inside.

"That we're talking without screaming and yelling at each other for a second time," she answered. "It's getting late. I should be going back to the house. If Aunt Hettie wakes up and finds me gone, she'll panic."

Brodie laid a hand on her arm. "Sit with me on the porch for a little while. Want a cold beer or a bottle of sweet tea?"

She slapped a mosquito only slightly smaller than a buzzard and left a small bloody mark on her arm. "I'm good. All the rain we've had is great for crops, but it breeds these vampire bugs like crazy. I'll see you in church tomorrow morning."

"I could walk you to your door," he offered.

Audrey shook her head. "We better not push our luck."

Brodie frowned. "Want to explain that?"

"Think about it. I'll see you in the morning, or maybe I should say later today, at church," she said, and blew him a kiss.

───────

Brodie felt like a teenager who had just broken curfew when he removed his boots at the door and tiptoed up the stairs to his bedroom. He carefully folded his shirt and jeans when he took them off and hung both over the back of the rocking chair. He sighed when he got into a bed where his feet didn't hang off the end and he could actually move around without fear of falling onto the floor. He laced his fingers behind his head and stared at the ceiling. Dark clouds drifting back and forth over the moon made for strange shapes on the ceiling and made him think of Audrey. She was like the fast-moving black cloud, but now a little light had shined through. And in that, he could feel the chemistry between them. He wondered if she felt it too, or if she was still angling to buy his farm.

The next morning, he was awakened quite abruptly by pounding on the double doors leading out onto the balcony. He groaned, looked at the clock to see that it was only six thirty, and crawled out of bed.

"What do you want?" he asked gruffly as he opened the doors wide.

"Well, good morning to you, too, Mr. Grouchy Ass," Knox smarted off. "Your alarm is going to go off in thirty minutes anyway, since it's your morning to make breakfast. If you will remember, you invited Ursula and Remy to come over and eat with us before we all go to church."

"But that would let me sleep another half hour," he said.

Knox pointed to a lovely sunrise. "Then you would have missed that. It reminded me and Tripp of Mother's excitement all those times when she showed us the beauty of nature."

"Come on out here and have a seat," Tripp said from the shadows. "Why are you so grumpy anyway. You are usually whistling by this time of the morning."

Brodie sunk down in a chair and propped his bare feet on the railing. "I couldn't sleep, so I got up and went to Walmart in Bowie to buy one of those igloo dog houses for Pansy. All these spring rains could make a mess under the trailer. The little igloo will keep her safe and dry. I didn't get home until late."

"Bet you that crazy pig won't even use the thing," Knox said.

"You'd lose that bet because she went right inside and was still there when I left," Brodie said. "And you are welcome. Especially you, Tripp."

"What'd I say?" Tripp protested. "I'm just sitting here looking at the sunrise and thinking of Mother."

"I ran into Aunt Bernie at the Walmart store," he answered.

"Why would I be thanking you for that?" Tripp asked.

Brodie told them a short version of the evening, ending with, "And she agreed to call off the matchmaking for all of us. She just wanted us to put down roots so Joe Clay wouldn't be sorry and sad when we left the area."

"Thank you, thank you!" Tripp said. "I'm sorry I let Knox wake you up. That's even better news than this sunrise."

"Amen!" Knox added. "But did she call it off forever or only for a few months?"

Brodie shook his head. "I'm not sure, but she might be

gunnin' for you, Knox, if you ever decide to take on a construction job outside of Montague County."

"Then I've got some breathing room," Knox said in a
serious tone. "It will take me months and months just to
get caught up on what all the sisters want done; and before
I even get started on their jobs, Joe Clay wants us to get
started on that new parsonage for Endora and Parker; and
then I've got to build a place for you."

"Is the parsonage a *for free* job?" Tripp asked.

"Yep," Knox answered. "It'll be a great tax write-off."

Brodie patted his brother on the arm. "Like I said, don't
ever mention moving away from here in front of Bernie, or
she'll have you saying 'I do' so fast it will make your head
swim. I'm going to get dressed and go downstairs. How do
frittatas sound?"

"With hot biscuits and gravy on the side?" Knox asked.

"Or maybe pancakes?" Tripp asked before Brodie could
answer.

"Since we're having company, I'll whip up all of the
above," Brodie said, and went on back into his room.

Will I ever make breakfast for Audrey? he asked himself
silently.

When Pansy sprouts wings and flies, the nasty little voice
in his head answered.

Chapter 13

THAT PRICKLY FEELING ON the back of Brodie's neck every time that Audrey was nearby let him know the very minute that she and Hettie came into the sanctuary. He glanced over his shoulder, locked eyes with her, and waited until she looked the other way before he turned slowly and stared straight ahead. But the image of her wearing an orange dress that hugged all her curves was branded on his brain. It didn't help when they sat down in the pew in front of the one that he and his brothers shared with Ursula and Remy.

Brodie didn't even try to pay attention to Parker's sermon that morning, not with Audrey sitting close enough that he could get a whiff of her perfume every time he took a breath. Even the voices of the old guys who added an amen every so often during the service sounded like they were far away. His thoughts bypassed all the bantering between him and Audrey in the past three months and landed on the two really great conversations they'd had the past week. The vibes between them had been strong, but he wasn't sure if she had felt the same thing.

Knox elbowed him in the ribs and jerked him back to reality. "Were you sleeping with your eyes open?"

"Yep," Brodie whispered, and looked down the pew at the family all bowing their heads. He dropped his chin to his chest, closed his eyes, and listened as an older man thanked the good Lord for the day and the good sermon and ended with a plea to keep everyone safe on their journeys home and said amen. Then there was the normal shuffling noise of people getting on their feet and conversations starting as folks walked down the center aisle toward the double doors, where Parker stood to shake hands with the folks as they left.

Brodie was last in the line, which meant Ursula, Remy, Tripp, and Knox filed out into the crowd before he did. As luck would have it, his shoulder brushed against Audrey's when they both stepped out into the aisle at the same time. Hot little sparks danced all around them, but he just smiled.

"Good mornin', Audrey," he said.

"Mornin' to you, Brodie," she replied.

"Don't you *even* be speaking to my niece," Hettie scolded. "And I'm still waiting for you to fix that fence. It's a rotten eyesore." She rolled her eyes toward the ceiling. "God, you can lay the sin of me swearing in church on Brodie Callahan. He made me say that word."

"Hey, now," Brodie said. "I didn't say anything to you, Miz Hettie, so don't go blaming me for your anger. And for your information, I'm not going to fix that fence. I'm going to take it down."

Hettie grabbed her heart and gasped, "You can't do that!"

"I own it, so I believe I can," Brodie said. "I won't get around to it this week, but I will before summer is finished."

"I hope God sends locusts to ruin your orchards," she barked at him.

"A barbed-wire fence won't keep locusts on my farm and not yours. They might have breakfast at my place, but when they see all those lovely corn plants, they'll have dinner on your land," he told her. "Speaking of food, can I take you and Audrey out for lunch? I promise it will be better than you having to scoot around in a chicken yard."

"You can go to…" she stopped herself midsentence, and with her chin tilted up so high that she could have drowned in a rainstorm, she headed down the aisle at a fast pace.

"When you bait her like that, I have to live with the consequences," Audrey whispered.

Brodie flashed his best smile at her. "You could go to Sunday dinner with me at the Paradise. That way Bernie would be as mad as Hettie."

"With that much hot anger, they could burst into spontaneous combustion and burn down the whole town," she whispered.

"I was a volunteer firefighter," he said. "With enough water, I could put the blaze out before it spread outside of their bodies."

"When you get ready to sell your farm, give me a call, and for goodness' sake, don't take down that fence," she said in a loud voice and hurried toward the doors.

"Why?" he raised his voice a little.

"My black dress is at the cleaners," she threw over her shoulder.

For a full minute, Brodie puzzled over what she said, but when he realized what she had meant, he laughed out loud. Joe Clay nudged him on the back and asked, "Was that Audrey Tucker that said something to tickle you?"

"It was," Brodie answered.

"Then I'm glad that Bernie is already outside. She likes it better when you and Audrey are arguing or rolling around in the mud while chasing after a pig," Joe Clay chuckled. "But I am very glad that y'all have come to an understanding about blind dates. That was a good thing to hear at breakfast this morning."

"Me, too," Brodie said.

Hettie had already settled into the truck's passenger seat and her seat belt was fastened when Audrey slid in behind the steering wheel. "Did you set Brodie straight?"

"I did," Audrey replied, and started the engine. "Shall we go to the café here in town or drive to Nocona or maybe go to that barbecue place in Bowie that you like so well?"

"I didn't sleep worth a"—she paused and sighed—"worth a *dang* last night, so let's just go to the local café. The Sunday special is always chicken and dressing, and I've been craving that for a spell now."

"Aunt Hettie, are you pregnant?" Audrey teased.

Her aunt slapped her on the arm. "I might ask you the same thing since you didn't come in last night until the wee hours of the morning. Who have you been meeting on the sly?"

"I told you the last time you asked that I was seeing all three of the Callahan brothers," she answered. "I think I might like Knox better. I do love a man with a little ponytail."

"That is enough!" Hettie growled. "It's a sin to even tease about such things, especially on Sunday."

Audrey started the engine and watched the three Callahan men walk across the parking lot and get into Brodie's truck. "Okay, then give me some advice," she said. "Which of the other two should I choose if it's a sin to be sleeping with Knox?"

"I told you that is e…nough!" She dragged out the last word into several syllables. "Take us to the café, and then I'm going home for a whiskey sour and a long nap," she declared, and gave Audrey a dose of the stink eye. "And don't you say a word about me drinking on Sunday. God understands that I need something to wash the taste out of my mouth when I have to be in the same room with Bernie or any of those Paradise people. And to have part of them sit right behind us? Lord have mercy! I couldn't even keep my mind on the sermon for wanting to turn around and swish a look down the whole pew that would melt all of them into a pile of nothing but boots and belt buckles."

"Even Remy and Ursula?" Audrey asked.

"I don't want to talk about that anymore," Hettie huffed.

Audrey didn't tell her aunt that she wanted to do a lot more with Brodie than just look at him over her shoulder or that the vibes she felt during the sermon were purely physical and didn't have a thing to do with spirituality. She drove straight to the café, which was less than half a mile from the church, and after making three rounds in the parking lot, she finally found a spot and pulled into it.

"At least Ophelia and Noah will be the only ones of the Paradise family that we have to worry about today," Hettie said as she unfastened her seat belt and opened the truck door. "I wish someone else owned the place, and then we'd be free of all of them."

If wishes came true, Audrey would want Ophelia and the rest of the seven sisters for friends, but she didn't voice that idea. Her aunt might actually combust right there in the truck and burn it to the ground.

"That's a mean thing to say. If it weren't for Ophelia and Noah, we wouldn't even have a café in Spanish Fort," Audrey said.

Hettie tilted her chin up and began to walk between the vehicles. "I've been good this morning. I didn't say a word to Bernie and only spoke to Brodie to warn him about talking to you," she said through gritted teeth, "so I can be mean if I want to. One balances out the other."

A young waitress met them at the door and led them back to the last available table in the dining room. "Can I get you something to drink? Water, sweet tea, coffee?"

"Sweet tea," Audrey answered as she sat down at the small table for two.

"Same," Hettie said with a nod.

"I'll bring that out with some corn bread muffins for

y'all to munch on while you are deciding what you want." She laid a menu in front of each of them and quickly hurried away when the bell above the door let her know more people were coming into the café.

"I don't need to look at this," Hettie said. "I want the Sunday special that was written on the blackboard inside the door."

Audrey had noticed the board, but she hadn't paid a bit of attention to what was on it. "And that is?"

"Chicken fried steak, mashed potatoes, and a side of my choice," she answered. "I can make a good chicken fried steak, but I hate cleaning up the mess. I can wait until another Sunday for chicken and dressing."

Audrey looked over the menu and then laid it down.

"Well?" Hettie asked.

"I'll have the same, and my choice of a side is fried okra," she said.

"Mine, too," Hettie said.

"And"—Audrey leaned over to whisper—"the waitress isn't even a Paradise person, so that should make you happy."

"It does," Hettie said with a sweet smile.

―――――――

All through Sunday dinner at the Paradise with most of the family gathered around the tables, Brodie kept replaying the conversations he'd had with Audrey, starting with the one in the store right after the tornado. He liked all her fire and determination even then. But what he liked even more was the heat that she generated in his body and heart when she kissed him during the fight with Linda Massey.

"We are buying the bar, and we're getting married the first Saturday in June. Nothing big. Just family with the wedding at the Paradise and a big reception out in the yard," Bo announced, and the dead silence that ensued after she made the announcement brought Brodie back to the present.

"Congratulations?" Brodie finally broke the quietness.

"That's a lot of news to spring on us all at one time," Joe Clay finally said. "What about the music store?"

"We're going to put that on hold for a while and move our trailer back behind the bar. Eventually, we want Knox to build us a house on the property where the music store was going to be," Maverick replied. "But we can live in the trailer or the apartment at the back of the bar until we get a house built, so there's no hurry."

"What made you change your minds?" Mary Jane asked.

"Dave is putting the bar up for sale and offered it to us at a good price—" Maverick started.

Bo held up a palm. "I hope we're not disappointing y'all, but we've been unhappy with our decision to put in a music store. When Dave called about selling the bar, we both came clean about how much we miss working together in the bar. So, we talked about it and jumped on the idea of owning the bar. We were so happy there, and we miss the excitement. But now we've got a half-redone store for sale. Anyone interested?"

"I am," Knox said. "I could run my construction business out of it."

"We'll sell it at a good price," Maverick said.

Bernie beamed across the table from him. "Remember that I'm available to relieve y'all anytime you want to take a few days off or for your honeymoon. I do know how to run a bar. When do you take over the business?"

"Thank you, Aunt Bernie. We may take you up on that, especially for the honeymoon. We take over tomorrow evening," Bo answered.

"Anyone else have a little earth-shattering news?" Mary Jane asked.

"Parker and I are having a baby right around Halloween," Endora blurted out.

"We might beat you to have the next grandchild," Luna said. "Shane and I are due in mid-October."

"Babies!" Daisy and Heather, twin daughters of Rae and Gunner, both squealed at the same time.

"Can I hold them first?" Heather asked.

"No need to argue about that," Rae said. "There will be at least two of them, and if history repeats itself, maybe one or both of my sisters will have twins, so there will be plenty of babies to go around."

That created enough of a stir to let Brodie sneak out the back door without having to answer any questions. Even if the new move took Bo and Maverick to Nocona, they would still be in the county and able to come to Sunday dinners.

He wandered out to the barn and sat down on a bench for a few minutes. His mind kept going back to the farm, so he finally walked back up to where all the vehicles were parked. He got into his truck and drove out to the farm, intending to give Pansy her walk early that day.

The pig must have recognized the sound of the truck because she was standing on her hind legs with her front ones up on the fence when Brodie arrived. She would have wiggled if she hadn't been so round, and if her tail had been long and straight, she might have wagged it. But there was no doubt in Brodie's mind that the little critter was glad to see him and probably ready for a nice long walk. He bent over and put her harness on and then attached the leash before he picked her up.

"I don't trust you to stay on our property without all this," he said, and set her on the ground.

She immediately started toward the back of the property. "Okay then," Brodie said, "evidently you are checking out the trees, so you'll know where the apples and peaches fall."

The pig just grunted and led him all the way to the back fence, then turned right like she had before.

"Don't tell me that pot-bellied pigs aren't smart," Brodie said. "You remembered the route."

He stopped for a while to let Pansy rest when he reached the corner of his property and Audrey's. He thought he was dreaming, but after blinking his eyes several times and swatting a mosquito from his arm, he realized that was really Audrey sitting on a blanket on the other side of the fence with a book in her hands.

"Hey," he said.

She looked up from her book and smiled. "Hey, yourself. What are you doing back here?"

"Evidently Pansy and I are disturbing your peace and quiet," he answered. "We'll just keep walking and let you get back to reading."

"Stay a while and let the poor little critter rest her short legs," Audrey said.

"Okay," Brodie agreed, and sat down on a bed of straw under a pear tree. "Why do you come back here to read?"

"It's peaceful, and I love the smell of the fruit trees when they're in bloom," she answered. "Are you really going to keep that pig for a pet?"

"Unless someone comes around to claim her, I guess I am," he said. "Do you have a pet hiding over on your farm?"

She laid her book to the side. "Not really. I've never had a real pet."

"I'll gladly let you adopt Pansy if you promise not to change her name," he teased.

"I'd rather adopt a rattlesnake," she said in a chilly tone.

"You called her a poor little critter just a minute ago," Brodie reminded her.

"That doesn't mean I want to take her home with me or deal with Aunt Hettie if I did," Audrey said.

"Would you rather have a dog or a cat? We could go to the shelter in Wichita Falls anytime and get you one of either or one of each."

"No thank you. The only thing that comes close to a pet on my place is a box turtle that has shown up every spring since I was a kid. Grandpa said that was the only pet a farmer needed." She lowered her voice. "'Audrey Rose,'" he said, "'a rancher needs dogs to help with the cattle, and old women need a lapdog to fuss over, but a farmer doesn't need a bunch of animals around to take their attention away from the crops.'" Then she went back to her normal tone. "But he didn't seem to mind that I named the turtle Mr. T, and he even let me feed it. The old boy will be coming around soon if he's still alive."

"I begged my mother for a pet, but I wanted a dog or a hamster," he said with a grin.

"And you got a pig," Audrey giggled.

Brodie nodded. "I did, but I'll be willing to give her up if she belongs to a family."

"Then you can get a dog or a hamster?" Audrey asked.

"I think I've outgrown pets," Brodie answered, and then silence filled the air.

"I should be—" he started to rise to his feet.

"No, stay a while," she said. "I've been living here permanently for two years, and I have yet to make friends. It's nice to visit with someone my age."

"You have met all my sisters. You see them every Sunday, and you must be involved with something at the church that could make them your friends," Brodie said.

Audrey frowned and shook her head. "I inherited Aunt Hettie with the farm, and she was already set in her ways when it came to the Paradise. Then the minute Bernie pulled her trailer into town, Aunt Hettie got more fuel for her fury.

I don't think being friends with your sisters would be such a good idea."

Brodie cocked his head to one side. "Explain the way that you inherited an aunt, please?" As soon as he asked the question, he thought about the way he and his brothers had inherited a whole family that included Aunt Bernie.

"When her husband, my Uncle Amos, died, she came to live with Grandpa and Granny," Audrey answered. "She more or less ran the house since Granny always had something wrong with her. If you looked up hypochondriac in the dictionary, you would find her picture right beside it. When Granny died, Aunt Hettie just kept doing what she'd always done—keeping house for Grandpa, cooking, and taking care of the flower beds out in the yard. When I finished college, Grandpa told me that I would inherit the farm when he died. Part of the deal was that I had to take care of Aunt Hettie as long as she was alive or until she decided to live somewhere else," Audrey explained.

Brodie tried to think of a question that would require more than a yes or no answer just to keep her talking. "Do you ever kind of resent that?" he asked.

"Nope," Audrey replied. "She's a lot of company, and I'd be lost without her, but some days she is a lot to deal with—like this morning in church. Now it's my turn to ask a question. How did you find out that Joe Clay was your biological father? And are Knox and Tripp really twins?"

"That's two questions," Brodie said. "Yes, they are really twins even though they don't look a thing a like—kind of like one set of my sisters, Rae and Bo. My parents adopted them when they were only a few days old. And as far as Joe Clay goes..." He told her about his mother revealing their biological parentage to all of the Callahan brothers.

Audrey reached under the bottom strand of barbed wire and laid a hand on his knee. "I'm sorry about your folks." After a gentle squeeze she took her hand away. "I can sympathize because I lost both of my parents in a trucking accident when I was in college. When I graduated from high school, Mama went on the road with my dad. They were killed when the truck in front of them jackknifed on the ice. Six people were killed that day. From then on, I just had Aunt Hettie and Grandpa. I'd spent all my summers here from the time I started kindergarten. I even came back to help Grandpa during holidays and summers after I started teaching vocational agriculture. From the time I was a little girl, I knew your sisters enough to say hello, but Aunt Hettie and Grandpa..." she shrugged.

"I understand," Brodie said.

"Now, it's my turn to ask a question. Other than a firefighter, what did you do before you moved here?"

"I spent two hitches in the army." He wished that she had not removed her hand. He would have loved to lace his fingers in hers.

"Doing what?"

He grinned and wiggled his dark brows. "I could tell you, but then I'd have to..."

Her laughter rang out over the cornfield behind her and

the orchard in front of her. "Really, what did you do?" she asked when she stopped giggling.

"Special ops, and I enjoyed my job, but Mother got sick about the time I should have reenlisted for a third time. I came home to help with her. Dad had died two years before that, and my brothers were both busy. They stepped in when they could, but that last year..." he swallowed the lump in his throat. "I wouldn't take for all the memories we made."

"Same with me and my folks," Audrey said. "I had finished college and had been teaching vocational agriculture at a little school out in the panhandle when I got the news about the wreck. I'd just spent a week with them over Christmas break, and I often think of all the fun we had."

"We hang on to the good," Brodie whispered.

She stood up and folded her quilt. "Yes, we do, and today has been a good day. But my time is up. Aunt Hettie will be waking up from her nap. She is as predictable as the sun when it comes to her schedule. She'll be ready for her afternoon snack and then she'll make herself a whiskey sour. I will fuss at her for drinking so early in the day because she likes to argue. But at her age, I really don't care how much she drinks or that sometimes she wants ice cream instead of healthy food."

"Shall we make a date for next Sunday right here at the same time?" Brodie asked.

"Brodie Callahan, are you asking me for a date?" Her tone attempted to be serious, but she had a smile on her face.

"I would, but..."

"Neither of us are ready to face the consequences, are we?" she asked.

"I'm ready when you are," he answered.

"Maybe someday," she told him.

He sat still and watched her until she disappeared into the cornfield and listened to her whistling until it faded away into the breeze that kicked up. He recognized the tune as "Would You Lay with Me," an old Tanya Tucker song.

The lyrics asked if he would walk a thousand miles through burning sand to get to her.

"Yes, I would," he said as he stood up with Pansy and walked all the way down the fence to the trailer with the song playing on a loop in his head.

Chapter 14

TEXAS FARMERS NEVER COMPLAIN about the spring rains, Brodie thought as he drove out to the farm on Monday evening.

The orchards, gardens, cash crops, and hayfields need all the water they can get before the summer heat arrives. But after a hard day's work in Tripp's barn, Brodie wished for a nice night with stars shining brightly and maybe a conversation with Audrey. The gray skies looked like they could open up with more rain anytime, but not even a fine mist had started yet. The air was heavy with the aroma of blossoms from the fruit trees as Brodie went from his truck to Pansy's pen.

"Are you ready for your evening stroll?" he asked.

She came out of her house and stood still for him to put the harness and leash on her. Brodie picked her up over the fence, set her down, and let her take the lead when she started off in the same direction that she always went—down between the trees to the back fence and then across to the fence separating the two farms. She stopped at the corner, found a little dry section of hay under a tree, and plopped down on her belly.

Brodie leaned on the fence post for a few minutes. He

visualized Audrey on the other side, sitting on a blanket with her book in one hand and a glass of cold sweet tea in the other. In his imagination, she had taken a shower after working in the fields all day, and her hair was still damp. He took a deep breath and imagined the smell of her perfume, but there was no Audrey, not that evening.

"Damned fence," he grumbled. "It's just a symbol of everything that keeps us apart."

Pansy stood up and tugged on the leash. He followed her down the fence row and back to the trailer. He lifted her over the edge, and as soon as he removed the harness and leash, she went right back into her house. With a sigh, Brodie walked back to his truck and stared at his toolbox in the back.

"I get the feeling you are trying to tell me something," he said.

Finally, he slapped his forehead and chuckled. "Now I get it. Fence first and then we'll tackle Bernie and Hettie." He opened the red metal box, removed the wire cutters, and grabbed a pair of work gloves.

He jogged back to the place where he and Audrey had visited the night before and snipped each strand of barbed wire from the corner. Then he moved eight feet down and clipped the wire from the wooden post, leaving a nice open space at the end of both farms. If there ever was a next time for him and Audrey to meet up, nothing would be between them but pure Texas air.

He whistled all the way back to his truck and tossed

the lengths of wire into the back and then headed over to the broken fence near the front of the property. He pulled up what was left of the rotted post out of the ground and threw it in the back of his vehicle. He stopped whistling and hummed Josh Turner's "Your Man" as he clipped away sixteen more feet of fence and added it to the pile.

"That should fuel Miz Hettie's anger," he whispered, and drove back to the Paradise.

As if Fate stepped in and took over his playlist, the very next song that came through the speakers was the same one that he had been whistling. The lyrics talked about locking the door and turning the lights down low. He turned down the lane to the Paradise and looked up to see that the dark clouds had moved to the northeast. Stars had popped out around a three-quarter moon.

He parked, got out of the truck, and met Joe Clay coming around the end of the house. "Looks like the clouds have parted, and we might have a good day tomorrow."

Brodie sat down on one of the rocking chairs. "Depends on who you are. I don't imagine it will be a good day for Miz Hettie."

"How's that?" Joe Clay eased down into the chair next to Brodie and propped his feet on the porch railing.

"I took out that sixteen feet of broken-down fence at the front of the property and eight feet at the back," Brodie answered. "I don't expect her to pitch a hissy about the back since she won't even know about it, but that front part is going to cause a stink."

"You get it started," Audrey said. "I've been cooped up all day. I need to get outside for some fresh air, and I'm living with a real feud right here in Spanish Fort. I've seen that series more than once, so I'll just sit in on it when I get back."

"You don't know jack squat about feuds, girl," Hettie snapped. "I lived with one for more than fifty years."

"Then you get the whoopie button for today," Audrey told her.

"I was out on the front porch a little while ago, and there wasn't anybody but a pig over next door," Hettie said. "So, who are you really sneaking out to see?"

Audrey winked at her aunt. "Like I said before, that is classified information. If I told you, I'd have to kill you."

"You are the most exasperating person that God ever let set foot on this earth," Hettie fussed.

"But you still love me," Audrey said.

Hettie set her glass on the table and popped her hands on her bony hips. "Of course I love you, but sometimes I don't like you."

Audrey slipped out the back door and let her aunt have the last word. She crammed her feet into the rubber boots on the back porch and headed along the edge of the cornfield toward the back corner. Even though nosy Hettie hadn't seen Brodie's truck in the driveway, it might have been parked out by the pigpen. She hoped that was the case, but she didn't get her wish.

She sighed with disappointment when she reached the end of the path. Her frown turned into a giggle when she realized that the back section of fence was gone. "Is that an open, no pun intended, invitation to go over to his place anytime I want?" she asked as she walked onto Brodie's property and up the trail between the trees to the pigpen.

If she and Brodie ever got serious without either Hettie or Bernie going to jail... The thought stopped when she remembered that there was something about a stolen pig in the series her aunt was watching that evening.

"Seems fitting," she said as she peeked into the pen.

Pansy poked her nose out of her house and then went back inside.

"You are kind of cute. If I stole you and put you out in one of my barns like one of the feuding families did in the show, I wonder what would happen?" She asked, and then laughed at the silly idea.

She turned around and intended to step over the broken part of the fence but found that the old wooden post was gone right along with the wire, leaving another open space. She walked through it, went back to her house, and left her rubber boots on the porch.

"You're back early," Hettie called out when she came in the back door. "Your feller must be afraid of a little rain."

Audrey took a bottle of sweet tea from the refrigerator and picked up the platter of cookies from the counter. "The rain has stopped, and the stars are shining. I guess all the Callahan boys are worn out from working inside the old barn today, and not a one of them has the energy to come make out with me."

Hettie ignored her and asked, "Did Brodie fix that fence?"

"Define fixed," Audrey said and set the tea and cookies on the coffee table.

"I'm going to watch my movie and ignore you," Hettie declared.

"Sounds good," Audrey whispered.

———————

Tuesday night, Brodie and Pansy made their evening circle out to the end of the property and through the orchard where the air smelled like peach and apple blossoms. There was no sign of Audrey, so they went back to the place where the broken fence used to be, and Brodie stared out across the open space for several minutes. Lights shone out the windows of the house, but off in the distance, he could hear the rumble of tractor engines.

"She must be working late tonight," he told Pansy and led her back to the pen.

Wednesday morning, Tripp had barely gotten breakfast on the table when Bernie and Pepper breezed in the back door. He reached up into the cabinet and set another plate on the dining room table. "Good mornin', Miz Bernie."

She stopped in the middle of the kitchen and shook her finger at Tripp. "I told you boys to call me Aunt Bernie. You are family."

"Yes, ma'am, Aunt Bernie," Tripp said with a grin. "We've got scrambled eggs and sausage plus waffles for breakfast. I hope you haven't eaten."

"Not since my midnight snack," she said, "and good mornin' to all y'all."

Brodie and Joe Clay nodded toward her, and both said, "Mornin'" in sleepy voices.

Mary Jane crossed the room and hugged Bernie. "What are you and Pepper doing out so early?"

Bernie unhooked Pepper's leash from his collar. He plopped down under the kitchen table and closed his eyes.

"He's a lightweight," Bernie said with a giggle. "He don't like to be woken up so early, but he also doesn't like to be left at home. And I'm out so early because I've got a full day. First me and Pepper have some last-minute details to work out with Vera and Gladys about the speed dating at Bo and Maverick's new bar. I'm almost as excited about that as I am about getting more babies in the family. Then we're going to take a walk to the barn to see what…" she stopped and looked at Joe Clay. "You go on and say grace so these boys can eat and get on about their day."

Joe Clay mumbled a quick prayer and then heaped his plate before passing the platter on to Mary Jane. "The barn is coming right along. We're hoping to hang sheetrock today in the apartment. The plumber came yesterday and set all the pipes for the bathrooms, and the electrician has finished up his part of the job," he told Bernie.

"Okay, then," Bernie piled up three waffles and poured warm buttered syrup on them.

How such a little woman could eat so much amazed Brodie. But then it probably took a lot of food to create all the brassiness that came out of her.

"I'll get to see some progress then," she said. "Knox,

when you get whatever all is on your list, I want you to put a deck on the backside, but don't attach it to my house. I want to be able to hitch it up to my house and pull it away. Me and the girls are going to take it and Pepper down to Florida come summertime, but not until after the wedding. Bo said I can be a bridesmaid, so I don't want to miss anything about helping get the wedding ready."

"It might be next summer before I can get around to doing anything for you, Aunt Bernie," Knox said. "All seven sisters have projects for me as soon as I get done with Tripp's barn, and then me and Joe Clay are going to build a new parsonage, and Brodie still needs a house. We hope to have the parsonage done by fall and maybe Brodie's house by Christmas. In between all that, I'm going to work on the old store building for myself."

"No rush," Bernie said, "but remember I'm old and might kick the bucket before you get it done if you don't get with it."

"Yes, ma'am," Knox said.

"Aunt Bernie, are you planning to go to Wednesday night church services?" Mary Jane asked. "Edits on my newest project came today, and I'll be working until midnight on them, so I won't be going or attending the quilting committee meeting afterward. You will be nice, though, right?"

"Of course, I'm going. We'll be deciding which missionaries get the money from our latest quilting bee project," Bernie said, and then narrowed her eyes. "I'll be as nice as Hettie is. That's all I can promise."

"So, Hettie will be there?" Joe Clay asked.

Bernie sighed so hard that it came out like a snort. "Probably, and she'll disagree with everything I suggest."

Mary Jane picked up the platter of waffles and passed them around the table again. "You two always disagree. Maybe it would be good to let her win once in a while."

Bernie laid her fork down and narrowed her eyes. "Not a chance. She's so bossy that God don't want her in heaven and the devil won't have her in hell. That's why she's lived this long, plus she's pickled. I hear she drinks whiskey sours like water."

"This coming from a woman who has Irish coffee for breakfast?" Joe Clay asked.

Bernie whipped around and glared at Joe Clay. "At least I don't go around with a drink in my hands all day long like I hear she does. Are you guys going to church tonight? I'll hitch a ride with one of you if you are."

"Don't know about the sons-in-law, but us four"—Joe Clay waved his hand to take in Brodie, Tripp, and Knox—"will be there. While you ladies have your quilting meeting, we're going to talk to Parker about the new parsonage."

"So"—Knox cleared his throat and changed the subject—"Tripp, what color are you going to paint the walls in your new apartment?"

"Something neutral," Tripp said, "and speaking of that, the lumberyard is delivering a load of sheetrock first thing this morning, so we probably need to get this kitchen cleaned up and get moving toward the worksite."

"I'll do cleanup," Bernie said. "You boys get on about your business. I may have another plate of waffles, and I don't like to rush."

"Thank you," Brodie said, and almost felt sorry for the two old gals if Joe Clay started something that evening that would help him get a real date with Audrey—but not sorry enough to tell his father to call it off.

Chapter 15

HETTIE HAD ALWAYS SAID that the good Lord would forgive her for not attending church on Wednesday night. Ranchers and farmers had to keep up with chores and crops late in the evening, so they didn't often have the time to get cleaned up and drive into town on Wednesday evening. But it rained all day that Wednesday and hadn't let up one bit when it was time to go to Bible study.

"We'll be attending church this evening," she announced at supper.

"I thought that God knows that ranchers and farmers—" Audrey started.

"He does!" Hettie butted in before she could finish. "But he also sends the rain on the just and the unjust. That tells me I need to be there, and besides, after we get done with the study tonight we're having a meeting to decide which of the missionaries get the money we made from the quilt raffle. We'll also be voting on the next quilt. I want it to be a double wedding ring, but you can bet pennies to cow patties that Bernie won't agree with a thing I suggest."

"What will do you about that?" Audrey asked.

"We'll have a vote, and if she wins this one, I'm never

setting foot in that church again. She can have the whole lot of it," Hettie said.

"You're going to let her win?"

"Yep, right after I mop up the church with her red hair," Hettie declared. "Now, you get ready to go. I've never been late to anything in my life, and I'm not about to start now. You probably ain't even read the study for tonight, but you might have time to glance through it. Matthew 5, it is."

"Isn't that about the meek inheriting the earth?" Audrey asked on her way out of the kitchen.

"It is, but I'm ninety years old. What would I do with the whole earth?" Hettie called after her.

Audrey took a quick shower, brushed her hair, and got dressed even though the last place she wanted to be that evening was church—for any reason. Just knowing that Bernie and Hettie would be in the same room made Audrey feel like she was sitting on a stick of dynamite with a short fuse. No, that wasn't right. Tonight was more like a whole barrel plumb full of C-4.

Why would I be so stressed about all this? The voice in her head asked.

"I have no idea," she whispered as she checked her reflection in the mirror. "I just feel like something is about to explode."

———

"This has been an amazing Bible study," Parker said when the service ended. "And now, there will be a committee meeting of the quilting ladies right here in the sanctuary.

The men will all meet in the fellowship hall to discuss the new parsonage. I'll hope to see you all on Sunday, and if any of you have a few hours to spare, the Callahan brothers could use your help with remodeling the old barn. I'll turn this over to my wife, Endora, now."

A dozen men followed Parker down the center aisle and disappeared through a side door. Endora left the front pew and went up to stand behind the lectern. "We made a thousand dollars on the quilt raffle, and now it's time to decide which of the three missionaries we plan to send the money to this time. I'll take suggestions."

Hettie raised her hand, then stood and turned to face the women sitting behind her. "I vote that from now on, we divide whatever money we raise with our quilting projects between the three. I personally like our little family in Peru, but it wouldn't be fair to always vote for them."

"That's a wonderful idea, Miz Hettie," Endora said. "That plan would also be fair since we never know how much money each of our quilts might generate."

Bo stood up from the pew right behind Hettie. "When y'all get the next one done, you can display it for a week in the foyer of my and Maverick's bar."

"And for a week in our winery," Ophelia offered.

"And in our store for as long as you need to," Luna added.

"That would get us a lot more bids," Endora said with a nod. "All in favor of going with Miz Hettie's suggestion to share our money with all three of our missionary families, raise your hand."

All hands but Bernie's went up.

"All in favor of letting our next quilt travel for more bids, raise your hands," Endora said.

All hands went up except Hettie's.

"It don't seem right to put a church quilt that's being sold in a silent auction in a bar," Hettie, who was still standing, protested.

"Why not?" Bernie popped up on her feet and glared at Hettie. "You carry around an alcoholic drink most of the time."

"What I do in the privacy of my home is different than owning or going to a beer joint or putting our church quilt in one of those evil places," Hettie barked right back at her.

"Nevertheless," Endora said with a loud sigh, "both ideas have been voted on and approved. This meeting is adjourned. We'll see you all at the next quilting bee. Y'all have a good night, now. Gladys has already made a log cabin quilt for us to work on next. We'll have it in the frame and ready to start on when we meet again."

"Let's get out of here," Hettie stepped out into the center aisle. "I don't want to even look at Bernie anymore."

The old gal's cane made a clicking noise as it hit the floor all the way to the foyer and out into the parking lot. Evidently anger fueled speed because Audrey had no idea her aunt could move so fast.

When she reached the truck, Brodie stepped out of the shadows and opened Audrey's truck door for her.

"Miz Hettie," he said.

"Go away," she hissed. "I don't need your help."

"My mama would haunt me if I wasn't a gentleman," Brodie said.

"I'll haunt you if you don't leave me and mine alone," she snarled.

"Yes, ma'am," Brodie said with a smile. "You have a wonderful rest of the evening."

Hettie plopped down in the passenger seat. "I'll have whatever kind of evening I want, young man, and it won't have a thing to do with you."

Just seeing Brodie had set Audrey's hormones into overdrive. She wanted to reach out and lace her fingers with his or maybe even throw her arms around him and kiss him right there in public.

"Miz Audrey." He tipped his hat toward her and turned to walk away.

"Wait a minute," she said.

He glanced over his shoulder. "Yes?"

"Meet me in the orchard tonight?" she whispered.

"I'll be there in a few minutes." He tipped his hat toward her and blew her a kiss.

"What did you say to that man?" Hettie asked as soon as Audrey was behind the steering wheel. "I saw him blow you a kiss. What does that mean?"

"I told him to please tell Knox that I couldn't meet him tonight and that he could take his brother's turn to court me," Audrey answered.

Hettie crossed her arms over her chest. "Am I going to have to get out my funeral hat?"

"Please don't wear that tacky thing to my funeral," Audrey said with half a giggle.

"That's enough out of you," Hettie growled. "You are spoiling my wonderful night. We should be celebrating my win over Bernie!"

"You won half of the argument. Bernie gets a star too," Audrey reminded her.

"For what?" Hettie asked. "For being a smart-ass about the little bit that I drink? I bet she put away a lot more whiskey than I do when she owned that bar."

"You fussed about putting the quilt in a bar, and she more or less advocated for it, so she wins that round," Audrey told her.

"But I won the big round," Hettie said with a big smile. "We're going to distribute the missionary funds the way I wanted—the fair way."

You are about to find out what fair is all about, Audrey thought as she drove back to the farm.

———

"What was going on out there?" Knox asked when Brodie finally got into the truck.

"Just a little argument with Hettie," Brodie answered.

"Who won?" Joe Clay asked.

"It was a draw," Brodie chuckled.

"That's better than a loss," Tripp said. "When are you going to stop thinking about what two old women think and ask Audrey out? I could feel the vibes between y'all all the way over here."

"When the time is right," Brodie answered as he made a right turn.

"Never will be," Joe Clay said, "if you're waiting on a truce between Hettie and Bernie."

"Or a good old-fashioned cat fight between them?" Brodie grinned and turned right into the lane. "I'm going out to the farm to let Pansy get out of the pen. See y'all later, and I'll be spraying the fruit trees tomorrow, so I won't be at the barn."

"See you at breakfast?" Knox asked.

"Of course," Brodie answered. "There's nothing at the trailer but pickles."

"And a couple of cans of warm beer," Knox said, and was the last one out of the vehicle.

How can a grown man be as nervous as he was on his first date and as excited as he was to come home from the last mission at the same time? Brodie asked himself as he drove to the farm.

He parked in front of the pigpen, got out of the truck, and shook the legs of his jeans down over his boots. Not sure where he might find Audrey, or even if he would find her; he wasn't sure where to even start looking for her. After all, she might have just been teasing him when she told him to meet her in the orchard. The fruit trees covered acres and acres of land, but on a whim, he started walking down the path toward the place where they'd sat across the fence from each other.

He hadn't gone far when he heard someone behind him and turned quickly to find the moon lighting up Audrey not six feet from him.

"Hey," she said.

"You came," he said.

"I did," she took a couple of steps toward him.

"And?" He couldn't take his eyes off her.

"I'm sick and tired of all this worryin' about what two bitter old women think of us." She took two more steps.

"Me, too," he said.

"So, you can either ask me out to dinner on Friday night, or I will ask you," she said.

Brodie's heart thumped around in his chest so hard that he thought it might jump out of his chest. He had been asked out by a woman more than once, and for some reason the dates had not gone well.

"Well, which is it going to be?" Audrey's tone was definitely impatient.

"Audrey Tucker, will you go to dinner with me on Friday night? I can pick you up at six if that works with your schedule," he said.

"Yes, I will, and can we please go to Bo and Maverick's bar in Nocona after we eat? I haven't been dancing in way too long."

"Yes, ma'am, but I have to warn you, I have two left feet," he teased.

Audrey reached out and took his hand in hers. "I don't believe that, but if it's the truth, I guess we better practice."

"Right here?" Brodie asked.

Audrey pulled her phone from her hip pocket and tapped the screen to start her playlist for two-stepping songs. She let go of his hand and wrapped her arms around his neck to one of Alan Jackson's older songs, "Livin' on Love."

When the song ended, she took a step back and frowned. "Don't you ever lie to me again, Brodie Callahan."

"What'd I say?" he asked.

"You said you had two left feet. I've never danced with anyone as smooth as you are. I can't wait to go to Bo's place now."

He laid a hand on his heart. "I promise to never lie to you again. Mama made all of us boys know our way around the kitchen and the dance floor, but Knox and Tripp are really better at the two steppin' and waltzin' than I am."

She tiptoed and kissed him on the cheek. "I do like a man with a little humility and who isn't all full of himself. Let's take a walk through the orchards. Did I tell you that I used to sneak away and sit by the back fence just so I could take in the sweet scent?"

She slipped her hand in his, and just that much contact warmed his whole body. "I don't remember if you did, but I've got a question."

"Shoot!" she said.

"Why did we wait so long to quit caring what Bernie and Hettie thought about us dating? And did you feel a connection between us from the beginning?"

"Mistakes are part of life," she said. "But it's what we

do *after* we mess up that is important. And yes, I did, but I thought it was anger, not chemistry."

"Are we ready to face the consequences, then?" he asked.

"We are going to go out Friday night and see if this attraction we both feel is a hot flash in the pan that will die after one date or if it's something worth pursuing," she answered. "You do feel something, right?"

"Yes, Audrey, I do," he answered.

She dropped his hand and sat down under an apple tree. Clouds covered the moon, putting the two of them in darkness, but Brodie didn't need to see her. All he had to do was close his eyes and a picture of her with the gentle breeze blowing her dark hair flooded his imagination. Now that they were this close and not arguing over land, he wasn't sure how to begin a conversation.

"Want to put your feelings in words?" she finally asked.

"Ladies first," he said.

Was this really happening, or was it another of his dreams? he wondered.

"I asked the question," she said, "so you go first."

"I've never liked wimpy women who need every minute of my time. One lady that I dated—only once—asked me to set the phone on the nightstand and aim it toward myself like a selfie—"

Audrey didn't let him finish. "What's wrong with a selfie?"

"Of me sleeping all night?" he asked.

"Holy crap!" Audrey said. "No wonder it was a one-night stand."

"It wasn't even that much. There wasn't even a good-night kiss," he said.

Audrey scooted over close enough that their shoulders touched. "I am not a wimpy or a clingy woman."

Brodie chuckled and draped an arm around her shoulders. "Amen."

"What's that supposed to mean?" she whispered.

The clouds moved, and the moon gave enough light to see her expression. Her eyes twinkled, and her smile was bright and beautiful.

"Think about…" he started.

"Linda Massey?" With a giggle, she finished the sentence for him. "I really didn't want her for a neighbor, but when I kissed you I felt something I had never felt before. I thought the rush was brought on by nothing more than pure old fury. But even after the anger was gone, something still drew me back here."

"Guys don't usually talk about feelings, but I felt it, too," he said.

Audrey locked eyes with him. "We're about to cause a big problem in both our houses. Are you ready for that?"

Brodie looked down at her lips and then cupped her face in his hands and kissed her—passionately.

"Does that answer your question?" he panted when the kiss ended.

"Oh, yeah," she smiled. "And on that note, I should be going. Many more kisses like that and we'll set the trees on fire."

"Friday night at six, then?" he said.

"I'll hide Aunt Hettie's sawed-off shotgun," she said as she walked away.

Chapter 16

AUDREY CHECKED HER REFLECTION in the long mirror on the back of her bedroom door. She'd put a few bouncy curls in her dark hair, and dragged out a lacy shirt she hadn't worn in years and a denim skirt with a flippy ruffle that ended right above her knee. She had two pairs of dress boots, but tonight she decided on the off-white ones with gold tips on the toes.

"Time to face the dragon," she whispered, and hoped that her aunt had already put away more than one whiskey sour.

"No, that's not right," she said with half a giggle. "If she's had that much alcohol, she will breath fire for sure."

Hettie looked up from the television show she was watching and frowned. "Are we going to a rodeo?"

"*We* aren't going anywhere," Audrey answered. "I have decided on which Callahan brother I want, and he asked me out. We are going dancing at Bo and Maverick's bar after we have dinner."

Hettie's frown deepened. "What about our supper?"

Audrey recognized the tone and refused to go on the guilt trip that it offered. "There is leftover spaghetti in the fridge and half a coconut pie. I don't think you will starve, but if you want something different, you can call Walter and ask him to drive you into town for supper."

"What if I fall down and can't get up or have a heart attack?" Hettie whined.

"Call me and then call 911. I bet I'll beat them home, but if you are faking either one, I'm going to be really mad at you," Audrey said.

Her aunt's tone and expression changed. She narrowed her eyes and set her mouth in a firm line. "I'm sorry I'm such a burden."

Audrey dropped a kiss on Hettie's forehead. "You are trying to guilt me into staying home, but it won't work. I'm going out. Brodie will be here any minute. I won't invite him in if you are going to be tacky to him. While I'm gone, you can call Bitsy and y'all can pray that I will have a miserable evening and hate him."

Hettie wiped the kiss away. "Are you trying to join the two farms with a marriage license? Just remember it was a marriage license that split things in two pieces in the beginning."

"No, ma'am," Audrey answered. "What is mine is mine. What is his is his. Never the twain shall meet, not even if there happens to be a wedding cake in the very distant future. The world today doesn't say that I have to give him what is mine. That ship sailed over a hundred years ago."

"And women still ain't got a lick of sense when it comes to men or the other way around either," Hettie huffed.

"I'm going to my room. I will not be a willing party to this thing, and if you ever do marry *that man*, I will not be at the wedding."

"It's a first date, not a proposal," Audrey argued.

———

Brodie found a whole party waiting for him at the bottom of the stairs—Joe Clay, Mary Jane, both of his brothers, Ursula and Remy, and their baby, Clayton. "What's this?" he asked.

Mary Jane brushed a bit of lint from his red-and-blue plaid shirt. "It's the first date you've been on since you arrived."

"I've been on half a dozen dates," Brodie argued.

"Those weren't real," Knox said. "Those were prearranged by Bernie. This one is important because you did the asking."

"Well, if y'all don't let me get out of here…" he started and stopped when Bernie came through the front door.

Brodie took one look at her and mentally compared the expression on her face to the tornado that had just recently created so much havoc on his farm. "Evenin', Aunt Bernie," he said.

"Don't you *evenin'* me, Brodie Callahan. I had to find out about this date through the Spanish Fort gossip vine. You should have told me yourself." She glared at him for a full twenty seconds, then broke out in laughter.

"Are you alright, Aunt Bernie?" Ursula asked.

"I'm just fine." She wiped her eyes with a tissue that she pulled from the pocket of her jeans. "I couldn't be better."

Brodie glanced over at his brothers. Both had that deer-in-the-headlights look in their eyes, and poor old Tripp was easing back a step at a time toward the kitchen. Remy slipped an arm around Ursula as if he was protecting her and Clayton.

"What is so funny?" Joe Clay finally asked.

"I win!" she raised both her fists in the air.

"You win what?" Mary Jane frowned.

"I bet Hettie is having a Southern hissy fit. She's made it clear that she doesn't want Brodie and Audrey to date."

"And that means if you don't put up a fuss that you win?" Brodie asked.

"Reverse psychology again?" Ursula asked.

"Bingo!" Bernie shouted. "Ursula gets a shot of Irish whiskey instead of a gold star. Come on out to the trailer anytime in the next week and claim it. I don't care who you boys date as long as you stay in Spanish Fort. But"—she paused and shifted her focus to Tripp and Knox—"it's my calling to try to help you two along. However, I knew it would make Hettie set her heels even more if I pretended to be against Brodie and Audrey. Now I can be all for it, and she'll dig in even deeper."

"You are a witch," Brodie whispered.

Bernie wrapped her arms round him, gave him a tight hug, and took a step back. "Thank you. That's the best compliment I've had in months. Now, go on and make me proud."

"Yes, ma'am," Brodie said with a grin.

Chapter 17

BRODIE PARKED IN THE driveway beside Audrey's truck and eased out of his vehicle. He'd only gone a few feet when a tall, lanky man wearing overalls rounded the end of the porch and nodded.

"Hello again, Brodie," Walter said.

"Walter, right?" Brodie asked.

"Yep, we met that one time." Walter backed up to Audrey's truck and propped a leg on the running board. "You kids know you are stirring up a hornet's nest, right?"

"Yes, sir, we do," Brodie answered, not sure if Walter was the first line of defense and would pull a pistol from his bib pocket if Brodie didn't leave.

"Audrey is facing down a dragon to go out with you, so she must like you. I'm sure that you are doing the same, and I just got one thing to say to you, son. Audrey is the granddaughter I never had. She's strong-willed, is as stubborn as a cross-eyed Missouri mule, and never backs down from a fight. I love her in spite of her faults. But she's also got a heart of gold, and if you break that precious heart, I will come for you. Are you still willin' to knock on that door?" Walter asked.

"Yes, sir, I am," Brodie answered.

"Then you are a brave man," Walter told him, and walked up on the porch with him.

Brodie wasn't sure what to do next, so he just knocked and waited. Audrey slung open the door and smiled. "You are right on time." Then she saw Walter and the grin faded. "Is something wrong?"

"Nope," Walter answered. "I just came to see my girl going out on the first date she's had since she took over the farm. You look mighty pretty tonight. You kids have a good time, but don't stay out too late. We've got work to do until noon tomorrow."

Her smile came back. "Thank you, Walter."

"I take care of what's mine," he said with a crooked smile. "See you in the morning." He turned and left.

"Are you ready?" Brodie asked.

"Yes, I am, and I'm starving," she answered as she came out onto the porch.

"Me, too, and Walter was wrong." Brodie escorted her out to his truck with his hand on her back.

"How's that?" she asked.

"You don't just look pretty, Audrey. You are downright gorgeous," Brodie answered, and opened the door for her.

"Well, thank you, and you clean up pretty good for an organic farmer," she teased.

"That's a bit of a backhanded compliment, but I'll take it," he said.

She tossed her purse over into the back seat. "Sorry that

Walter kind of hijacked us, but I've got to admit, I was glad to get some support. Aunt Hettie sure didn't give me any."

"I'm willing to fight the odds against us." Brodie closed the door and jogged around the back of the truck. When he was in the driver's seat, he turned to her and asked, "Where do you want to go for dinner? Looks like we've got a choice in Nocona of Mexican, pizza, barbecue—"

"I'm a cheap date," she said. "I would love a cheeseburger, fries, and a chocolate milk shake."

"Then Dairy Queen it is," he said, still feeling like he might be dreaming.

"Music?" he asked.

"Let's just talk," she answered. "Other than the dates that Bernie set up for you, how many times have you been out in the last two years?"

"In the last fifteen months, none. Maybe twice in the months before that. I went on a couple of dates the last year that I was in the army. Then it was time for me to put my name on the paper for a third enlistment, and my mother got terminal cancer. She required all of my attention. I'm not complaining. We had a beautiful year together. Then this last few months, I've been busy with the farm," he said. "That's a long explanation when I could have just said two."

"I already told you that when my grandpa passed away two years ago, I resigned from the school where I was teaching Vo-Ag and came to Spanish Fort to take over the business. With Aunt Hettie constantly underfoot, there was no time"—she paused—"no, that's not right. I could have made time, but there were no guys around that interested me or, for that matter, seemed interested in me."

"Then I interest you?" Brodie tried to bite back the grin but it was impossible.

"Yep, you do," she said.

He made a turn onto Highway 82, which led to the Dairy Queen. "Why is that?"

She giggled softly and said, "Aunt Hettie says that men don't want an independent woman who is full of spit and vinegar—whatever that means. In her opinion most men want a woman who makes them feel all macho, but you didn't back down from me, so that means you aren't looking for a wimpy woman."

"Guess I'm not most men, then," Brodie said. "In my book a little spit and vinegar adds a lot of spice to a relation-ship." He made a left turn into the Dairy Queen parking lot and parked not far from the entrance.

Brodie and Audrey found the place totally packed except for one booth at the very back of the smallest of the three dining areas off to the side.

"I'll go take up homesteader's rights on that table if you'll order for us," Audrey said.

"Double cheeseburger with bacon, fries, and a chocolate shake?" he asked.

"Just a single cheeseburger and no bacon. The rest is good."

He was still watching her walk away when the lady behind the counter cleared her throat and asked, "What can I get you?"

"Two of the cheeseburger meal deals with fries and

chocolate shakes, and add two sweet teas to that, also." He took out his wallet and paid for the food, then started back to join Audrey.

He had just settled into the booth across from Audrey when Knox and Tripp slid in beside him. He gave both of them a dirty look and asked, "What are you doing here?"

"We just finished ordering some nachos. When we get done eating them, we're going to the bar for a few beers and to flirt with the ladies," Tripp answered. "Figured we'd better have something on our stomachs before we start drinking."

"What are y'all doing here?" Knox raised his eyebrows and asked. "If I was going out with a woman who looks like Audrey does tonight, I'd take her somewhere fancier than the Dairy Queen on the first date."

"This is my choice. I love burgers and fries," Audrey told him.

Brodie bit back a groan. To be honest, he had only told his brothers that he and Audrey were going out to dinner. He had not mentioned the bar or dancing, but still, of all the rotten luck.

"Guess that's our cue," Knox said and nodded toward the window. "I see half a dozen vehicles leaving the parking lot. We can probably go get our own table now and not interfere with y'all's date anymore."

Tripp slid out of the booth and tipped his hat toward Audrey. "Y'all have a good time. See you tomorrow morning at the barn, Brodie."

"Enjoy your nachos," Audrey said.

"Sorry about that," Brodie said, "but in their defense I didn't tell them where we were going or that we were going to the bar for some beers and dancing afterward."

Audrey sighed and pointed out the window. "No need to apologize. Looks like maybe we might as well have told *everyone* where we were going."

Brodie followed her finger to see Hettie and Walter getting out of his truck and heading into the Dairy Queen. "The Universe appears to be testing us this evening."

"We passed the first round. I'm not so sure about this one—or that one." She pointed in a different direction.

"Holy smoke," Brodie groaned when he saw Bernie and her friend Gladys getting out of a compact car.

"Fire sirens will be sounding any minute," she said.

"You think the café will be blazing soon?"

"Yep, and we're boxed in," Audrey said. "The waitress is bringing our order to us right now."

A young girl smiled and set the tray in the middle of the table. "Y'all enjoy. Can I get you anything else?"

"Yes," Brodie said quickly before she could walk away. "We would like a sack to take this food with us."

"Yes, sir, coming right up," she said, and hurried back to the counter.

She brought a sack and a cardboard container to hold the drinks back to the table in only a few seconds. "Sorry to be in a hurry, but my shift just began, and it looks like we've got more customers. Mabel, the lady who was on the counter before me, said that we've really been hopping."

"Looks like it," Brodie said as he packed the burgers and the fries into the sack.

Audrey placed the tea and milk shakes in the carrier and picked it up. "I'll take care of these."

"Come back to see us," the girl said, and ran back to the counter, where Hettie and Walter waited.

There were two ways out of the café. Brodie would have taken the back door, but Audrey led the way and marched right past Hettie and Walter.

"I didn't know y'all were out tonight," she said.

"I told you Brodie was a dud," Hettie hissed. "A man should take a woman to a nice place to eat. Not just expect her to be happy with hamburgers."

"Don't you call Brodie a dud," Bernie said as she crossed the room and got in line behind Hettie and Walter. "Just because we're in a public place don't mean I won't slap the fire out of you for talking like that."

Hettie bowed up to Bernie, looked her right in the eye without blinking, and said, "You better think twice before you do something stupid."

"Let's get out of here," Audrey whispered.

"Lead the way," Brodie said.

They had barely gotten seated inside his truck when Bernie tapped on the window. Brodie rolled it down and raised an eyebrow. "We decided to forego the burgers and go have Mexican food before we hit the bar. I want to see how Bo and Maverick are doing. I'm buying if you kids want to join us, and I'll spring for the first round of beers if you want to go dancing afterward."

"No, thanks," Brodie said. "We've seen enough family for one night."

"It will be a date neither of you ever forget." Bernie giggled and hurried off to get into the car with Gladys.

"She didn't say a mean word to me," Audrey gasped.

"She knew we were going out tonight and doesn't have a problem with it. Seems that she wants to one-up Hettie, but to be honest, I figure that is the only reason she isn't flaming mad." Brodie started the engine but didn't know where to go after that. "What now? Looks like family will be at the bar tonight. We can still go if you want to, but it won't be the date I'd hoped for."

"I want to go to the park, have a picnic while we watch the sunset, and then dance barefoot in the grass until we absolutely have to leave," she said.

"That sounds amazing," he said, "but I will need to make one quick stop by the Dollar General Store."

"What for?" she asked. "The burgers are probably already getting cold."

"A blanket and one of those candles in a jar," he answered. "How far is the park?"

"Probably five minutes," she answered.

He pulled into the parking lot, stopped the truck, and leaned over and kissed her on the cheek. "You are not only gorgeous but also amazing."

She touched his cheek with her open hand. "I don't know about all that, but I am adaptable when I want to be, and tonight, I really want to spend time with you. It doesn't matter if we're on the dance floor at the bar or in the park."

Brodie gently moved her hand and kissed the knuckles. "Then thank you for being adaptable. I'll be back as soon as I can."

Luck might not have been with him before, but it made up for lost time in the store. He found a throw with a beach scene printed on it and a candle with a label that guaranteed it to smell like fresh ocean air. He paid for them and rushed back out to the truck, tossed them in the back seat, and started the engine.

"Navigate for me. Which way are we going?" he said.

"Go that way," she pointed, "to Seventh Street, and then turn west onto Mesquite Street, and it's only a little ways to the park."

He followed her directions and, like she said, in less than five minutes he had parked the truck at the edge of a nice, big park complete with a picnic table under a pavilion. The sun had just begun to dip down to the tops of the trees in the distance and was painting the sky with brilliant pinks, purples, oranges, and yellows.

"It's gorgeous, isn't it?" she said.

"Yes, but when it comes to beauty, it can't compare to you," he answered.

"That's a good pickup line," she giggled. "Did you just make it up on the spot, or have you used it in the past?"

Brodie got out of the truck and opened the door for her.

"I don't have pickup lines, and I call it like I see it. Right now, I'm lookin' at the prettiest woman in Texas, who is hungry, so let's lay this blanket out and pretend that we're at the beach."

She picked up the drinks, slid out of the seat, and said, "Maybe someday we can go to the beach. I've never seen the ocean or even been to the Gulf."

He grabbed the sack with their food inside and the one from the Dollar General. "I would love that."

Maybe on our honeymoon, he thought and then shook his head at such a silly notion on a first date.

Audrey set the drinks on the ground and helped spread the blanket out. She was impressed by the beach scene but even more so by the fact that Brodie had a lighter in his pocket for the candle.

She sat down on one end of the quilt. "Looks like we are ready for a romantic dinner on the beach."

He sat down beside her and handed her the first burger and container of fries. "I couldn't pull out a chair for you, but I can serve your supper."

"Do you wish we would have stayed at Dairy Queen?" she asked.

"Do you wish we were going to the bar for beers and dancing?" He fired back at her.

"I was happy meeting you in the orchard," she replied. "We should do that more often."

"I agree, or I've heard there's a lake near here. We could go swimming when the weather gets warmer," he said.

She bit into her cheeseburger and eased a french fry out of the container and threw it over Brodie's shoulder. "Squirrel was begging. Guess there haven't been many folks out here to feed them today, and yes, I love to swim. Haven't been in a couple of years."

"Me, either," Brodie said.

"I lied," she said. "I really want to go have some beers and dance, but if we do that, one of us will have to stay sober to drive home."

"Let's watch the sunset and feed the squirrels," Brodie said, "and then we'll go to the bar. Bernie might close the place down, but my brothers will leave fairly early. They want to get a full day in at the barn tomorrow."

Audrey ate a fry and then tossed another one to the squirrel. "That sounds great, and I won't lie to you again. If we're going to date, we need to be honest with each other."

"Then you didn't like meeting me in the orchard?" he teased.

"Yes, I did, and that's great, but let's go out sometimes."

"Then you are going to go out with me again?" he asked.

Audrey loved the way that the candlelight and the setting sun put a gleam in his eyes. She had read her students as well as the men she had dated long enough to know that Brodie was honest, spoke his mind, and was funny all in one package.

What made you change your mind about him? You hated him in the beginning, the pesky voice in her head asked.

A woman can change her mind, especially when her hormones are involved, she answered.

"Well?" Brodie asked.

"I'm sorry," Audrey said. "I was fighting with the voice in my head. Yes, we will go out again if you ask me, and if you don't I'll ask you because I'm impatient that way."

He leaned over and kissed her on the cheek. "Will you go out with me next Friday night? Maybe we'll go to Wichita Falls or Gainesville and hope that Fate doesn't put our families in our path."

"Yes," she answered. "Pick me up at six?"

"I'll be there." He carefully threw one of his fries out to the squirrel, who quickly buried it in the ground. "I guess we'll come back here next year to find a french fry tree growing right there. Maybe it will give us some shade. But we were talking about the voice in your head. Who won the battle?"

She took a long drink of her tea and remembered that she had promised not to lie to him again. "It was a close tie but not an easy race."

"I understand," Brodie said. "The sun has set. The food is gone. The squirrel has gone to bed for the night. Shall we head to the bar?"

"Yes, and I get the first and last dances," she said as she crammed all the trash down into the paper bag; she stood up and tossed it all in the trash.

"You can have all the dances," he told her.

"What if there's a beautiful woman there who tries to cut in?"

"That's when you remember what happened with Linda," he chuckled.

"I can do that, but what if there's a sexy cowboy there who wants to dance with me?" she asked.

"Then me and Mr. Sexy Cowboy will go outside and have a duel." Brodie blew out the candle, picked it up, and tossed the blanket over his shoulder. He laced his fingers with Audrey's, and together they walked across the park to his truck.

Forget about vibes or even sparks—the warmth of his hand set off a fireworks show in her body. A vision of throwing that blanket down on a bed of straw up under an apple tree flashed through her mind. She imagined his hand sliding up under her short skirt and his kisses on her lips.

"Am I walking too fast?" he asked.

You can't lie. This time it was Walter's voice in her head.

"No," Audrey answered. "I was just enjoying the visions in my head."

"Want to share?" Brodie helped her get into the truck.

"Not tonight, but maybe someday they'll come true."

"Then I won't tell you about the video that was playing in my head," he said.

"Maybe someday?" Audrey asked.

"Here's hoping both will be a reality," Brodie answered.

"The look in your eyes says that if it does, it will be pretty good," she said.

"Not pretty good. It will be amazing!" he promised.

———————————

Brodie scanned the Busted Spur—the new name for Bo and Maverick's place—when he and Audrey walked inside, but he didn't see Knox or Tripp anywhere. Bernie and Gladys were sitting on barstools and talking to Maverick. Bo was taking a pitcher of beer to a table with two couples seated around it.

"We're going to need music if we're going to dance," Audrey said.

"You better come up on the stage with me and help pick out what you want to hear." He took her hand and led her up to the jukebox.

He plugged several dollar bills into the jukebox, and they took turns picking songs. Brodie wondered if the ones she picked were supposed to have meaning. He was sure that his choices—mostly older songs—had lots of underlying significance.

"Okay, let's see who gets tired first," Audrey said when they had finished.

Brodie led her to the far end of the bar from where Bernie and Gladys were sitting. "But first a cold beer to get us started. I figure lots of dancing will wipe out just one beer, so I can still drive home."

"Hey, you two!" Bernie called out when she caught sight of them.

Brodie waved at them and waited until Audrey was

seated before he sat down. Maverick smiled and brought over two longneck bottles of icy-cold beer. "First drink is on the house. I saw y'all plugging money into the jukebox. Thank you for that. It's been pretty quiet here for a Friday night..." He paused when a dozen young people pushed their way into the place. "Guess I spoke too soon."

Every barstool and all of the tables were soon filled, and the dance floor began to get crowded—and on Brodie's dollar.

"Ready to dance?" he asked when the first guitar licks of "Your Man" started.

"I thought you'd never ask," Audrey said, "and this is a good song to start off the night since you chose it. I know that you can two-step in an orchard when it's just the two of us. Let's see if you are as good on a wood floor with lots of people around."

"Oh, honey, that's a challenge if I've ever heard one." He grinned and led her to the edge of the floor. He put one arm around her and held her hand close to his chest with the other one. Her body fit against his better than anyone he had ever danced with before, and her steps matched his like they had danced with each other since they were kids.

The song ended, and Shania Twain began singing "Any Man of Mine." He stood still and crossed his arms over his chest. Audrey teased him by dancing all around him. Everyone backed up and gave the two of them the whole floor, clapping in time with the beat. She swayed and dipped, put her hands on his cheeks, and blew him kisses until he was almost sweating from sheer heat that had absolutely nothing to do with the temperature of the bar.

When the song ended, she walked into Brodie's arms and wrapped both arms around his neck, swaying to the soft Blake Shelton song "Who Are You When I'm Not Looking."

"Want to answer that question?" he asked.

"It will take a lifetime, Brodie Callahan, for you to get those answers," she whispered.

"I'm willin' to get the answer one date at a time," he said softly for her ears only.

Brodie didn't even know when Bernie and Gladys left the bar, and all the people that filled up the dance floor were nothing but blurs. As far as he was concerned, he and Audrey were the only couple in the bar, and they didn't even need anything more to drink.

"It's getting close to midnight, and I really do have to work tomorrow," she said.

"I don't want the night to end," he said as they finished the evening with "I Hope You Dance."

"Me, either, but there will be other nights, right?" she said.

"Oh, yes, there will be," he promised.

Bo waved from behind the bar when they started out the door. "Y'all be careful."

"Will do," Brodie replied. "See you in church on Sunday."

Bo nodded and raised her glass of beer.

"This has been a perfect night," Audrey said on the way back to Spanish Fort.

Brodie reached across the console and took her hand in his. He brought her knuckles to his lips and kissed each one. "Absolutely."

He didn't need words to fill the silence in the cab of the truck. The quietness was comfortable, which was something he'd never known with other women. When they reached her farm, he got out of the truck, helped her out, and walked her to the door.

She wrapped her arms around his neck, tangled her fingertips in his dark hair, and tiptoed. His lips closed on hers in a passionate kiss that ended a perfect night.

"Meet me in the orchard tomorrow night?" he whispered when the kiss ended.

The porch light flickered on and off several times. "Aunt Hettie is telling me that I've been out past curfew and to cut the good-night kisses short. She's making up for never having daughters by treating me like I'm still sixteen."

Brodie brushed one last kiss across her lips. "Good night, Audrey. See you tomorrow night."

When he got home, he stood on the porch a full minute, but no one turned the porch light on and off several times. He chuckled as he made his way up the stairs to his bedroom. Raising girls, at any age, must involve more than bringing up boys.

Chapter 18

HETTIE SHUFFLED DOWN THE hallway and slammed her bedroom door with such force that it rattled the picture of Audrey's grandparents taken on their wedding day that hung in the hallway. Audrey had expected some attitude, but she'd thought it would come in the form of pouting, yelling, or maybe even a few threats about her moving out to live in the retirement home with Bitsy. But it looked like Hettie might be trying her worst tactic—called silence.

"Well, darlin' aunt," Audrey whispered as she went into her bedroom and eased the door shut. "Nothing you can do or not do is going to ruin my evening. It was straight out of a romance book, and I'm meeting him in the orchard tomorrow evening."

She awoke the next morning to find that not even the aroma of coffee was drifting down the hallway, much less bacon or maybe cinnamon toast. She found Hettie sitting on the porch with a cup of coffee in her hand and half a dozen cookies on a plate next to her.

"Good morning," Audrey said cheerfully.

"Is it?" Hettie barked.

"Did you only make one cup of coffee this morning?"

She tilted her head up so far that if another tornado came through Spanish Fort, she would have spun around like a whirligig. "This is instant coffee with a shot of whiskey to cut the horrible taste. You can make your own coffee and breakfast."

Audrey went back to the kitchen and put on a full pot of coffee, made herself a bowl of cereal and a piece of toast, and sat down at the table. If her aunt wanted to act that way, she would take a sack of sandwiches to the barn and not come back to the house until after dark. Maybe she would even sleep in the equipment barn that night. That would give Miz Barky Britches time to settle down and stop pouting.

She finished her breakfast, washed her bowl and spoon, and set about filling a paper sack with enough snacks and sandwiches to last all day. That done, she dressed in a pair of work jeans, a T-shirt, and boots. She grabbed her old straw hat from the rack inside the back door, crammed it down over her hair, and headed outside with the sack in one hand and a small cooler of sweet tea in the other.

"Mornin'," Walter said from the bottom of the steps.

"I wouldn't go in there," Audrey said. "She's on a warpath."

"Got coffee in the pot?"

"Yep, but I had to make it. She's drinking instant," Audrey answered.

"Then I'll make a pot out in the barn," Walter whispered and nodded toward the sack of food. "Do you plan to be gone a week?"

"Maybe," she answered.

"I understand there's an empty trailer next door," Walter chuckled.

"I'll give her a couple of days to get in a better mood, but that *is* an option. I'm sure that Brodie will rent it to me, especially if I offer to walk his pig every day," she said with a smile. "We should get going before she comes outside and decides to unleash on us."

"You betcha," Walter said and followed her out to the equipment barn. "How did the date go last night?"

"Good," she answered. "No, it went great, and we're going out again next Friday night."

"Just don't rush into anything," Walter advised. "Take time to learn all about each other. Ira and his brother got into a big squabble because neither of them really got to know Clarice. You know the story and how miserable that woman made both their lives."

"I do, and I will be super careful, Walter," she told him. "Brodie and I fought a lot in the past, but looking back, I was running from what my heart was telling me. I knew he wouldn't sell me his farm, and I didn't really want it for myself, but Aunt Hettie had her heart set on putting the two farms back together."

"And you've never been a good loser, have you?" Walter slid the barn door open.

"Nope, I have not," she replied, "but in this case the loser just might be the winner after all."

"Funny how things work out like that, ain't it?" Walter said.

Several local men had shown up to help with Tripp's barn on Saturday morning. They were determined not only to get the dry wall put up in the apartment and the workroom but to also do the bedding and taping. They had met their goals by the end of the day, but it was well past quitting time when everyone stood around to visit about what Tripp wanted to do with the large portion of the barn that would be used for a store. Brodie would have gladly skipped supper and gone straight to the farm, but Joe Clay had made chili and Tertia sent over a chocolate cake for desert—two of his favorite foods. He impatiently sat through the meal, helped with the cleanup, and then raced upstairs to get a quick shower and change from his work clothes into a pair of jeans and a T-shirt.

Dark had settled in by the time Brodie made it to his farm. He quickly harnessed Pansy and set her outside of the pen and started down through the orchard on their nightly walk. He would have been disappointed if Audrey had given up on him and gone home, but he would not have blamed her. His whole mood lifted when he saw her sitting on a blanket on his side of the place where the fence used to be.

"Hey, I was hoping I didn't miss you," she said. "Walter and I worked all day and past suppertime on tractors. I figured you would give up on me and go home."

Brodie tied Pansy to an apple tree and sat down beside Audrey. "I was thinking the same thing about you. Glad that we are both here, though. We put in a long day, too. Had some local help who were good at bedding and taping, so we kept at it until the job was done."

Audrey scooted over and laid her head on his shoulder. "I thought about you a lot today."

Brodie draped an arm around her and kissed her on the forehead. "It seems like a week has passed since last night. Did I tell you that Aunt Bernie has planned a speed dating night at Bo and Maverick's bar? It starts at six and is over at seven. She wants all three of us guys to be there, and you of course, but if you would rather go somewhere else, I'll bow out."

"I'd love to go," Audrey said. "That sounds like a lot of fun, but are you going to be jealous of the men who will sit down at my table?" Audrey asked.

"Not at all, because I'm going to be the only one that sits with you," he said. "Are you going to attack any women who flirt with me?"

"I will mark my territory with a long, sexy kiss on your lips when we first arrive," she teased.

"I can live with that." He grinned.

A little seed of doubt floated into his mind and planted itself right in the middle of his heart. What if Bernie wasn't really good with him dating Audrey. Did she have something up her sleeve with this speed dating thing? Was she really trying to keep them apart?

"Your expression tells me that the wheels are turning in your head," Audrey said.

"Yes, they are," he agreed with a slight nod. "I'm

wondering if…" He went on to tell her about his thoughts on Aunt Bernie.

"Well, we'll just have to ruin her plans if that is what she is thinking," Audrey said. "I do not intend to give anyone my phone number except this organic farmer that I have a slight interest in getting to know better."

"Slight?" Brodie raised both eyebrows.

She snuggled in ever closer to his side. "For now, but you never know what the future holds. That *slight* could turn into something more in a few weeks or months. Are you in a rush to see where this relationship is going?"

"Relationship?" he asked.

"What would you call it?" she answered with another question. "We're a little old to say we're going steady, and even if we weren't, I don't see a class ring on your finger."

"Relationship suits me just fine. I lost my class ring on my first deployment to the Middle East. I would like to know if we are exclusive," Brodie said.

She didn't answer for a few seconds and then nodded. "I'm not planning on seeing anyone else, and besides, I don't have time to even get to know two men at once. But I have to admit that I have teased Aunt Hettie about seeing all three of you Callahan brothers."

Brodie chuckled and a sense of relief washed over him. "I bet she loved that. I've got so many irons in the fire that I couldn't possibly throw another one into the blaze."

"Okay then, but before we get into this relationship, let's lay out some ground rules. Number one. We will always be honest with each other. Number two. If at any time one of us decides that we aren't happy, we don't let things rock on. Number three. We don't let anyone else influence us in the way we feel."

Brodie loved her forthrightness and honesty. "I agree. Shall we seal our deal with a kiss?"

"It might take two or three to seal a deal this big. But not a whole make out session because I need to get back to the house," Audrey replied, and moved over to sit in his lap.

With her arms around his neck and her fingers tangled in his hair, she brought her lips to his in a steamy kiss that sent sparks dancing all around them. After five minutes, she pulled back and wiggled out of his embrace. "Anymore and I'll drag you back to the trailer or out to one of your barns," she panted.

Brodie's words came out between gasps for breath. "And just what would be wrong with that?"

She stood up. "I don't sleep with anyone after just one date. That would be moving our relationship too fast."

"But you want to?" Brodie stood and folded the blanket for her.

"Of course, I do," Audrey answered. "That tells me we are on the right path. See you in church tomorrow."

"Can we sit together?" Brodie asked.

She blew him a kiss. "Maybe after the sixth date."

Audrey was almost to the door leading out of the church and felt like she had dodged a bullet. Hettie and Bernie had not crossed paths even once, but then someone touched her on the shoulder. Expecting it to be Brodie, she turned around and flashed her brightest smile—only to find Endora standing behind her.

"I'm so glad I caught you before you left," Endora said. "Parker and I would love to have you and Brodie come to our house for lunch today."

"Don't you go to the Paradise for Sunday dinner?" Audrey asked.

"Not today." Endora smiled and whispered, "Brodie said he would be glad to join us."

Hettie had moved on a few feet, but she whipped around and gave Audrey a dirty look. "Our pot roast is going to burn if you don't hurry up," Hettie said.

"I'd love to, but Aunt Hettie already made lunch," Audrey said, and then lowered her voice. "And she only stopped giving me the silent treatment this morning. Why don't you and Parker come home with us?"

"I'm not that brave," Endora said. "I've already invited Brodie, so I wouldn't feel right telling him that we've changed our minds. Why don't you come to the parsonage for dessert with us after you have dinner with Miz Hettie?"

"Now that I can do," Audrey agreed. "About one o'clock?"

"That would be great," Endora said. "See you then."

Audrey caught up to her aunt and looped her arm into Hettie's. "I'm starving, and I love pot roast."

"Why were you talking to Endora?" Hettie hissed after they had shaken hands with Parker and were outside.

"She invited me for Sunday dinner at the parsonage, but I told her that you had dinner in the oven," Audrey answered, and changed the subject. "Isn't it a lovely day? That sun should feel good on your old bones."

"Don't call me old, and stop trying to change the subject," Hettie snapped. "I was the one who got up early this morning and put dinner in the oven."

"But you had instant coffee again, didn't you?" Audrey reminded her.

"I wasn't ready to talk to you, but this *is* Sunday, and if I don't forgive you for going out with that Callahan boy, then God won't forgive me for having more than one whiskey sour on some days," she said.

Audrey opened her truck door and helped Hettie inside, then hurried around to get into the driver's seat. "According to Parker, it's not what we eat or drink or wear on our bodies that will either open the Pearly Gates or keep them closed. It's what's in our hearts. I'm glad you've accepted that I'm dating Brodie."

"I haven't accepted a thing," Hettie told her. "I will pray that another tornado comes and sweeps him away to Canada, and when he wakes up he has amnesia and doesn't remember where he came from. I figure we only get so much forgiveness on the books in heaven, and I don't want to use up all of mine forgiving you for bad choices."

"Look at it like this," Audrey said as she started the

engine. "If that's the way things work, then as many whiskey sours as you've been drinking will need lots of a merciful heart."

"What does that mean?" Hettie asked.

"From what you said, God pardons your drinking if you forgive me, so the more I go out with Brodie, the more you can drink, right?"

"I'm not going to talk about this anymore. I'm hungry, and I'm sleepy. So, drive us home so we can eat and I can get my Sunday nap," Hettie told her.

"After we finish dinner, I'm going to Endora's to have dessert," Audrey said as she turned down the dirt road leading back to the farm. "You won't have to ask God to pardon your whiskey because I'm going to the parsonage. That should be a freebie for you. You are welcome."

"I said that we aren't talking about this anymore," Hettie huffed. "Next thing you'll be doing is going to the Paradise for Sunday dinner."

"I thought we weren't talking about this anymore." Audrey parked the truck, got out, and slammed the door.

Hettie was out of her seat, feet on the ground, and stomping toward the house before Audrey could help her. "I can smell the roast from here," she said.

"Hmmph," Hettie growled.

─────

Brodie's heart skipped a beat—as usual—when he heard a vehicle driving past the church. When Audrey parked in the driveway, he walked out to the truck and opened the door for her. She unfastened her seat belt, put her hand in his, and stepped out onto the ground.

"I'm so glad that you came." With her hand tucked into his, he headed toward the porch with her.

"Welcome," Parker said, and set a tray with four glasses of sweet tea on a small table in front of the swing. "Endora is on her way... There she is now."

Endora opened the door and brought out a platter stacked high with an assortment of cookies that all looked homemade. "Hello, Audrey. I'm so glad you could make it, and you are right on time. Since it's such a beautiful day, I thought we would have dessert out here on the porch."

"Sounds wonderful," Audrey said. "I spent all of yesterday in the equipment barn working on tractors, so I'm glad to get some air that doesn't smell like motor oil."

Endora set the cookies on a small table with the tea and sat down. Two rocking chairs made up a nice little conversation group, and since Endora sat down beside Parker, Brodie figured the rocking chairs were for him and Audrey. They sat down at the same time, but he would have far rather been sitting beside her on the swing, so he could feel her shoulder against his.

"In a couple of months, it will be too hot to sit outside except in the late evening," Endora said, and reached for a glass of tea. "Texas gives us four seasons: drought, flood, blizzard, and twister, and then it starts all over again. We've made it through the blizzard that hit in December and the twister that took Brodie's house, and now it'll start all over again. It's going to get hotter than—"

"A blister bug in a pepper patch?" Audrey finished the sentence for Endora.

"You got it, sister!" Endora laughed.

"Amen to that," Brodie said. "I've heard that the four seasons are almost hot, hot, hotter, and hottest. We're hoping to get Tripp moved into his apartment before the *hotter* part hits us."

"We'll get it done," Parker said. "Tripp's and my goals are to have it finished before Bo and Maverick's wedding in June. They said they only want a small ceremony and a reception at the Paradise, but you know how that goes."

"Bo's the last of the sisters to get married, so Mama will do it up right, no matter where it is," Endora said with half a giggle. "And you can bet it will be hot, or maybe raining, so they'll have a backup plan for that."

"They have said that they are having the wedding in the late evening, but it wouldn't hurt to start praying for a nice cool breeze for that day," Parker said.

"Peanut butter cookies are my favorite." Brodie reached for one with one hand and picked up a glass of tea with the other.

"Mine, too," Parker said, taking two, "and Endora's are the best. She's got a secret special ingredient."

She leaned over and kissed him on the cheek. "No secret, sweetheart. It's just a double dose of love baked into every one of them."

Brodie envied his youngest sister for what she had with Parker. They made a cute couple. She had blond hair and big blue eyes and looked like a model for a magazine cover. On first glance, Parker looked so plain with his light-brown hair and hazel eyes that he could disappear into a crowd. But when he smiled or looked at Endora, everything changed.

If eating peanut butter cookies baked with love would make Audrey look at Brodie like that, he would feed her a dozen at every meal.

"I want to apologize for never inviting you to one of our family gatherings, or even here to the parsonage," Endora said.

"No apology necessary," Audrey said. "I had to jump a big hurdle called Aunt Hettie before I could get to know any of y'all, and until now…" she shrugged and glanced over at Brodie.

"Our aunts need a lesson in love," Endora said.

"Find out where they are giving those, and I'll enroll Aunt Hettie!" Audrey declared.

Brodie took a long sip of his tea and said, "I'll be next in line to fill out the form for Aunt Bernie."

"Maybe a miracle will happen, and they'll work it out themselves, but that does give me an idea for my sermon next Sunday," Parker said.

"For those two old gals to get along, we'd have to call down some pure magic," Endora laughed, and then focused on Audrey. "Brodie tells us that you were a Vo-Ag teacher. Do you ever think about going back to that?"

"Nope, not one time," Audrey answered. "Do you ever wish you were teaching again?"

Endora shook her head. "No, I love being Parker's wife, and the work we're doing together at the church is so fulfilling. Plus, I'm selling my children's books as fast as I can write and illustrate them." She laid her hand on her stomach. "And I can't wait for this baby to be born. Life is good."

Brodie slid a sideways look over toward Audrey. They hadn't talked about anything beyond a relationship, but could she possibly be yearning for what Parker and Endora had like he was?

"I'm jealous," Audrey said.

"Of what?" Endora asked.

"The happiness that you and Parker have, the gleam in your eyes when you look at him, and all this." She waved her hand to take in the parsonage and the whole scene.

Does that answer your question? His mother's voice popped into his head.

Brodie almost expected his mother to laugh like she did when he was a little boy and learned how to ask *why, when,* and *what for.*

Parker took Endora's hand in his. "Thank you for that, Audrey. I like the way she looks at me, too. Makes me feel ten feet tall and bulletproof, as the old country song says."

"Just tellin' it like I see it," Audrey said.

"I like honesty," Endora said. "Whatever made you go into Vo-Ag?"

"I always came to the farm during holidays and the

summer months, and I loved it more than living in the city. Studying about farm life and ranching life seemed to be a natural path for me. I've got to admit, I would love to have a little bit of ranching thrown into the business. I've eyeballed that forty acres just north of my and Brodie's properties. It would be an ideal place to run a few head of cattle," she said.

"We'll have to get together with Ursula sometime," Endora said. "She's the rancher in the family."

Audrey picked up another cookie. "I thought she was a novelist."

"She is, but Remy is a rancher, and she helps out with that a lot," Parker said. "She puts baby Clayton in one of those things that she straps on her body, and away they go. The kid is going to know more about ranching when he starts to school than most foremen know when they're forty."

"I'd love to talk to her, but it'll be years before I can afford to buy that acreage," Audrey said with a sigh, and bit into the cookie.

Brodie had never thought of raising cattle until that moment. Organic beef might be something to research. His mother usually bought half a steer from a local rancher who only used natural food for his herd.

"I wouldn't mind running a small herd in the future," Parker said. "I helped build a couple of barns and put an addition on to a ranch house before I moved to Spanish Fort."

"What made you decide to be a preacher?" Brodie asked the question that had been on his mind for months.

With Parker's tattoos and his choice of clothing—jeans and T-shirts—he could easily be mistaken for a biker rather than a minister.

"I ran from my calling for years," Parker answered. "I tried many things to get God off my back, so to speak. I was a member of a small biker gang that supported a shelter for homeless kids. I became a carpenter and roamed around the country building houses or, like I said, barns for ranchers. But there was no peace until I finally submitted to what my heart was telling me. And look at all the benefits I've been given because I did. I've got Endora, a baby on the way, and a wonderful family. I've got sisters and brothers and new babies coming along to go with Clayton, Heather, and Daisy."

"We all have a calling," Endora said. "Some of us, and I'm talking about myself, just take the long road around to find it."

"Amen to that," Brodie said, and checked the time on his phone. "It's already two o'clock. I should be going. Pansy didn't get her walk last night, and she'll be fussy if she doesn't get one this afternoon."

"Me, too," Audrey said.

"Y'all haven't eaten nearly enough cookies," Endora said. "Let me put some in a couple of bags for you to take home."

"My brothers will love that," Brodie said.

"Aunt Hettie probably won't touch them, but Walter and I will love having them for lunch tomorrow," Audrey added.

"I'll get those bags for you, darlin'," Parker said and headed into the house.

"This has been great," Endora said. "We should do it again, only next time plan to come for dinner and stay longer."

Audrey and Brodie stood up at the same time. "I'd like that a lot and thank you for inviting me."

"Don't stand on formality," Endora said. "You are welcome anytime. I know you are too busy to come to the quilting bees, but know that we'd love to have you."

"Maybe someday," Audrey replied. "Aunt Hettie will be there every time though. She is like the old saying about the mail: she wouldn't miss a quilting bee even if it rains, snows, or another tornado blows through Spanish Fort."

"Neither would Aunt Bernie," Endora said. "That's their time to banter back and forth or else give each other dirty looks. I really think they enjoy that more than anything in their lives."

"That's their spice," Audrey agreed. "Without it, their lives would be bland. Then when we go home, Aunt Hettie calls her friend Bitsy, over in Wichita Falls, and tells her all the gossip."

Parker returned with two small paper bags and handed them to his wife.

"I remember Bitsy. She made the best cookies and pies for church potlucks when I was a little girl," Endora said as she loaded the bags with cookies. She handed one to Audrey and one to Brodie. "Have a great rest of the afternoon."

"You, too," Audrey said.

Brodie escorted Audrey out to her truck with his free arm draped around her shoulders.

"Want to take a walk with me and the pig?" he asked, and then laughed. "Never thought I'd ask a woman out with that line."

"I would love to, and I never thought I'd be asked out on a date to walk a pig. Do you think I passed?" she whispered.

Like always, Brodie opened the truck door for her. "Passed what?"

Audrey slid in behind the wheel and started the engine. "The test to see if the sisters were going to like me or join Hettie's side in trying to break us up?"

"Oh, honey, I believe you got a solid A." He grinned. "Endora doesn't send cookies home with someone that she doesn't like."

Chapter 19

BRODIE HAD MIXED FEELINGS about taking Audrey to a speed dating event. One side of the argument he had in his head was a worry that Bernie was indeed cooking up something to try to end their relationship. The other side assured him that he was showing Bernie that she couldn't do anything to upset the chemistry between him and Audrey.

"Well, here we are," he said when he found a place to park out at the far end of the bar's gravel lot. "Do we want to run or go inside?"

"Go inside and prove to Miz Bernie that not even a dozen men are going to make me throw you out to the curb," Audrey answered and leaned over and kissed Brodie on the cheek. "We are going to leave this shindig together."

"You've had the same thoughts I did?" he asked.

"Yep, I did, and you better not let one of those hussies in there split us up," she teased as she opened the door and stepped out of the truck.

"Hey, you are supposed to wait for me to do that," Brodie said.

"I've got my big-girl, sassy panties on tonight. I've got things to prove to your aunt," she told him.

He hurried around the truck and took her hand in his. "What color are those sassy britches?"

"Red," she answered without hesitation. "That's the color for battle."

"We'll win this one, darlin'," he said as they entered the foyer together.

Bernie met them right inside the door. "Welcome to the speed dating event of the year," she said, and handed Audrey a name tag with *Number Five* written on it.

"What's this for?" Audrey asked.

"You will see that number on the table where you will sit. You'll find a pad and paper to take notes on or to use to write numbers down should any young man impress you enough to get his information for your phone," Bernie explained.

"How many tables are there?" Audrey asked.

"Twelve," Bernie answered. "The hour will go by quick with five minutes allotted to each guy."

"I've never been to one of these. Are there any rules for me?" Brodie asked. "Do I get a number?"

"You are number thirteen," Bernie said as she peeled the back off a name tag and slapped it on his chest. "You can't visit one table more than twice. That's the only rule you have to follow. Here is your notebook. Use it to write down names and numbers, if the lady at the table wants to give them to you, for later use."

Brodie glanced around the dance floor, where twelve card tables had been set up in a semicircle with two chairs at each one.

"A bell will ring at the end of five minutes, and you'll have thirty seconds to move," Bernie went on. "There are more guys than women, and y'all will line up at the bar and have until straight up six o'clock to check out the women that you want to get to know. Looks like we've got more coming in now, so take your seat Audrey, and Brodie, your brothers are waiting for you."

Brodie kissed Audrey on the forehead and said, "I will be your number twelve because the lucky guy who gets the last dance goes home with the lady."

"What happens if some good-lookin' feller slips in ahead of you and sits down in the chair?" Audrey teased.

"I'll just have to challenge him to a duel," Brodie said, and headed toward the bar.

Audrey followed his line of sight to the table where she was supposed to be seated, and there was Linda Massey sitting at table number four. "Sweet Jesus!" she gasped.

Brodie whipped around to see what had happened and saw that she was looking at Linda Massey at table number four and Wanette was taking her place at number six. That put Audrey right in the middle of them.

Brodie hurried back over to her side and whispered, "Do you want to fake sickness?"

"Who says I'd be faking?" Audrey asked. "But no, I've taken care of those two before, so I know I can do it. If things get too rough, I'll just wipe up the bar floor with them and send them crawling outside whimpering. Do you think that Miz Bernie did this on purpose?"

Brodie gave her a sideways hug. "No, because she was handing out the numbers on a first come basis."

"Then I do not like the Universe, or Fate, and Jesus and I might even have a long talk before this evening is over," Audrey declared as she started that way.

———

Linda gave her a dirty look when she sat down. "If you start anything, I *will* finish it this time," she snapped.

"Did you bring a pig with you?" Wanette asked.

"Not tonight, but I know where to find Pansy if you want to pet her," Audrey answered. "What are you doing here, anyway?"

"I like speed dating, and I'm still looking for the right man to take to California with me," Wanette answered.

Audrey gave her a curt nod and turned to Linda. "What are you doing here?"

"I might ask you the same thing since everyone in the county knows that you and Brodie are dating," Linda replied.

"His Aunt Bernie needed a few extras," Audrey replied. "But you can bet your muddy butt, I'm the one that will be going home with him."

Wanette tucked a strand of red hair back behind her ear. "You can have him and his pig. He will not be getting my phone number. Not even Brodie Callahan can make my little heart flutter after that incident in the café. That stupid pig ruined an expensive shirt and embarrassed me at the same time."

Audrey turned to Linda.

"Don't look at me. I don't want him, either," she barked. "If he thinks he can come crawling back to me after cheating on me, then he's got cow patties for brains. And one more thing, if he cheated on someone like me, he *will* cheat on a mousy person like you."

Wanette spoke up from the other side. "She's got a point there, and you've got to consider that a man with a pig for a pet isn't much of a catch and you aren't the prettiest woman in the room. I'm wearing that crown."

Linda whipped her hair over her shoulder. "I beg your pardon!"

Before the two women started something that would have Audrey ducking under the table, Bernie whistled shrilly into a microphone. "This event is about to kick off in one minute. Everyone heard the rules at the door when they picked up their numbers. Ladies are seated. Guys have had time to look around."

Suddenly, Audrey felt like a prize cow at a barn auction. She wouldn't have been at all surprised if Bernie had started the bidding in a fast-talking auctioneer's voice.

"When I ring this bell, you guys can find a seat and visit the lady of your choice for five minutes. When the bell rings again, you'll have time to move to another chair. Then it's like the shampoo commercial—wash, rinse, repeat. The countdown begins now. Ten…"

Everyone clapped like she had just delivered the winner of an Oscar.

"Nine, eight, seven, six, five, four..." she stopped for a breath.

"Three, two, one, go!" she said and rang the bell.

A tall, lanky red-haired man beat Brodie's time and sat down at Audrey's table first. "Hello, I'm Denison Walker. I'm from Gainesville, and I'm a lawyer. You are definitely my number one choice for the evening."

Audrey hoped that Wanette and Linda heard him say that.

Too mousy for Brodie, my ass, she thought.

"What do you do for a living?" Denison asked.

If that's your best line, I wouldn't even hire you to represent me for tossing trash out my window, Audrey thought. "I'm a farmer," she said. "I have several hundred acres of corn and sunflowers up near Spanish Fort. I live with my ninety-year-old aunt, who is bossy and mean as a rattlesnake when she doesn't get her way, and I think she might be the devil's sister."

"What do you like to do for fun? When you aren't doing whatever farmers do," he asked.

"I like to go visit my neighbor. He's got this cute little pot-bellied pig. We go for walks with her. I don't have a picture on my phone, or I could show it to you. Her name is Pansy. She has to stay in a pen because she rooted up my aunt's flower bed. She was ready to grab her shotgun and shoot the poor little thing, but I shooed Pansy back over to her own land. What do you like to do for fun?"

Surely that will send this lawyer running for the hills, Audrey thought.

Watching Denison's face turn pale told Audrey this could very well be more fun than she thought possible.

"I like to read, to work on my model train collection, and cook," he answered, but he was already scanning the room looking for the next woman. Only a minute had gone by, and he still had to sit there for four more. So far, Audrey would give him a solid C minus for at least trying.

————————

Brodie was surprised to see so many men at the event. He quickly figured out if he was a little slow when the last bell rang, some other guy would beat him to the chairs. When Bernie announced the last chance of the evening, he hurried over and got ready to sit down across the table from Audrey.

Another man beat him to the chair and smiled at Audrey. Brodie heard him say that he loved farming and had a pot-bellied pig at his place he would love to show her.

Brodie smiled and blew a kiss toward her. She pretended to catch it and put it in her shirt pocket. "Hey"—Knox interrupted the moment—"I got two numbers and plan to call one of them. That should make Aunt Bernie happy. I noticed that you didn't sit down a single time. That surprises me. What happened?"

"I moved too slow," Brodie answered. "How did Tripp do?"

"Strange enough, the women loved him. He's got a whole notepad full of numbers that he says he's going to burn as soon as he gets home—but me and you are both in trouble if we mention it to Aunt Bernie," Knox said with a chuckle.

"He wants her to think that he's going to call several of them."

Audrey left her table and motioned to Brodie that she was going to the ladies' room. He nodded and turned back to Knox. "Are y'all sticking around for a couple of beers?"

"Yep, want to join us?" Knox asked.

"Nope. I could hear rain on the roof, so please tell Audrey I'm going to bring the truck up to the door, so she doesn't get wet," Brodie said.

"Will do, and y'all have a wonderful evening," Knox told him.

"It's always great when I get to spend it with Audrey." Brodie grinned and waved. "Looks like there's a line at the ladies' room, but she should be out soon."

"No problem," Knox assured him. "I'll make sure she gets the message."

The gray skies guaranteed that the rain would be coming down for a while. He jogged out to his vehicle, drove it right up to the door, left the engine running, and got out. He peeked inside the doors to see how far Audrey had moved up the line. She saw him and held up two fingers. Brodie took that to mean there were two people ahead of her.

Before he could even nod, Bernie caught him and asked if he would take a couple of tables out to her vehicle. When he finished that, he headed outside to stand under the porch roof, and noticed that Audrey was standing right in front of him. He took a couple of steps and slipped his arms around her waist, pulled her back to his chest, and sunk his face in her hair.

Audrey must have changed shampoo because that night

it didn't smell like it usually did. He was about to say something when the lady whipped around, wrapped her arms around his neck, and planted a kiss on his lips that tasted like cigarette smoke and whiskey. He didn't remember seeing Audrey drink anything but water from the bottle on her table during the event, and she dang sure didn't smoke.

Then the whole world seemed to crack like an earthquake had struck north Texas. One minute he was kissing a woman he thought was his girlfriend. The next an arm was wrapped tightly around his and someone spun him around. He was shocked to see Audrey standing there, but even more so when she slapped him soundly across his face.

"What…how…" he jerked his head from one woman to the other. "Good Lord! Let me explain."

"I don't need you to explain what my eyes saw. I guess Linda Massey is right. Once a cheater, always a cheater," she said, and stormed back into the bar.

Stunned, Brodie looked down at the dark-haired woman who had kissed him. She had a big smile on her face and said, "Darlin', I don't remember you being at my table, but that was a helluva good kiss. Let's bypass all the formalities and go to my hotel room. My name is Valerie and honey, not one of the men I talked to tonight made my heart feel like it does now. What is your name?"

"My name is *Taken*," he muttered, and went back into the bar. He scanned the whole place but couldn't find Audrey. A line of ladies still waited in the foyer to get into the restroom, and she wasn't among them.

"Are you looking for Audrey?" Bo asked from the other side of the bar.

Brodie nodded.

Bo wiped down the counter and set two beers out for Tripp and Knox. "She came through here about a minute ago looking like she was about to burst into flames. Did y'all have a fight or something?"

"I'm not sure." He explained what had happened.

"Hey." Maverick waved as he came out of the storeroom with a bottle of wine in his hand. "Audrey just left with Gladys. They went out the back door. What happened?"

"You tell him," Brodie said and hurried outside.

The rain had gotten serious by the time he made it to Audrey's place. He jumped out of his truck as soon as he parked and jogged up onto the porch. He knocked and the door immediately swung open. Hettie stood on the other side with a look meant to kill him.

"You've got two minutes to get off this farm," she said through gritted teeth. "I told Audrey you were no good from the beginning, but she had to go and find out herself. She don't want to see you ever again, so take your sorry ass home and never show your face here again."

Brodie crossed his arms over his chest. "I'm not leaving until I talk to her and explain what happened."

"Tell her more lies? I don't think so." Hettie slammed the door in his face.

"I meant it," Brodie said, and sat down on the porch swing to wait—in the pouring-down rain.

Chapter 20

AUDREY SLEPT FITFULLY, DREAMING about Brodie, waking up to toss and turn, going back to sleep only to have him invade her subconscious mind again and again through the night. She awoke early on Saturday morning and found her aunt in the kitchen stirring up a batch of blueberry muffins.

"Thank you for making my favorite breakfast." She poured herself a cup of coffee.

"Do you want to talk about last night?" Hettie asked, her voice all sweet and kind.

"Nope," Audrey replied. "What's done is done. I learned my lesson."

Her heart felt like a rock in her chest, and tears formed behind her eyelids, but she refused to let them fall. She would miss that breathless feeling she had every time that she was around Brodie, and she would *really* miss having Endora for a friend.

That's what you get for tempting Fate, the annoying voice in her head said.

Better to learn the truth now than later, she argued.

Hettie slid the pan of muffins into the oven. "You are

strong. You don't need any man who treats you like that rotten Callahan did."

"You are right," Audrey headed for the front door.

"Where are you going?" Hettie asked.

"Out to the front porch to suck in the fresh scent after a spring rain," she answered.

"That's a good sign that it's time for you forget all about Brodie Callahan," Hettie agreed. "But fifteen minutes is all you get. The muffins will be ready, and they're best eaten right out of the oven."

Audrey forced a smile. "Slathered in butter."

"That's right," Hettie answered.

She stepped out onto the porch and sucked in the smell of a nice morning breeze after a hard rain. "Nothing better than…" she whispered, and then gasped when she realized Brodie was curled up on the porch swing.

He opened his eyes, sat up, and rolled the kinks out of his neck. "Good mornin'."

"Get off my porch and off my property," she growled.

How did she not see his truck parked in the driveway beside hers? Or even get that tingle she always felt when he was anywhere around? Had he completely ruined everything they had had in their short-lived relationship?

Water droplets hung on to his dark hair, and his jeans and jacket were both soaking wet. "Not until you hear me out," he said. "Remember the three rules that you laid out? We'll always be honest. We will tell the other one if we want to date other people. We won't let anyone influence the way we feel. Well, I'm adding a fourth one. We will trust each other, even when the circumstances tell a different story than the truth."

"You erased all those rules when you kissed that woman," Audrey snapped.

"Even in a court of law, the guilty party gets his time in the witness stand," Brodie shot back and shivered.

"How long have you been here?" she asked.

"All night. I told Hettie I wasn't leaving until I talked to you," he answered.

She was astonished to the point that her words came on in a whisper. "You slept in that swing in the pouring-down rain?"

"I just sat here and huddled up against the wind and rain. I fell asleep about an hour ago," he admitted. "I'll sit here all day if you don't let me explain what happened."

"Okay, then," she said with a sigh. She dragged a ladder-back chair from the other end of the porch and sat down. "You've got about ten minutes."

"Why ten minutes?" he asked.

"That's when the muffins come out of the oven, and Aunt Hettie will yell at me to get in the house," she answered. "So, talk fast."

"I thought that woman was you," he said. "She had long, dark hair and the same jacket you wore last night. I walked up behind her and put my arms around her. I thought something was strange when her hair didn't smell like yours did, and I didn't get any vibes like I usually do when you are around. Then *she* turned around and kissed *me*. I was about to push her away when…" he paused. "It sounds like a lame excuse, and if I knew her last name, I would tell you to go ask her what happened. She said her first name was Valerie, but that's all I know. I expected you to tie into her like you did Linda Massey instead of accusing me of something like cheating."

"O…kay…eee," Audrey dragged the word out into several syllables. She wasn't sure that she believed him, but she would give him the benefit of a huge doubt after she had time to think about his excuse. "Can we talk about this more after I've had my breakfast? Meet me in the orchard this afternoon?"

"I'll be there," Brodie stood up. "What time?"

"We quit work at noon. I'll bring sandwiches and cookies," she said.

"One o'clock?" he asked.

"Yes," she said with a nod.

"I'll see you then," Brodie said, and slowly walked out to this truck.

Audrey's heart told her to drop her coffee mug, run after him before he could leave, and apologize for being so hasty and not trusting him. Her mind told her that any man worth his salt would have told her he was sorry and promise to never again make out with an old girlfriend or maybe a woman that he had just met that night. Aunt Hettie would agree with the intelligent side of the argument, not the happy-ever-after side that her heart presented.

She sat in the chair and watched him drive away and dreaded seeing him that afternoon—and at the same time couldn't wait.

"Hey, who was that leaving so early?" Walter seemed to appear out of nowhere.

"Brodie Callahan," Audrey answered.

Walter sat down on the swing. "He's alive after spending the night with you. I figured Hettie would fry him with a look and finish him off with a tongue-lashing if she ever found him in the house at breakfast time."

"He slept on the swing," Audrey said, and then told him the whole story.

———

Brodie drove over to his farm, then sent Knox and Tripp a text telling them that he had had a rough night and wouldn't be at the barn that morning. Then he went inside the trailer, dropped his boots right inside the door and his jeans and shirt beside the table, and crawled into the cot-sized bed. Compared to the porch swing, it was pure luxury. He was thinking about talking to Audrey again when he closed his eyes and drifted off to sleep.

When he first awoke, he thought that another storm was brewing but soon figured out that it was Pansy rooting around under the trailer. He sat up in bed, checked his phone for the time, and found that it was past noon. He'd been sleeping for more than five hours and still felt like he could fall back on the narrow bed for another five.

"Who needs an alarm clock when you've got a pot-bellied pig?" he said as he got out of bed and went into the tiny bathroom to take a quick shower and brush his teeth.

His stomach grumbled while he was shaving and let him know that he hadn't eaten since lunch the day before. He and Audrey were supposed to go to the Mexican restaurant in Nocona after the speed dating event, but that had blown up in their faces.

"If it wasn't for bad luck, I'd have no luck at all," he said, quoting something he'd heard in the past.

He dragged out the coffeemaker from under the sink in the kitchen but couldn't find a pod, so he wound up making a cup of instant. "Tastes like motor oil mixed with mud," he grumbled, but he drank every bit of it while he checked his texts.

Knox wanted to know if he had patched things up with Audrey. Tripp asked if he was going to stay in the trailer until he got over his heartache. Audrey asked if he liked mayo or mustard on ham and cheese sandwiches. He ignored his brothers and sent a text back to Audrey with one word: mustard. Not even a please or thank you until they figured out where each of them stood.

And where you stand as a couple? his mother's voice asked.

"That is first and foremost," he said as he dragged the quilt off the bed and threw it over his shoulder. He had only taken a few steps when a slow drizzle started again. He sent Audrey a text and asked if she would meet him in the equipment barn to the west of the orchards.

Brodie kept running until his senses picked up that very

familiar tingle that said Audrey was nearby. He looked over his shoulder to see her coming behind him with a cooler in one hand and a paper bag in the other. He didn't wait but kept jogging all the way to the barn.

She came in right behind him and set the sack and cooler on a worktable, then removed her yellow slicker and looked him right in the eye. "I guess we need to talk."

He spread the blanket out on the floor. "Do you believe me?"

"My heart told me that no one would sit in the rain all night if they weren't being honest, but my mind says that you are crazy for doing that and such a person will make up excuses," she said.

"Which one are you going to believe, and can we please eat while we talk? I haven't eaten in twenty-four hours, and I'm starving. My girlfriend didn't even offer me a cup of coffee this morning. Or maybe she's not my girlfriend anymore and didn't want to waste good coffee on me?"

"Mama used to say that nothing ever got resolved on an empty stomach." She sat down on the far edge of the quilt and carefully arranged all the food.

Brodie sat down beside her but kept his distance. She handed him a sandwich and a bag of barbecue potato chips. He opened the chips and ate one while he unwrapped the sandwich. "My mother said the same thing. Seems they were both right. Aren't you going to eat?"

"I can't—not just yet," Audrey answered. "But you go on and enjoy the food. I've got muffins and cookies for dessert, and there's tea and a couple of beers in the cooler."

Brodie opened the cooler and took out a bottle of sweet tea. "Why can't you eat?"

"What you said has been going over and over in my mind all morning," Audrey answered. "Until we get this settled, my appetite is gone. I ate two of Aunt Hettie's muffins this morning, but they tasted like sawdust. And by the way, Walter thinks I'm right to talk to you. Aunt Hettie is giving me another dose of the silent treatment."

"Seems like one of the rules that you laid out was that we wouldn't let other people influence us," Brodie said between bites.

"Walter says a man who is lying wouldn't sit in the rain all night and couldn't possibly sit here and eat sandwiches with me," she said. "Aunt Hettie says that you can't trust a man whose family lives in a brothel."

"Well, let's get this over with so you can eat," Brodie said. "Have I ever given you a reason not to trust me?"

Audrey shook her head, inhaled deeply, and let her breath out slowly. "No, but you've got to know where I was coming from. You saw that I was sitting between two of your blind date women."

Brodie finished off his sandwich and unwrapped another one. "I did, and I also saw you talking to twelve different guys. The last one was trying to woo you away with his love of farms and pot-bellied pigs."

She giggled nervously. "Who uses the word *woo* in this day and age?"

"I do because I don't know any other word that fits," he answered.

Audrey had trouble reading Brodie. One minute he seemed like he wanted to make up. The next she wasn't sure that he wasn't about to tell her to take a hike back to her own side of what fence was left.

"Okay, then," she said. "I'll give you that, but I told them all the same story. That I had a neighbor who had a cute little pot-bellied pig that I dearly loved. That was a little bit of a lie, but I was trying to put them off. Then I got a farmer who must've heard the story from one of the others."

"I was a little jealous of that last one," Brodie admitted, "but I didn't worry about it, because we both know and understand that every relationship is built on trust."

Audrey absolutely hated to apologize to anyone for anything, but she also had always taken pride in the fact that she was honest with herself above all else. "I'm sorry that I didn't trust you. What happened was my fault. I shouldn't have let Linda Massey plant a seed of doubt in my heart. You didn't cheat on her—not by any stretch of the word."

"No, I did *not*. I didn't even go out with her," he said, and finally smiled. "Thank you once again for saving my country ass with that woman."

Audrey laid a hand on his knee. "Am I forgiven?"

"If you will sit with me in church tomorrow." He grinned.

"Yes," she said. "But not with your family or with Aunt Hettie. We'll sit together without either one."

"Will you go to Sunday dinner with me?"

Audrey wasn't sure she was ready to be that sorry, but she nodded. "Can we maybe just go to Tertia's café? I'm not quite ready to be thrown in the middle of the whole Paradise family."

"Yes, we can," he answered. "And you don't have to meet the whole family until you are ready. Maybe you'll come to Bo and Maverick's wedding with me and meet them at the reception."

"That's in June, right?" Audrey asked, and reached for a sandwich.

"Yes, it is," Brodie answered.

"Then yes," she answered.

"Why does it matter when the wedding is?" Brodie asked.

Audrey had never been good at really opening up to anyone, especially someone who could possibly break her heart. But if, in spite of all the obstacles, this was going to work with Brodie, she had to give a little. "You said to be honest, so I will. That gives me a little while to get ready to be thrown in with your whole big family. I've been an only child as well as an only grandchild for my whole life. I don't have relatives, so I have mixed feelings about being around all those folks. It took a lot for me to go to Endora's, but I want to be friends with her. And a little more about me: I talk too much and too fast when I'm nervous."

Brodie scooted over closer to her. "We've got our first argument behind us."

She shifted her position until their shoulders were touching. "Is it time to make up?"

"I think it just might be." Brodie turned slightly, tipped

up her chin with his fist, and kissed her. The first time his lips met hers, the kiss was sweet. The second time it deepened, and the third had them both panting when it ended.

"How many dates have we been on?" he asked.

"Tomorrow in church is number six," she whispered, and kissed him again.

"How are you counting?" he asked.

"I guess from the first time I kissed you to make Linda Massey leave you alone." She managed to really smile for the first time since the night before.

"Then number six, it is." He grinned and kissed her one more time.

Chapter 21

CHURCH SERVICES STARTED AT eleven o'clock, so Brodie arrived fifteen minutes early and took a seat in one of the wingback chairs in the foyer. Five minutes later the buzz of conversation mingled with laughter filled the sanctuary as folks left their Sunday school classes. He recognized Endora's and Rae's voices, but the rest of them blended together. In another minute Ursula and Remy came through the doors.

"Hey, where's the rest of the brothers?" Remy asked.

"They've already gone inside. I'm waiting for Audrey," Brodie answered.

Ursula patted him on the shoulder as she passed by and went into the nursery. "Good luck with that. We need to get Clayton into the nursery, or we'd stick around to give you some moral support."

She and Remy were barely in the nursery when Hettie and Audrey arrived. Brodie stood up and smiled at both of them. "Good mornin', ladies. Y'all both look very pretty this morning."

Hettie narrowed her eyes, snarled her nose like she was smelling a skunk, and shook a veined fist at him. "I don't like this, and I won't ever accept you into the Tucker family.

If Audrey doesn't put an end to this, I will move to Wichita Falls to the retirement village where my best friend Bitsy lives."

Family was everything, and Hettie was Audrey's only living relative. No matter how strange the bickering relationship between the two of them was, there was every possibility that Audrey would resent him if she was forced to choose either him or her aunt.

"Aunt Hettie, you are in church," Audrey scolded.

"You don't have to accept me, Miz Hettie," Brodie said in the calmest voice he could muster up. "But it would be very nice if we could be civil to each other."

"Hmmph," she huffed, and headed into the sanctuary alone.

"I'm so sorry," Audrey whispered. "She's had a burr in her saddle for months and seems to get worse with every passing day. No, that's not right: with every minute, not day."

"Things could have been the same at the Paradise if Bernie hadn't been agreeable," Brodie said. "Are you sure you're ready for this, and I don't just mean today but in the future as well?"

"I am if you are," Audrey answered.

He planted a kiss on her forehead and took her hand in his. "I've been ready ever since you kissed me and then rolled around in the mud with that woman—what was her name?" he teased.

"We need to forget all about who she was and just focus on what we are, and that's a couple," she informed him, "whether Aunt Hettie is happy with the idea or not. She's always fussy about something, it seems."

"Since I moved in next door?" Brodie asked as the two of them walked hand in hand down the aisle.

"More like since I moved in," Audrey answered. "And according to her, if we share a hymnbook, we are a set-in-stone couple."

"My mother said the same thing about the folks who went to our church in Bandera," Brodie said. "I never understood how two people holding one songbook was indicative of two people looking at wedding cakes."

"Don't be getting any ideas about a cake-tasting evening. This is just our sixth date," Audrey said out the corner of her mouth.

"I do like wedding cake, but I can get that when Bo and Maverick tie the knot. However," he said, stopping in the double doors, "how many dates do we need to go on before we do think about that kind of thing?"

"A hundred at the very least," she answered before he could finish.

"Sounds good to me. Who's going to keep count? Me or you?" Brodie stood to one side to allow her to be seated on an empty pew ahead of him. He wasn't sure if the quietness that filled the room was just his imagination or if everyone had gone silent when they saw Brodie and Audrey were together. He could almost read their minds by the expressions on their faces. *Run for the hills. World War III is starting right there in the Community Church of Spanish Fort.* The fight between

Bernie and Hettie wouldn't leave a single splinter behind when it was all said and done. The poor congregation looked like they didn't know whether to drop down on their knees and pray or to really panic and run for the Red River.

"What is going on?" she asked as she sank down on the pew.

"Everyone is in shock, but don't worry"—he sat down beside her—"by next week, it will have worn off and someone else will be the headline of the Spanish Fort gossip vine."

"Fame and glory never last long," she teased.

"Good morning, everyone," Parker said. "If you will open your hymnbooks to page thirty-nine, we'll all sing together. Pay attention to the words about love conquering all."

Brodie pulled a hymnal from the back pocket of the pew in front of them and opened it. Audrey slid over even closer to him and whispered, "Seems appropriate, doesn't it?"

"Yep, it does," he answered. "But I can feel the heat from Hettie trying to fry me into a pile of ash right here in the church."

A loud crack of thunder sounded as if it rolled right over the top of the church, then rain pelted down so hard that it looked like fog out the side windows. Brodie leaned over and asked, "Do you think Hettie called that down?"

"I don't reckon she's got that much power," Audrey giggled softly.

"Good thing we didn't plan a picnic in the orchard and decided to eat at the café—unless you want to drive down to Nocona and have lunch at the Mexican place?"

Audrey shook her head. "That place is bad luck for us. Remember what happened the last time we planned to go there."

Brodie nudged her gently with his shoulder. "We could have a trailer picnic."

"That sounds wonderful for another time," she said. "But, today, let's just go to the café."

———

Parker called on Remy to give the benediction at the end of the service, and he had barely gotten the amen said when the sound of sirens got louder and louder until they stopped in front of the church. Two EMT's ran through the doors and yelled, "Where is Henrietta Morris?"

Audrey left Brodie's side and rushed across the church to the pew where her aunt was sitting with her chin dropped almost to her chest and her cell phone in her lap. "Aunt Hettie, what's wrong? Why did you call 911?"

"I've got chest pains," she panted. "I think I'm having a heart attack, and *you* caused it."

"You ate a lot of salsa on your eggs this morning," Audrey reminded her. "Are you sure it's not heartburn?"

"It's my heart! I know my own body, and this is not heartburn!" Hettie raised her voice to a yell as the EMTs helped her onto a gurney. "It's broken because of the way you treat me."

Audrey tried to take her hand, but Hettie pushed her away. "I don't need you."

"I love you and want to go with you," Audrey said.

Hettie crossed her arms over her chest and prayed loudly, "Our Father in heaven, don't lay this to Audrey's many sins. Forgive her for killing me, and please make her break up with that evil man. He has brainwashed her, and she will be miserable if she chooses him over me, and don't let me die before I see her open her eyes and see what a mistake she is making. Amen."

The last word came just as the EMTs wheeled her outside.

Brodie seemed to appear out of nowhere and said, "I'll follow the ambulance. Y'all will need a ride home if she's okay."

"Thank you," Audrey said, and crawled into the back of the ambulance with her aunt.

"Get out!" Hettie yelled, and then groaned. "Until you break it off with that Callahan man, I don't even want to look at your face."

"Aunt Hettie, you don't mean that," Audrey said, "and I don't care what you say; I'm going with you. If you aren't able to sign papers, I'll need to be there."

"Why? You ain't my keeper," Hettie argued. "And besides, Bitsy is meeting me at the hospital and sitting with me until I either die or get well. Until that man is out of your life, I don't need you in mine."

Audrey held on to the bar beside the narrow seat. "How did Bitsy even know that you were being taken to the hospital?"

"I called her when I first started having chest pains.

She told me to call 911 and said that she was on her way. Did you know that at her retirement village, the people can have a car?" Hettie asked, and then moaned, "I feel like an elephant is sitting on my chest."

"Miz Morris, I'm going to put an IV in your arm. If this turns out to be a heart attack, we can get medicine in to help you—"

"Do what you can," Hettie said. "I can see a white light up ahead of me. I hope Bitsy makes it to the hospital in time to tell me goodbye."

Audrey patted her on the shoulder. "What you are seeing is the ambulance light right above your eyes."

"I know what I'm seeing, and it's my precious Amos shining a flashlight to show me the way to him," Hettie argued.

Audrey had absolutely no doubt that her aunt was faking. Was there nothing Hettie wouldn't do to ruin her relationship with Brodie? And would he get tired of the old gal's shenanigans before long?

The ambulance stopped under the awning at the emergency room entrance. The EMTs opened the back doors, and in seconds they were rolling Hettie inside. When Audrey started to follow them, one of them reached out with an arm and said, "You will need to stay in the waiting room until we get her settled and figure out what's going on. Someone will keep you updated and let you know when you can go back to see her."

Brodie parked right behind them, jumped out of the truck, and opened up his arms. "What happened?"

Audrey walked into them and said, "I really think she is faking."

Brodie buried his face in her hair. "Why would she do something like that?"

"In my opinion, she's bored with farm life and wants to go live close to her friend in a retirement village," Audrey said. "But she wants it to be my fault."

"Good Lord!" Brodie gasped. "Why?"

"Who knows?" Audrey took a step back and shrugged. "If she was really having a heart attack, she wouldn't argue with me or have the breath to pray like she did as they wheeled her out of the church. But, hey, I could be wrong, and that's what's scary. She *is* ninety, so maybe a cardiac arrest affects people her age different than it does anyone else."

"I need to move my truck, but I'll be inside as fast as I can," Brodie said.

She tiptoed and kissed him on the cheek. "Thank you for coming."

"I wouldn't want to be anywhere else," he said.

She wasn't surprised to see Bitsy already in the waiting room, but she was shocked when the older woman patted the chair beside her. "Sit down. We need to talk."

Audrey slid down in the chair. "Do you know what is going on?"

"I told her that she should move to Wichita Falls with me when I left Spanish Fort years ago. She kept saying that Walter needed her. Then her excuse was that you needed her," Bitsy said. "She hasn't been happy since Amos died and she moved to the farm, but honey, I do not believe there's a thing wrong with her today. Other than the fact that she wants to leave the farm, but she needs"—she reached over, patted Audrey on the knee and then went on—"she needs someone to be the blame, and she really doesn't like Bernie or the people at the Paradise, so she can't let them think that they are running her off. I intend to take her home with me today for a week or two. She's going to try to make you feel guilty, but don't let her. A little cottage right next to mine is empty, and I've put in a good word with the folks who run the place. I'm hoping that she'll take it, and we can spend our last years together."

Brodie came into the room and sat down beside Audrey. "Any news yet?"

Audrey shook her head. "It'll take a while, I'm sure. They'll run tests to be sure, and that doesn't happen in an hour."

"How about I go into town and get some burgers? I know you must be starving," he offered.

"First let me introduce you to Bitsy, Aunt Hettie's friend. Bitsy, this is my boyfriend, Brodie Callahan. Brodie, this is Bitsy."

"Pleasure to meet you, Miz Bitsy," he said.

"Same," Bitsy said, "and yes, I could use something to eat. I left services at the chapel in our village before they ended and came straight over here. I'd like a cheeseburger, no onions, and an order of fries."

Brodie stood up. "Something to drink?"

She held up a bottle of root beer. "Got plenty of that right here."

"You know what I want," Audrey said.

"Yes, ma'am," Brodie said with a smile.

Bitsy pushed her glasses up on her nose and watched him walk away. "Hettie hates him, but I'm going to reserve judgment. He's a handsome feller and seems like he's got a good heart, but that can be deceiving. But back to Hettie. I'll take her back to Spanish Fort to gather up a few of her things, but don't try to talk her out of going with me. She needs this, and so do you."

Bitsy had always reminded Audrey of Marie on the television show about Raymond. Except for her curly hair and her stout body shape, she and Hettie were alike in the fact that they had no filter on their mouths.

"Yes, ma'am," Audrey agreed. "And I've got broad shoulders if she needs to blame me for moving out. I love her and want her to be happy."

"She can't let Bernie win any other way," Bitsy said with a long sigh. "If you happen to marry that sexy hunk of a man, just run off to Las Vegas. That way she won't have to come back to Spanish Fort for the wedding."

"I'm not in a hurry to take that big of a step," Audrey said.

"Meals in a bag is here," Brodie said as he came into the waiting room. "Any news yet?"

"Not a peep, but me and Audrey have had us a good talk," Bitsy answered.

Audrey smiled at Brodie. "Thank you for the food. I really was getting hungry. Maybe we'll know something soon."

"I'm here for as long as it takes," he promised.

She had taken the last bite of her burger when a nurse came out and asked for Bitsy instead of her. "Hettie Morris wants me to tell you that she didn't have a heart attack, but she had a really bad case of indigestion that can present as the first signs of a heart attack. She's been released, and as soon as the papers are signed she will be ready to go home with you—in about half an hour. She was adamant in saying that she would only leave with you and not someone named Callahan."

"When you wheel her out, I'll get my car and bring it up to the doors, and thank you," Bitsy said.

"It was all that picante sauce that she piled on her eggs this morning. She probably did this just so she *would* have heart attack symptoms," Audrey groaned.

"You are most likely right." Bitsy grinned and focused on Brodie. "I'd like to give you some advice."

"Which is?" Brodie asked.

"Y'all go on to Spanish Fort, but stay out of sight until you are sure my car is gone from in front of your house, Audrey," she said. "She'll gripe and complain about no one caring enough to beg her not to go, but she really wants to leave, and this will make it easier on both of you."

Brodie shook his head. "Audrey, I'm not so sure about this. She needs to know that you love her, and I sure don't want to come between you and family. We can take a step back and let things cool down. I don't want to put you in a position to choose either me or your aunt."

"She won't stay even if Audrey gets down on her knees and begs her—or if she offers to never see you again," Bitsy informed them.

"Are you sure about that?" Audrey asked.

"Absolutely," Bitsy said. "Give her until tonight and call her. Tell her you love her and that you want her to live with you, but you aren't going to bend to her will."

"I'll feel guilty if she moves out and dies in a month," Audrey said.

"Honey, we all are born with an expiration date," Bitsy said. "It's not stamped on our bare butts or tattooed on the bottom of our foot, but it's there. When it's my time to go, there's nothing anyone can do to prevent it, just like when it's Hettie's turn. Let her do this her way and then move on with your life."

"Yes, ma'am, but—"

Bitsy shook her head and put up a palm to stop her. "There are no buts in real love. You are showing that you love her by taking the blame onto yourself for her doing what she's wanted to do for years."

Audrey took a deep breath and nodded. "Okay, then, we'll do it your way, Bitsy. Take good care of her."

"Always," Bitsy said. "That's what good friends do for each other."

Chapter 22

AUDREY STOOD IN THE doorway of the trailer and watched Bitsy park next door. Hettie looked absolutely spry as she got out of the old Cadillac and marched up the porch steps. She didn't even use her cane, but she did shake her fist toward Brodie's farm.

Brodie came up behind Audrey and put his arms around her waist. She leaned back against his chest and listened to his heartbeat. "She wasn't like this when I was a little girl, or when I was in college, or even later when I came home for holidays. She was always so sweet and kind to me. I can't help but wonder if she has dementia or if she has always had a mean streak like her brothers had."

"Mother always said that unhappiness can cause bitterness to come out," Brodie said. "I'm sorry you have to go through this, but, darlin', you have the right to walk right over there and talk to Hettie if you want to."

Audrey said with a long sigh. "Your mama was right. Looking back, I can pinpoint when she got so cantankerous, but I thought it was brought on by grief when Uncle Amos passed away. When she threatened to leave the farm,

I thought she was trying to win an argument. I had no idea that I was holding her back."

"She'll have a few days to figure it all out. Once she gets away from the forest, she may even see that the trees aren't a bad thing," Brodie said, and then backed away and took two beers from the refrigerator. "You probably need something stronger, but this is all I've got to offer."

"Is it cold?" she asked. "After today, I don't think I could handle warm beer."

Brodie nodded, twisted the top off one bottle, and handed it to her. "The generator is running. It can't produce enough power to keep the place air-conditioned, but it keeps the refrigerator running and the little hot water tank going. When Knox took the trailer with him on jobs, he always parked in places where he could plug in to electricity."

"Thank you," Audrey forced a smile.

"Hey, now." Brodie kissed her on the forehead. "I can always fill in for Hettie if you need a good argument."

"I'm confused, Brodie. She has never had any trouble speaking her mind, so why didn't she tell me she wasn't happy?"

"She's old, darlin'," he answered.

"Old, yes, but—" she started.

"Hey, is anyone home?" Walter's voice floated across the yard.

"Come on in," Brodie called out.

Walter opened the door, wiped his feet on the welcome mat at the top of the stairs, and went inside. "I thought I might find you in here, Audrey. Did Hettie really have to go to the hospital?"

"She did," Audrey moved over closer to Brodie and patted the seat beside her.

Walter sat down and raised an eyebrow. "Why is Bitsy over there?"

Audrey told him the whole story, from the time the ambulance showed up at the church to that moment. "I feel horrible. She's blaming me for almost having a heart attack and for leaving Spanish Fort. This has been her home her whole life."

"That makes sense, but you shouldn't go on a guilt trip," Walter said.

"Can I get you a beer or a bottle of water?" Brodie asked.

"I'd love a beer," Walter answered, and then reached over and patted Audrey on the cheek. "Even eating a nice, big, grilled T-bone steak gets old after a while if you have it on the table every day for a month. You'll get to craving a bologna sandwich or even a peanut butter one just to have something different."

"I understand where you are going with this," Brodie said.

"Well, I don't," Audrey declared.

"Your aunt has been in Spanish Fort on a ranch or a farm her whole life," Brodie explained as he got a beer out of the fridge and handed it to Walter. "She's sick of the same old thing. Maybe getting out of this area is on her bucket list, but she feels guilty, like she is leaving her late husband. So, she needs someone to blame for her move. Also, if you have to shoulder the cause of her decision if it doesn't go right, then that's your fault, too."

"Yep, that's it," Walter said.

"Did you talk to her?" Audrey asked.

"That's not just a no, but a hell, no, all in capital letters," Walter answered. "Her bedroom window was up, and I could hear her rantin' and ravin' and sayin' something about not stickin' in Spanish Fort until she had a stroke. Bitsy told her that today was a wake-up call and that she needed to do what she should have done years ago. I thought maybe you would be over here at Brodie's place tryin' to stay out of the way of flyin' bullets."

"I feel like I'm still teaching school and having to listen to all the drama of high school girls," Audrey said with a long sigh.

Walter took a long gulp of the beer and then said, "It'll do her good to get away for a while. If she comes back, it will be with a new attitude, and if she doesn't, she'll be happy. It's win-win either way."

"But why did she have to make a big scene in church of all places?" Audrey asked.

"That way, she's leaving on a win. She beat Bernie on the missionary thing," Walter reminded her. "And Bernie knows now that she didn't run Hettie out of town but that it was your decision to date Brodie that caused the whole problem. I'm going to leave now. Thank you for the beer. I'll just take the rest of it with me and sneak back over to the barn the way I came. You kids enjoy the rest of the day. See you bright and early tomorrow morning, Audrey."

She wiped a tear from her eye and nodded. "Thank you for everything, Walter."

He stood up, bent down, and gave her a tight hug. "It might not seem like it now, but in a couple of weeks, you'll see that you are both a lot happier. In time she will be glad to see you coming around to visit, and"—he smiled as he opened the door—"don't forget to take her a bottle of her favorite whiskey."

When Walter left, Audrey scooted over and laid her head on Brodie's shoulder. "Thank you for being here with me through this."

"Always," he whispered.

Chapter 23

As Brodie finished putting the last pancake on the platter on Monday morning, Pepper pulled Aunt Bernie into the kitchen like a miniature Adirondack dog hauling a sled all by his tiny self. She was fussing at him to slow down the whole time that he stretched the leash to the limit. If it broke, Brodie could see Bernie flying across the room to the far wall. He had never thought the little feller had that much strength, but then when it came to chasing the family cat, Pepper was only slightly smaller than a Saint Bernard—at least in his mind.

"Who's leadin' who?" Joe Clay chuckled.

The dirty look that Bernie shot Joe Clay made him laugh out loud. "Y'all looked like a cartoon coming out across that yard. Take a look." He held out his phone.

Bernie glanced at the video he had taken and frowned. "If you ever show that to anyone else, I will put a hex on you. My hair is a mess, and I look terrible."

"Too late," Mary Jane said. "He let me see it while you were taking the leash off Pepper."

Bernie shook her finger at him. "No one else. Not a soul, do you hear me? I could lose my reputation as a matchmaker if you put that on the internet."

"Well!" The twinkle in Joe Clay's eyes contradicted his fake sigh. "I guess I could delete it if that's the case."

"Thank you," Bernie said. "Now, let's get breakfast started and talk about what happened yesterday."

"What happened?" Mary Jane feigned ignorance.

"I'm tired of playing games with you two. What made everyone in such a good mood anyway?"

Brodie carried the platter of scrambled eggs and sausage links to the table. "Well, for one thing, Hettie did not have a heart attack."

"That's not good news," Bernie fumed. "Will someone please say grace so we can eat, and Brodie can fill me in on all the details. Everyone made a quick run for their vehicles after the ambulance took Hettie away. Did she lose her mind?"

"What makes you ask that?" Knox asked.

"The way she was praying one minute and yelling at Audrey the next made me wonder if maybe Parker needed to do an exorcism right there in the church," Bernie answered. "Somebody pray, please, before my food gets cold and I drop dead myself from worrying about what really happened."

Mary Jane said a quick prayer, and as soon as she said amen, Bernie locked eyes with Brodie. "Well?"

"That's a deep subject." He smiled and handed the plate stacked high with pancakes across the table to Bernie.

"Don't you get funny with me," she scolded.

"Evidently, she wanted to go out on a win against you, Bernie, so she faked a heart attack and left town with her friend Bitsy," he answered.

"A win?" Mary Jane asked.

Brodie told the tale from start to finish and hoped the whole time that it would be the last time he had to go over it. "And that's what happened."

"I will gladly let her *think* she won," Bernie said, "but that was cruel of her to accuse Audrey like she did. I wouldn't do that to a single one of my nieces—not even Clara, and I liked her least of all of them for the most part. We've kind of made up now, but she's still not my favorite."

"My apartment is going to be ready to move into by next weekend," Tripp said.

"Are you trying to change the subject?" Bernie growled.

"Yep, how did I do?" Tripp flashed a grin across the table toward her.

"You did great," Mary Jane answered. "I can't believe that Easter is coming soon. The girls and I have a date tonight to stuff candy in hundreds of eggs. Audrey is welcome to come to help if she doesn't have other plans."

"Okay, okay, I get the hint," Bernie snapped. "We will talk about Tripp moving out of the Paradise and stuffing Easter eggs for Sunday afternoon. I'll let this thing with Hettie stew a while before I bring it up again. On a different note, I love to see all the little kids out there in the backyard with their baskets. I missed so much when the nieces were growing up, but I'm trying to make up for it now. I'll be here to stuff them plastic eggs tonight, Mary Jane. Have you got plenty of candy? I can always make a run to the store if you need me to."

Brodie could have kissed Mary Jane for helping get the spotlight off him.

═══════════

Audrey waited until after work Monday to call her aunt and was about to hang up when Hettie finally picked up. "What do you want?" she growled. "Have you already moved that Callahan man into the house now that I'm gone?"

"No, I have not," Audrey answered. "I don't want anything. I just called to tell you that I miss you and love you."

"Don't bother begging me to come back and take care of the house and cook for you," Hettie snapped. "I might consider it if you lay your hand on your grandpa's Bible and promise to never see or talk to anyone from the Paradise again, but anything short of that, and you can stay away from me."

Audrey fought back tears and giggles at the same time, which seemed totally weird. "I can't do that, but I do hope you are happy in the retirement home. If you decide to stay there, I can bring over the rest of your things and the rest of that case of whiskey I found in your room."

"Don't you dare go through my things," Hettie raised her voice higher with every word. "If I decide to stay, I'll come get my stuff."

"What if Brodie is here when you do?" Audrey asked. "Are you going to be civil to him?"

"I will not," Hettie declared. "Don't you dare let him sleep on my bed, with or without you, and I don't believe you. The minute I was out of the house, you probably moved him in."

"If we *were* cohabiting," Audrey said, all hope of a nice, peaceful conversation gone out the window, "it would be right here in this house in my bed, not yours. The tornado took his place, and there's no way we can both sleep in that little cot-sized bed in the trailer. If you need to come after the rest of your belongings, please let me know in advance so Brodie and I can both be out of the house."

The phone screen went dark. Audrey tossed it over on the other end of the sofa and paced the floor for a few minutes. Then she picked it up and called Brodie. "If I'm going to have the name, I might as well get the game," she muttered as he waited for him to answer.

"Hey, are you done for the day?" Brodie asked.

"Yep, how about you?"

"On my way to the Paradise right now," he answered.

"You owe me a fried chicken dinner," she said. "I thought I'd collect tonight."

"I'll order it now, so it'll be ready to pick up as soon as I grab a quick shower," he said. "Thirty minutes?"

"I'll be waiting on the front porch," she said and headed for the kitchen.

Half an hour was exactly what she needed to make a small Texas sheet cake for dessert. She muttered about the way Hettie had acted the whole time that she whipped up the cake and slid it into the oven.

"Why doesn't she want me to be happy?" she asked.

She's old and wants her way, the annoying voice in Audrey's head answered.

"I can agree with that," she said with half a giggle.

When the cake was done, she poured the icing on it and put the dirty bowls and the pan she had used into the dishwasher. She had only been sitting on the porch swing for a few minutes when Brodie parked in the driveway.

"When are you going to get that truck to a body shop?" she asked when he opened the driver's side door.

"Soon as Tripp gets his out of the shop," he answered. "Are you ashamed to ride with me?"

"Not if you brought fried chicken," she said with a smile.

He held up a large paper bag and sniffed the air. "Do I smell chocolate?"

"Yes, you do," Audrey answered, and held the door open for him. "Come right inside and we'll have supper and finish it off with chocolate cake."

Brodie followed her through the living room and into the kitchen/dining area. "This place is laid out exactly like my house was," he said.

Audrey took two plates from the cabinet and cutlery from a drawer. "No surprise there. From what I see around town, a lot of the houses that were built at the same time as this one are pretty much the same."

Brodie set the sack on the table and removed containers of fried chicken, potato salad, baked beans, and hot rolls. "What would you do different if you could build a house any way you wanted?"

"Kind of like you have to do after the storm took your place?" she asked.

"That's right," he answered. "My brothers and I were putting together a design for a new house, but now that Tripp is going to live in the old barn and Knox is buying the old store for his construction business, I'm not sure what I want to build."

"I'd start with"—she said as she set the plates on the table, then turned and placed her hands on his chest—"a long, steamy hot kiss from the sexy organic farmer who lives next door to me, and then we'd discuss the design for his new house."

Brodie took her in his arms, tipped up her chin with his fist, and lowered his lips to hers for several fiery kisses. "What number is this date?" he asked breathlessly when she pulled back.

"I'm not sure, but I'm two ways about what I want next. I'm starving, so I need sustenance for a make out session, but at the same time, I want to skip the food and..."

"We've got all night," he whispered, "or until you tell me to go home, whichever comes first."

She tiptoed and kissed him one more time. "Then let's eat, but we'll save the cake for later."

"Dessert before dessert?" Brodie teased.

"For an organic farmer, you ain't so dumb," she smarted off.

"Thank you, darlin'." He grinned and held out a chair for her. "You never did answer my question about what kind of house you would want."

"Sweet tea?" she asked before she sat down.

"Yes, ma'am," he answered.

She filled two glasses with ice and tea and carried them to the table, then sat down. "I would want a ranch house that could be added onto as needed. Someday I want a big family, so it might have to have more than one addition. What about you?"

He passed the chicken to her. "That sounds good to me. How many dates do we have to go on before we can start designing a house like that to be built over on my land?"

She laid two pieces on her plate and then gave it back to him. "Probably a hundred and fifty."

He raised a dark eyebrow. "What number is tonight's date?"

She tapped her chin with her finger. "Maybe eighty. I lost track during those hot kisses."

"I like the way you count." He grinned.

"I never was real good at math," she smiled back.

"Would another kiss or two or ten make that number shoot up to a hundred?" he asked.

"It's worth a try," she answered.

She missed Hettie, but a sense of total freedom washed over her when Brodie had kissed her. She could say what she wanted, flirt with him, and possibly even more later on that evening without any repercussions from her aunt.

"But," she went on, "I'm not sure I know how to make out in this house."

"You never brought a boyfriend home to meet your grandparents or even Hettie?" Brodie asked.

Audrey shook her head. "Grandpa and Granny threw a

fit if I even flirted with the summer help. I can't imagine ever asking a boyfriend to come for supper. And Hettie... Well, enough said there."

"We had a little taste of making out before we sat down to supper," Brodie reminded her.

"I bet Grandpa is twisting in his grave, and Hettie is packing up her things to come back here to scream at me," Audrey said.

"Let's lock the doors."

"And turn the lights down low," she answered with the lyrics of a song that started out that way.

"I'm game, but only if it's been enough dates," Brodie said.

She finished off the last bite of food on her plate, stood up, and took him by the hand. "I don't need music or candles, but I do need you, Brodie Callahan."

She locked the back door and then the front one before she led him down the hallway to her bedroom. She didn't even bother to close the door but wrapped her arms around his neck and started a string of kisses as she walked backward to the bed.

Chapter 24

BRODIE RAISED UP ON an elbow and watched Audrey sleep for several minutes before she finally opened her eyes and smiled. "Ready for dessert?"

"I thought we already had it, but I'd go for seconds if you're still hungry," he answered.

She pulled his lips down to hers and groaned when the phone rang. "It's Hettie," she whispered.

"Answer it," Brodie said. "This time she might really be having a heart attack."

"Hello," Audrey said and then hit the speaker button.

"I'm sending movers to bring the rest of my things to me. They'll be there between noon and four tomorrow afternoon," Hettie said. "I like it here even better than I thought I would. Bitsy and I played bingo tonight, and I won several times. Tomorrow, the shuttle is taking us to the mall to shop, and Wednesday, we're going to a museum. Sunday, they're having a big Easter egg hunt for all of us senior citizens. And they have a massage lady that comes in once a week for any of us who are interested. Bitsy gets one real often, and I'm going to give it a try."

"You sound happy," Audrey said, "but don't you want

to wait a few days or weeks before you make a definite decision?"

"I do not!" Hettie's tone turned cold. "The only opening they have is a little cottage right next door to Bitsy's, and I had to tell them today whether I would take it or not. And if and when I get too old to take care of myself, there's a nursing home right here on the grounds that they can move me into."

"You told them that you would take it on the spur of the moment? How many whiskey sours did you have before you put your name on the papers?" Audrey could hardly believe that her aunt would make such an impulsive decision when it took her two days to decide whether to wear her good blue dress to church or her black pantsuit.

"Not a single dang one. I would have done this when Frank died, but I had to help finish raising you," Hettie argued.

"Am I raised up good enough to make my own decisions now?" Audrey asked.

"Seems like that day ain't never comin', and I ain't gettin' no younger," Hettie said. "If you make a mess of your life, it's on you, Audrey."

"Am I allowed to come see you?" she asked.

"Maybe on Mother's Day, but don't bring Brodie with you. He's not welcome," Hettie said, and the screen went dark.

"My mother said that chocolate cake cures anything, even cantankerous old gals who don't have a bit of love for a man who loves her niece," Brodie said.

Audrey threw a pillow across the bed toward him. "How did your mama know my Aunt Hettie?"

Brodie caught the pillow in one hand. "Darlin', she probably dealt with dozens of women like Hettie. I'm going to try the old 'kill her with kindness' act and see if that works. I'll have a couple of bottles of her favorite whiskey delivered to her a week before Mother's Day and maybe some chocolates, also."

Audrey tackled him in the middle of the bed. "I just might be falling in love with you."

"Well, darlin', I'm already in love with you," Brodie drawled.

———

"Good mornin'!" Walter carried his thermos into the kitchen and stopped right inside the door. "Who's cookin' breakfast this morning?"

"It's a joint effort," Audrey answered.

Walter set the thermos down and got a coffee cup from the cabinet. "Then I'm inviting myself to join y'all."

"What's that supposed to mean?" Audrey asked.

"It means that you aren't fighting or arguing." Walter poured himself a cup of coffee. "I quit eating breakfast in this house when Frank and Ira started their bickering over Clarice. If y'all can agree in the kitchen, then things just might work out for you."

Audrey took a pan of biscuits from the oven and set them on the table. "I got a call from Aunt Hettie last night."

"And?" Walter asked.

"She's sending a mover to take her stuff to Wichita Falls. A cottage next to Bitsy was up for grabs and she took it," she answered.

"Is she still mad and blaming you?"

"Yep," Brodie answered. "She says that Audrey can't come see her until Mother's Day, and I'm not welcome."

"That shouldn't surprise any of us," Walter chuckled and sat down at the table. "But both of you seem happy this morning, so I'd say that it's time for Hettie to move on and for y'all to do the same. When I move to Florida, you are both welcome to come see me anytime you want. My back door will open right out onto the beach, and when the children come along, they'll need a great grandpa."

"Thank you," Brodie said.

Audrey felt tears welling up behind her eyes. She stood up, rounded the table, and gave Walter a hug. "You can never know what that means to me."

"Honey, you've been the granddaughter I never had, so it stands to reason that your children will be my great-grands. I'd be very sad if you didn't bring them to see me a couple of times a year," Walter said. "I see Brodie cooked something in a skillet that looks real good. So, let's eat and talk about what we're doing today. The hired hands will be here in thirty minutes, ready to fertilize and spray for bugs."

Audrey swallowed the lump in her throat on her way back to her chair. Brodie set the cast-iron skillet on the table and sat down. He reached over, laid his hand over Audrey's, and then leaned over and kissed her on the cheek.

"I've learned that family doesn't always share DNA," he whispered. "I couldn't ask for a better person to fill in for my mother than Mary Jane, and my brothers and I don't share a bit of blood."

"Amen to that. I'll say grace," Walter said and bowed his head. "Father, I thank you for the peace that I finally feel in this house, and for this food, and for the love I see in these two kids. Amen."

Audrey grabbed a paper napkin and wiped her eyes. "That was beautiful."

"The truth often is." Walter smiled and slathered two biscuits with butter. "Now, I've got a question that I bet neither of you have thought about. You've been so wrapped up in each other and being able to finally spend the night together that you didn't even think about what lies beyond today."

Audrey frowned. "How do you know that Brodie spent the night?"

"You just told me," Walter chuckled.

Brodie turned to Audrey and laughed. "He will bear watching for sure."

"I agree," Audrey said with a nod. "Now what is this question?"

Walter scooped out a big helping of the omelet, took a bite, washed it down with coffee, and said, "This is delicious. But back to my question. What religion do you intend to raise your children in?"

"We haven't talked about children," Brodie said.

"Yes, we did," Audrey corrected him. "When we were discussing building a house, I told you that I wanted a bunch of kids. I do not want to raise an only child. It's too lonely."

"That's right," Brodie agreed. "But that's not going to be a problem since there's only one church in Spanish Fort."

"And we both go there, so…" Audrey started.

Walter shook his head. "That's your spiritual religion, and children need to be raised in church. I'm talking about your farming religion. Brodie goes to the everyday organic church, and you go to the commercial one. Which way are you going to raise the kids? Brodie, do you intend to change?"

"Nope," Brodie answered.

"Audrey, do you?" Walter asked.

"No, I do not," she answered, "and I'm not going into this relationship with thoughts of changing one thing about Brodie."

"Well, then," Walter said, "I'm glad I'm leaving in the fall because bickering and arguing are sure to come back to this house."

Audrey had been so happy that she had finally admitted that what she felt for Brodie went beyond lust and into love that she had not seriously thought about raising a family. Even though she hadn't put it into words like Walter did in his prayer, the peace in the house really had wrapped around her that morning like a warm sweater on a cool day.

"I don't want fighting…" she started, but a lump the size of a grapefruit in her throat kept her from finishing.

"Me, either," Brodie said. "So, let's compromise. When

the children want fruit as in what I grow, then they can go to the organic church that day. When they want corn on the cob or sunflower seeds, they can eat from the commercial table."

Audrey sucked in a lungful of air and let it out slowly. "I can agree to that with no problem."

"Got that settled over a good breakfast," Walter said with another chuckle. "Now let's move on to another question."

"Are you trying to start a fight?" Audrey asked.

"Nope," Walter answered. "I'm trying to get everything laid out so there ain't no problems when I'm in Florida. Which farm are you going to live on?"

"We'll cross that bridge later," Audrey replied. "We've made a compromise about any future children, and that's enough for one day."

She really didn't care if they lived in her house or if they built a brand-new one over on Brodie's farm. As long as she could be with him, it didn't matter where they lived. But she did want to enjoy the place they were in right then for a while before they set the plans for a house in stone. She was in no hurry to go to the courthouse and stand before a judge to make things legal in the eyes of the government, or to start a family. She just wanted to go slow and enjoy the journey before they tackled those decisions.

Walter put a thick glob of butter on his plate and poured honey on top of it. "Fair enough. Just one more question, though. I plan to go to the Easter egg hunt at the Paradise on Sunday. Are you going, Audrey? I understand that you've been reluctant about going there for Sunday dinners, and I can well understand, but things are different now."

"I haven't been invited," she said.

"If you go to the same church as the Paradise folks, then you are invited. The egg hunt starts after the Easter potluck at the church, and the whole community goes. Mary Jane puts out snacks, and everyone brings lawn chairs or quilts. The menfolk hide the eggs, and the ladies help with serving punch and cookies," Walter told her.

"And you are definitely invited," Brodie said, "but in case you need me to say the words: Will you please let me be your escort for the potluck and then out to the Paradise?"

Audrey's giggle turned into a laugh, then she couldn't stop. Tears rolled down her cheeks and left spots on her T-shirt when they dripped off her jaw. "That's why..." she grabbed another paper napkin.

"Why what? And what's so funny?" Brodie asked.

"Why Aunt Hettie"—she took a deep breath and finally got control—"faked a heart attack and moved this week."

"Yep," Walter agreed. "She couldn't not go to the Paradise or Bernie would declare it a win, and she couldn't go, or else she would be going back on her vow to hate anything that has to do with that place."

"Hasn't she gone before?" Brodie frowned. "I understand it's been a tradition for about twenty years."

Audrey glanced over at Walter for an answer.

"She's always made excuses. First she volunteered to stay with Clarice because she was sickly. Then it was Frank, and last year, she said she was feeling poorly," Walter explained. "She didn't agree with me going, and she refused to speak to me for a week."

"How'd you help her get over it?" Brodie asked.

"It's amazing what a bottle of her favorite whiskey will do to patch things up," Walter chuckled.

"We didn't even stay for the potluck last year," Audrey remembered. "She planned this escape very well. She figured I would go with Brodie if he asked me."

"Does that mean you're going to let yourself end the guilt trip you've been on?" Brodie asked.

"Yes, it does," Audrey answered. "I'll still call her every week and tell her I love her. If she changes her mind about you coming with me, I'll go see her on Mother's Day."

"Don't look for any miracles," Walter said as he pushed back his chair and carried his dirty dishes to the sink.

"I'll talk to Bitsy," Audrey said. "Aunt Hettie listens to her."

Walter waved from the door. "That's almost a month from now. Maybe the whiskey sours, or finally being happy, will soften her up by then."

Audrey moved from her chair to sit in Brodie's lap. "We've got half an hour before I need to leave. Got any ideas about what we should do with the thirty minutes? Wash dishes together, maybe?"

"Well, we never did get around to eating that chocolate cake," he teased.

"I've got another dessert in mind." She pulled his face down to hers and kissed him. "If we do things my way, I promise to meet you in the orchard at noon with some sand-wiches and chocolate cake."

He stood up with her still in his arms and carried her to the bathroom without breaking the string of kisses. He turned on the water in the shower and then slowly undressed her. "Ever had shower sex?"

"No. Have you?" she asked.

"Nope, but today's the day," he answered.

Chapter 25

"YOU LOOK ABSOLUTELY GORGEOUS." Brodie's breath caught in his chest when Audrey came out of the bedroom dressed for church in a pretty yellow dress and high-heeled sandals to match. Sometimes he still had trouble believing that he was actually dating the woman who gave him so much grief for three months after he had bought the farm.

"Well, thank you," she said. "You clean up pretty good yourself."

"I do the best I can with what I've got to work with," Brodie said. "Without a doubt, you will be the prettiest woman at the egg hunt and at the potluck. But I do have one problem."

Audrey glanced down at her dress and then up at him. "What's wrong? The dress isn't new. I didn't have time to shop. Is there a stain on it somewhere?"

"No, darlin'." Brodie took her in his arms and held her close. "My problem is that I won't be able to hear a word Parker says this morning with you sitting so close to me. I'm going to be undressing you with my eyes all day."

She raised up on her toes and kissed him. "I will probably have the same problem."

Brodie picked up the backpack he had brought into the house every day that week, and Audrey shook her head. "Why don't you just leave that here? You are coming back tonight, aren't you?"

"Yes, but that would mean..."

"It would mean that I'm asking you to move in with me," Audrey said with a sexy little grin. "Unless you're afraid to actually live on a farm with commercially grown crops."

Brodie dropped the backpack. "I'm not afraid of anything but losing you. Should I bring more stuff, or do I just get to move in what I've got in there?"

"Bring everything. You can have the closet in Aunt Hettie's old bedroom, and store whatever else you need to in the empty room. I've already cleaned out a drawer for you in our bedroom," she answered.

He held the door for her, and they walked out to his truck together. "Is this so you don't ever have to deal with Hettie again?"

"Not at all," Audrey replied. "She called and apologized for being so hateful. Evidently, Bitsy and Walter both had a 'come to Jesus' talk with her. But enough about her. Isn't it a beautiful day for an Easter egg hunt?"

Brodie helped her into the truck and then hurried around the back end and settled in behind the steering wheel. "Yes, it is. Are you absolutely sure about us moving in together? We only stopped fighting a few weeks ago."

"Never been surer about anything in my whole life," she answered. "Are you having doubts that we are ready?"

"Nope, no doubts or second thoughts," Brodie answered. "I love waking up to see you beside me every morning."

Audrey blew a kiss across the console. "Me, too."

———

Brodie took a half-bushel basket filled with plastic eggs to the far corner of the massive backyard and began to hide them in the tall grass. His thoughts were on how much he dreaded telling Joe Clay that he was moving out of the Paradise when, as if on cue, the man appeared right beside him.

"Seems like more and more kids show up to this every year, but then Rae works at the school now, and she put out the word that all the children were invited. Not that I'm complaining. Holidays are the Paradise highlights. We love having folks come here to help us celebrate," Joe Clay said. "And on a different note, I'm glad to see Audrey's smiling face over there with the sisters."

"They're making her feel right at home, and I appreciate that," Brodie said and carefully dropped an egg with every step he took.

"Speaking of home, lately you haven't been spending many nights here," Joe Clay said. "When are you two going to officially move in together?"

"Today," Brodie answered. "She asked me this morning."

"Congratulations, but always remember if things were to go south, you have a home here," Joe Clay said.

Brodie wondered what that had to do with him and Audrey or with the egg hunt, and then it dawned on him.

"We are comfortable in Audrey's house for a while, but eventually I'd like to build something on my property."

"Are you keeping the organic and chemical farms separate?" Joe Clay asked.

"We are," Brodie answered. "I'm not going into this relationship thinking that I will convince her to come over to my side of farming. And she's said the same about me."

"That's a good thing," Joe Clay said. "Looks like we're out of eggs and the kids are lining up. Don't be a stranger around here, son."

Brodie slapped a hand on his father's shoulder. "Same goes for you and all the rest of the family. Our door is open all the time."

Joe Clay wiggled his eyebrows and grinned. "All the time?"

Brodie laughed out loud. "Most of the time."

"Hey," Audrey ran over to him and gave him a quick hug. "I can't believe how much fun having a big family is. Let's have at least seven kids and give our new house a name, like The Orchards, when we get it built. Maybe Pansy will still be alive for them to walk around both properties."

"I can manage the name business, and I'll even buy another pot-bellied pig if Pansy doesn't make it that long, but seven kids?" Brodie asked. "Someone will be fighting, crying, or giggling all the time."

"Sounds like fun, don't it?" Audrey wrapped her arms around his neck and brought his mouth down to hers for a long kiss. "But let's wait a little while to start building a house or a family. Endora needs her new home finished first, and Luna and Endora should have the spotlight until they have their first babies."

"You are amazing," Brodie whispered.

"You and this family bring out the best in me," she said.

Epilogue

AUDREY CROWDED INTO ONE of the Paradise bedrooms with the seven sisters on that hot evening in June. Bo looked like she walked off the cover of a country western music CD in her white eyelet off-the-shoulder, wedding dress and white lace cowboy boots. Bernie bustled around making sure that Bo's veil was straight and she was holding her flowers right for the picture the photographer was trying to capture in the full-length mirror.

Audrey was glad to be included in all the excitement, but at the same time she couldn't help but think about the day she would get married. Walter might be persuaded to come back to Texas to walk her down the aisle, but there would be no family on her side of the church.

"Just think," Bo said and looked over her shoulder at Audrey, "I'm the last of the seven sisters to get married, and that means you and Brodie are next."

"Yes, they are," Bernie said. "When can we start planning?"

"Y'all do know that Aunt Hettie is my last living relative, other than a cousin that I hardly know. We probably should just go to the courthouse or maybe to Las Vegas and let an Elvis impersonator marry us," she said.

"Oh, no!" Bernie declared. "That won't do at all. We love weddings, and honey, you've got lots of relatives right here at the Paradise. We don't stand on ceremony. Folks can sit on either side at a wedding here in Spanish Fort."

"Thank you," Audrey said. "I hear the music starting, so I'm going to go find y'all's handsome brother and sit with him."

"Talk to him about setting a date," Bo said. "Mama will need something to plan after Luna and Endora have the babies."

Audrey gave her a thumbs-up sign and escaped down the stairs to the living room, where Brodie waited. "Is all this giving you wedding fever or cold feet?" she asked.

"I told you a while back that I love wedding cake, and I definitely love you, so no cold feet here," he answered with a grin. "This is the first of the sisters' weddings that my brothers and I have got to be a part of, so I guess I'm getting a dose of wedding fever. Do you have cold feet?"

"I do not, and Bernie wants us to set a date," she answered.

"I'm ready when you are. How about sometime around Christmas? This place is amazing during that holiday."

"I love it," Audrey said.

"Reckon we could seal that deal with a kiss?" he asked.

"A kiss for now. More than just a kiss later," she whispered.

Keep reading for an excerpt from
Carolyn Brown's *Coming Home to Paradise*.
AVAILABLE NOW!

Chapter 1

Nine whole days of freedom.

Bo kept repeating five beautiful words to herself—*nine whole days of freedom*—when she awoke to the smell of bacon and coffee floating up the stairs and into her bedroom. Tomorrow morning it would be the aroma of cinnamon that wafted up to her bedroom. Lots of things changed with time, but not her mother's special Thanksgiving and Christmas Day breakfast sweet rolls.

People changed. She thought of her youngest sister, Endora, and her messy breakup a couple of years before. She had always been such an outgoing person, and after she found out her fiancé and best friend were sleeping together, she went into a deep depression. Now she was engaged to the local preacher and had turned her life right back around.

Dreams change. That brought on a sigh when Bo remembered the dream she chased for ten years, and finally gave up a few months ago. She had gone to Nashville right out of high school and thought she would be the next big country star. She found out really quickly that she wasn't the only young girl in Tennessee who wanted to sing for a living.

A decade later, she finally gave up and came back to Spanish Fort and now helped her great-aunt out with her advice blog and speed-dating events business.

"What are you thinking about?" Her twin sister, Rae, peeked into her bedroom. She was wearing an oversized T-shirt from the police department, where she'd worked in Boise City, Oklahoma, for several years.

Bo sat up and inhaled deeply. "I was thinking about how things change. We can always depend on Mama's cinnamon rolls on Thanksgiving Day. That never changes."

Rae sat down on the edge of the bed. "What has changed?"

"All seven of us sisters," Bo answered.

"Amen to all of that," Rae said, "but it seems strange to have just three of us living here. Every time I've been home for the holidays, all the bedrooms were full."

"You've only been here a week," Bo told her. "It took me at least a month to get used to not having Ursula, Tertia, Ophelia, and Luna in their bedrooms."

"But we do have Aunt Bernie!" Rae giggled.

"Don't remind me," Bo groaned. "Don't get me wrong. I love our great-aunt, and she was quick to give me a job when I came home, dragging my tail behind me."

"Don't say that!" Rae scolded.

"It's the truth," Bo said with a long sigh as she threw back the covers and stood up. "All six of my sisters fulfilled their dreams. If I'd been fishing for my supper, I would have gone hungry. I didn't even get a nibble of a singing contract the whole ten years I was in Nashville."

"Crap on a cracker!" Rae fussed.

Bo whipped around and stared at her sister. "What brought on that Sunday school cussin'?"

"What you said," Rae answered. "Think about the dream we each had and look where we are now. We all couldn't wait to get away from the Paradise. Now, one by one—well, Luna and Endora came back at the same time, so that was two— we are coming home to Spanish Fort. Seems to me like we just made a big old circle."

Bo slipped a hot-pink robe over her red pajama pants and matching shirt. "Kind of like that Rascal Flatts song about God blessing the broken road."

"Yep, only this isn't a boy-comes-home-to-girl song," Rae said with a nod. "It's a girl…" She paused.

"It's seven girls coming home to find happiness," Bo finished for her. "And the last two—that's me and you…"

Rae laid a hand on her sister's shoulder. "Are going to have to run from Aunt Bernie's matchmaking."

"You got that right." Bo nodded. "I hate to say it, but I'm glad she's going to be gone for a few days. Freedom from her trying to hook me up with every eligible bachelor in Montague County sounds like heaven right now. You might as well wipe that smile off your face. As soon as she gets back, she will start her campaign to find you a husband."

"I figure I've got a few weeks." Rae gave her sister a gentle push toward the door. "She's still scrounging up every available male in a forty-mile radius for *you* right now."

Bo stepped out into the hallway and got an even stronger

whiff of cinnamon. "Not every single one. She's already warned me that I cannot even look crossways at the bartender at Whiskey Bent. She found out that he doesn't stay in one spot more than a few months or a year at the most."

"Isn't his name Maverick?" Rae asked.

"Yep," Bo answered. "What kind of guy comes to mind when you say *Maverick Gibson*?"

"Bibbed overalls, a dip of tobacco and gray hair," Rae said with a giggle. "How about you?"

"Not what you said." Bo started down the stairs. "That sounds a lot like Henry Marshall, who has that orchard and truck farm south of town. I imagine him being middle-aged, round-faced, and with a three-day-old beard. I used to wonder how some men were always somewhere in between a clean shave and a real beard."

"Then you had a relationship with a guy who put a guard thing on his electric razor that gave him that sexy look, right?" Rae followed her to the bottom of the stairs.

"I don't kiss and tell"—Bo stopped in the middle of the foyer—"but a one-night stand does not a relationship make. Tell me all about how you found out how men could do that."

Rae's crystal-blue eyes twinkled. "I read it in a magazine."

"Yeah, right," Bo said. "And FYI, I'm going to steer Aunt Bernie toward you. I'll tell her that I always wanted to be the last one to get married so I could have the biggest wedding of all seven of us."

"You are a rat from hell," Rae snapped.

"Yep, and I will own it," Bo giggled and took a step

forward. "Since I work for Aunt Bernie, I can always tell her what kind of man you prefer. Do you want tall, dark, and handsome? Policeman or rancher? Cowboy or combat boots? Sensitive or alpha male?"

Rae pushed her into the kitchen. "Mama, Bo is picking on me."

Their mother, Mary Jane, and stepfather, Joe Clay, both looked up from the table at the same time. A little bit of salt had sprouted in their dark hair for both of them, and crow's-feet had showed up around their eyes, but they would always be young to Bo—even if they were in their late fifties.

"Do you both want to have dry toast for breakfast instead of the spread over there on the bar?" Mary Jane teased.

"Or worse yet, have to go stand in the corner?" Joe Clay's grin left no doubt that he was joking.

"We'll be nice," Bo answered, "but for the record, Rae started it."

———

The hour hand on the old alarm clock that had sat on Rae's bedside table since she was a little girl moved slowly to the eleven o'clock position. Two weeks ago, she was getting into her squad car and making her first rounds for her shift. Before she left, her partner had warned that leaving the graveyard shift and going back to a normal sleep pattern would take a severe adjustment. He had been right. She was still wide-awake at this time of the night and got sleepy sometime around eight in the morning.

She wandered out onto the balcony that was wrapped around three sides of the house and figured out quickly that it was too cold to sit out there in nothing but a thin nightshirt. She went inside and wrapped a quilt around her shoulders, then went back outside, closing the French doors behind her, and sat down in the ladder-back chair. Three more were lined up down the length of the balcony, and there were four on the other side of the house.

A brisk wind made eerie music when it rattled the bare limbs in the pecan trees around the house. Rae scooted her chair back against the wall of the balcony just off her bedroom. She had thought the balcony was the best thing about the Paradise when Mary Jane moved the girls to Spanish Fort.

The old brothel must have been built on a solid foundation because it had stood like the last silent sentinel of the cattle-run days for a century and a half now. Twenty years ago, it had been put up for sale, and Mary Jane learned about it from a friend. The house and the location were exactly what she wanted, so she moved her girls without even taking them to see the place first.

"And the older sisters threw a pure old southern hissy fit because there was only one electrical plug-in their bedrooms." She giggled at the memory.

That vision in her mind faded and another image appeared. Mary Jane had hired Joe Clay to remodel the whole place—room and board included and a bonus if he finished the job by Christmas. He moved in before he knew he would be living in a house with seven bickering and conniving little girls.

The sound of a door opening next to her brought her back to reality, but only for a few seconds when a visual popped into her head of all seven of the sisters spending time on the balcony in times past.

Bo came out of her room and dragged her chair over close to Rae's. "This is a whole new ball game for us. It's our first holiday to be home and not leave at the end of the weekend. Think we'll have to fight the urge to pack our suitcases and get ready for the long trip home after church on Sunday?"

Rae shook her head. "Not me. I'm glad to be here, to have time with family and figure out what I want to do with my life from here on out."

"You've got more options than I have. You can always go back to working for a police force or maybe for the sheriff's department in Montague," Bo suggested. "Or maybe you can put in your own private investigative business. Or even teach since you have that double degree. You covered your bases better than I did when it comes to getting a job."

"Hey, now! You are still singing," Rae argued.

"Playing the piano and singing in church doesn't bring in money," Bo said in a grumbling tone.

"But it makes Endora and Mama happy, so that counts for something," Rae reminded her. "Aunt Bernie keeps you busy with her advice blog and the matchmaking events she's getting into. At least you aren't bored while you are trying to figure out your place in life."

Bo slapped her on the arm. "Don't say the word *bored* out loud. Mama can hear it from a mile away on a day when there's not even a breeze to blow it to her ears."

"I forgot," Rae whispered.

Bo shivered. "I'll never forget washing all the downstairs woodwork and washing down the entire porch."

"Floor and walls both, and there were spiders in the corners," Rae remembered.

"Took the two of us all weekend," Bo said.

"We never said we were bored again," Rae said with a chuckle. "And the others learned from our mistake."

"What's going on out here?" Endora asked. "Are y'all having a preholiday party without me?"

"We were just reminiscing. Come on out and join us," Rae answered. "It's late for you to be working on your next children's book, isn't it?"

Endora brought her chair over to join them. "I wasn't working on that. I still have time before the deadline, and right now I'm concentrating on the Christmas program at the church. Seems like the holidays always bring out memories. What you thinking about?"

"The day when we first saw this place, and when Daddy first met us," Rae answered.

The wind seemed to carry Bo's and Endora's giggles out across the land.

"I remember Mama promising us that our bedrooms would look different by Christmas," Endora said. "Luna and I had always shared a room, and it took a long time for me to be able to sleep in my own room, even after it was remodeled and ready for me."

"I loved the balcony," Rae said. "I used to sneak out here late at night and look at the stars."

"You always were the night owl," Bo reminded her.

"Yep, and the graveyard shift these past few years has suited me well," Rae admitted.

"How are you adjusting?" Endora asked.

"Slowly, but then—on a different level, and a very different situation—it took you more than a year to get your sea legs back under you and figure out things," Rae reminded her.

"Yes, it did, and I have to admit when I found out my fiancé and my best friend were having an affair right under my nose, it knocked me for a loop and shattered my heart." Endora pulled the hood of her jacket up over her head. "But Parker Martin has put all the pieces back together, and we are going to have a wonderful life together. I just wish March wasn't so far away."

"It will be a beautiful wedding"—Bo reached across the distance and patted her baby sister on the knee—"and we're all here to help you plan it."

"You've made new memories," Rae said.

"Yes, I have, and Parker gets the credit," Endora said. "I'm going inside. I'm freezing."

"Me too," Bo said. "Good night to y'all. Tomorrow is going to be crazy with all of us here, so we should get some sleep."

"Thanksgiving is always crazy and so much fun," Endora said and disappeared down the balcony.

"Think she's really all right?" Rae asked.

"I believe she is," Bo answered and closed the door to her room.

Rae wondered if she and her twin sister would be able to say that they were all right with their decisions to move back to Texas. Would another year bring happiness, or in her case, would she finally be able to adjust to a normal sleep pattern?

"Will Aunt Bernie succeed in her attempts to marry us off, so we'll settle down somewhere in this county?" Rae muttered to herself.

Acknowledgments

I've often said that it takes a village to take a book from an idea to the finished product you hold in your hands today. I would like to thank everyone in my village who has had a hand in that job: First, my readers for supporting me through the *Sisters of Paradise*. Then Deb Werksman and all the folks at Sourcebooks for giving me the opportunity to write more stories about the Paradise. My gratitude to Folio Management for representing me, and to my agent, Erin Niumata, who has been on this journey with me for more than twenty-five years. Thanks to my family and to the memory of Mr. B, my husband and soulmate, who would be so happy to see that I'm still writing. Every one of y'all has made me the author I am today, and I'm sending out virtual hugs to each and every one of you.

About the Author

Carolyn Brown is a *New York Times, USA Today, Wall Street Journal, Publisher's Weekly*, and #1 Amazon and #1 *Washington Post* bestselling author. She is the author of more than one hundred novels and several novellas. She's a recipient of the Bookseller's Best Award and the Montlake Romance's prestigious Montlake Diamond Award and a three-time recipient of the National Reader's Choice Award. Brown has been published for more than twenty-five years. Her books have been translated into twenty-one languages and have sold more than ten million copies worldwide.

When she's not writing, she likes to take road trips with her family, and she plots out new stories as they travel.

Website: carolynbrownbooks.com
Facebook: CarolynBrownBooks
Instagram: @carolynbrownbooks

Also by Carolyn Brown